An elegant debut? Hardly!

"I find that most amusing, don't you?"

"Not really," I said, and spilt my chocolate on her.

She dropped the chocolate pot, which instantly became the drabbest earthenware bowl imaginable, and overset her chair as she leapt to her feet, slapping at the dark stain on her dress, which rapidly spread to her hands. It seemed to burn her, for she kept jumping and slapping. The pins and needles vanished. I swept my skirts up and found I was able to get to my feet and run, stumbling and gasping, for the little door. It was latched but not locked, thank goodness, and I slammed it to behind me, then leaned against it to catch my breath. And realized every onlooker in the hall was staring, for I had slammed the door at the very height of the smallest choirboy's solo.

I don't need to tell you the rest, do I?

PATRICIA C. WREDE
AND CAROLINE STEVERMER

SORCERY

being the correspondence of
two Young Ladies of Quality
regarding various
Magical Scandals
in London and the Country

and Cecelia

OR

THE
ENCHANTED
CHOCOLATE
POT

Magic Carpet Books
Harcourt, Inc.

ORLANDO AUSTIN NEW YORK SAN DIEGO TORONTO LONDON

www.HarcourtBooks.com

First Magic Carpet Books edition 2004
First published as *Sorcery and Cecelia* in 1988

Magic Carpet Books is a trademark of Harcourt, Inc.,
registered in the United States of America and/or other jurisdictions.

The Library of Congress has cataloged the hardcover edition as follows·
Wrede, Patricia C., 1953–
Sorcery and Cecelia or the enchanted chocolate pot:
being the correspondence of two young ladies of quality
regarding various magical scandals in London and the country/
Patricia C. Wrede and Caroline Stevermer.
p. cm.
Summary: In 1817 in England, two young cousins,
Cecelia living in the country and Kate in London, write letters
to keep each other informed of their exploits, which take a sinister
turn when they find themselves confronted by evil wizards.
[1. Cousins—Fiction. 2. Wizards—Fiction. 3. Supernatural—Fiction.
4. Letters—Fiction. 5. London (England)—Social life and customs—
19th century—Fiction. 6. England—Social life and customs—
19th century—Fiction.] I. Stevermer, Caroline. II. Title.
PZ7.W915So 2003
[Fic]—dc21   2002038706
ISBN 0-15-204615-1
ISBN 0-15-205300-X pb

Text set in Fournier
Designed by Lydia D'moch

A C E G H F D B

Printed in the United States of America

The authors wish to dedicate this book to
Jane Austen, Georgette Heyer,
J. R. R. Tolkien, and Ellen Kushner,
all of whom, in their several ways,
inspired us to create it.

SORCERY and CECELIA

OR

THE ENCHANTED CHOCOLATE POT

8 April 1817
Rushton Manor, Essex

Dearest Kate,

It is dreadfully flat here since you have been gone, and it only makes it worse to imagine all the things I shall be missing. I wish Aunt Elizabeth were not so set against my having a Season this year. She is still annoyed about the incident with the goat, and says that to let the pair of us loose on London would ruin us both for good, and spoil Georgy's chances into the bargain. I think this is quite unjust, but there is no persuading her. (I believe the fact that she would have been obliged to share a house with Aunt Charlotte, should she and I have come to London this year, may have contributed to her decision.) So I rely on you, dearest cousin, to write and tell me everything! If I am not to be allowed to enjoy a Season of my own, I can at least take a vicarious delight in your and Georgina's triumph! I am quite convinced you will take London by storm.

Not that we are without amusement in Essex; quite the contrary! Aunt Elizabeth and I called at the vicarage yesterday and spent a stimulating afternoon listening to the Reverend Fitzwilliam discoursing on the Vanities of Society and the Emptiness of Worldly Pleasures. Aunt Elizabeth hung on every word, and we are to return and take tea on Thursday. I am determined to have the headache Thursday, if I have to hit myself with a rock to do it.

There is, however, a ray of hope. Lady Tarleton is to have a party for her niece next week. The invitation arrived this morning, and Papa says we are to go! And Aunt Elizabeth approves! She thinks it is to be an informal hop, as Lady Tarleton's niece is not yet out, but Patience Everslee told me in the greatest confidence that there is to be waltzing! I only hope Oliver will stay long enough to accompany us. He has been moping around the house like a sick sheep ever since you and Georgy left, and yesterday he asked Papa, very casually, whether Papa did not think it would be a good idea for him to go to Town this year for a week or two. He thinks he is being very sly, but if he puts off making his arrangements for another day or so Papa will have accepted Lady Tarleton's invitation and Oliver will be obliged to stay here until after the party. I have not, of course, pointed this out to him. Oliver has stated many times his dislike of hearing advice from his younger sister, so it is his own fault if he has not got sense enough to see which way the wind is blowing.

Aunt Elizabeth intends for the two of us to pay a call on Lady Tarleton and her niece on Monday, by way of improving our acquaintance before the ball (which is to say, she wants to have a look at the niece). I shall be on my best behavior, even if the niece turns out to be quite odious. There is no point in *looking* for difficulties the day before a party.

And there may be more excitement to come. Sir Hilary Bedrick has just been named to the Royal College of Wizards; the whole village is buzzing with the news. I suspect he was chosen because of that enormous library of musty old spellbooks at Bedrick Hall. He left yesterday for London, where he will be installed, but all of us expect great things when he returns. Except, of course, for Aunt Elizabeth, who looks at me sideways and says darkly that magic is for heathens and cannibals, not for decent folk. Perhaps that is why she holds Sir Hilary in such dislike. I would wager my best kid gloves that if it were not for Papa's interest in the historical portions of Sir Hilary's library, Aunt Elizabeth would have cut the connection ages ago.

Do, please, try to find me those silks I asked you about before you left, and if you should happen to see a pair of long gloves that would match my green crape, please, please send them at once! I should so like to look well at Lady Tarleton's party.

Give my love to Georgy and Aunt Charlotte, and do try not to let Aunt Charlotte bully you too much. And do, do write and tell me everything you are doing!

Your loving cousin,
Cecy

Dear Cecy,

If you've been forced to listen to Reverend Fitzwilliam on the subject of the emptiness of worldly pleasures for hours together, I feel I ought to write something bracing to cheer you up. But after three days of a London Season I find it hard to come to the defense of frivolity with any spirit. Perhaps it will make Rushton seem more amusing to you if I complain *vigorously.* (Don't worry, I haven't said a word to anyone else, not even Georgina.)

First, there was our arrival in Berkeley Square, a very welcome event after a day spent in the coach with Aunt Charlotte complaining of her migraine and Georgina exclaiming, "Only look, a sedan chair!" at every opportunity. It was very late and we were very tired and soiled with our travels, too weary to feel the proper emotions on entering such a grand house for the first time. (Horace Walpole is by no means Aunt Charlotte's favorite author, but the opportunity to hire the genuine Mayfair town house he genuinely died in for the Season has given her a new appreciation of him and his works.)

Make no mistake, it is very grand. On the outside it is a high, narrow, polite-looking house built of brick. On the inside there is a high-ceilinged entrance hall with a marble staircase winding up two flights. On either side of the hall are reception rooms. The one on the right is called the blue saloon. It is very comfortable with a bow window overlooking the Square. On the left side of the hall is the drawing room, much grander than the blue saloon, furnished with lyre-back chairs, delicate sofas, and a spinet. There are velvet curtains in the windows and a highly polished marble floor, upon which I slipped and sat down hard as we were being shown about the house. This was my first piece of clumsiness in London, but I suspect it will not be my last. The general effect of the marble floor and ivory curtains is almost arctic. Only touches of primrose and black relieve the whiteness. At the top of the two flights of stairs are the bedrooms. Georgina's looks out over the Square and mine faces back into the lane behind the house. If I crane my neck I can see down into the kitchen garden—but there is nothing much to look at. Nothing to compare with the gardens at Rushton.

It seemed like a dream to me, following Georgina up and up the stairs—she like a kind of angel climbing to her proper place, her golden hair bright in the light from the lamps—me like a ramshackle shadow lurking after her, shedding hairpins and stumbling over the hem of my skirts.

The bedrooms are lovely, but that night they seemed grand and cold and I was a little dismayed to find myself in my own room all alone—can you credit it, after I schemed for years to get a room to myself? So I slipped in to Georgina to say good night and get my top buttons undone.

Georgina was sitting at her window, trying to guess from the darkened glass what direction she was facing so she could say her prayers toward home. I turned her around and didn't tease her, even when I saw the lock of hair she had clenched in her moist little palm—Oliver's, tied up in a bit of pink ribbon. Can you believe it?

Well, as I say, I got her pointed in the right direction and she got me unbuttoned and told me that I had a smut rubbed clear across my forehead and a spot coming on my chin. (As if I hadn't been driven half-mad feeling it coming out *all day long* in the coach . . .) So we parted, she to her prayers and I to my bed, the highest, hardest, narrowest, dampest bed on four lion's paws (London would be grander still if they knew how to air their sheets).

Our first day in London was spent shopping, which means I kicked my heels while Aunt Charlotte and the modiste went into raptures over Georgina. The second day, we were taken to see the Elgin Marbles, which was interesting, and to listen to other people see the Elgin Marbles, which would make the eyes roll right back in your head with boredom. The third day, we went back to shopping and I was able to get gloves. Please find enclosed a pair that I think will suit your pomona green crape to perfection. I bought a pair for myself and have spilt coffee on them already. So you see London hasn't changed me yet.

I feel quite envious about Lady Tarleton's dance. Aunt Charlotte has spoken of Almack's but never yet without looking at me and giving a little shudder of apprehension. She intends to call on Lady Jersey tomorrow. If their acquaintance has been exaggerated (and you know that sometimes people do not care quite as much for Aunt Charlotte as she thinks they do), I don't know how we will obtain vouchers. It is plain, however, that without vouchers for Almack's Assembly, Georgy will never truly shine in Society, no matter how lovely she is. For my own sake, I hope I get to go, too. It would be a shame to have trodden Robert Penwood's feet black and blue learning to dance and then never to get a chance to put it to the test.

Do you think a wizard's installation would be a ladylike thing to attend? We passed the Royal College on the way to the Museum and I'm sure I could find my way.

Do tell me all about the dance and mention Oliver a little so Georgina doesn't sigh herself away entirely.

Love,
Kate

14 April 1817
Rushton Manor, Essex

Dearest Kate,
Your letter arrived this morning, and I refuse to believe it. London cannot possibly be as dreary as you make it seem! I am quite persuaded that you are roasting me, in

order to make me feel better about being left behind. Pray do not; I am most eager to learn what I may look forward to next year.

Yes, Kate, it seems I am to have my Season after all! This afternoon Aunt Elizabeth took me to call on Lady Tarleton, to make the acquaintance of the niece, Miss Dorothea Griscomb. I was determined to dislike her, for I had seen her driving through the village the day before, and she is nearly as lovely as Georgina! Her hair is paler than Georgy's, and I am sure that without crimping it would be quite straight, but Dorothea's eyes are a deeper blue and her figure is already elegant and graceful. I was sure she would be odious, for you must admit that females as pretty as Georgy are, in general, quite spoiled. I was, therefore, expecting the worst.

When we arrived, Lady Tarleton and Dorothea were already ensconced in the drawing room with Mrs. Everslee and Patience. Mrs. Everslee was looking quite put out; I believe she was hoping that with Georgy in London, Patience would come into her own. Dorothea was sitting in a corner, staring down at her teacup with a miserably uncomfortable expression, Lady Tarleton was looking stiff, and Patience was casting about desperately for a way to persuade her mother that it was time to go. I conclude from this that Mrs. Everslee had been saying something cutting.

Our appearance provided the opportunity Patience had been seeking, and Aunt Elizabeth and I soon found ourselves the only callers. I felt rather sorry for Dorothea. So I sat down beside her and tried to engage her in conversation.

I was not, at first, successful. Dorothea turned out to be quite shy, and I was reduced to insipid commonplaces about the weather and how good the cream pastries were. I was about to abandon the attempt in despair, when by the luckiest chance she said something about India.

"India!" I said. "You mean you have lived in India? Oh, do tell me all about it!"

My excessive enthusiasm was as much the result of relief at having finally found a subject of conversation as it was due to any desire to hear about foreign climes. However, Dorothea opened up wonderfully to such encouragement, which gave me the opportunity of replenishing my supply of tea, ginger biscuits, and cream pastries. Dorothea was, apparently, born in India, and did not even see England until she was eight years old. Her Papa, of whom she seems touchingly fond, made a great fortune there, and she showed me a carved ivory bracelet she had brought back with her. By the time she finished telling me about her childhood, we were fast friends, and she brought herself to ask me very softly about the people she would see at Lady Tarleton's party.

I did the best I could to explain who she was likely to see, as well as who would not be present. "My cousins, Kate and Georgina Talgarth, have already gone to London for the

Season," I said (with considerable regret). "And Sir Hilary Bedrick is away as well; he is to be invested as a member of the Royal College of Wizards this very week!" I glanced at Aunt Elizabeth and lowered my voice. "It is a great pity that the Mysterious Marquis is not in residence, for I am sure your aunt must have sent him an invitation card. But then, he never *is* in residence."

"The Mysterious Marquis?" Dorothea said warily. "Who is that?"

"The Marquis of Schofield," I said. "He owns an estate about ten miles from Bedrick Hall, but he never visits it. I suppose Waycross is too small a property for him to bother with, compared to Schofield Castle."

"Oh, that's not it at all," Dorothea said, then looked very frightened. It took me several minutes and two ginger biscuits to persuade her to tell me what she meant by such a comment. Apparently her Mama has some acquaintance with the Mysterious Marquis, and Dorothea overheard her say that the Marquis and Sir Hilary had some sort of falling-out long ago. The reason the Marquis never visits Waycross is that it is too near Bedrick Hall. I was disappointed to discover that Dorothea knew no more than that, but I did not like to press her. Her Mama must be a veritable dragon, for Dorothea was quite terrified of telling me even as much as she did.

Aunt Elizabeth overheard us and said quite sharply that the Marquis of Schofield's affairs were not a proper topic for young ladies, so I think it very probable that the Marquis is a great rake. I find this somewhat comforting, for I was quite cast down to discover that his reasons for avoiding Essex are so ordinary. Anyone who is known as the Mysterious Marquis ought to have far more interesting reasons for his behavior than a stupid dispute with Sir Hilary.

Lady Tarleton seemed quite pleased that Dorothea and I got on so well. She went so far as to inquire from Aunt Elizabeth whether I was to make my curtsey to Society next year, saying that it would be pleasant for Dorothea to have some acquaintances in Town when she makes her come-out. Well, what could Aunt Elizabeth do but agree? I made sure to bring it up to Papa as soon as we got home, and I shall keep talking about it until everyone takes it for granted that I am to be presented next year. I only wish that it could have happened sooner, so that you and I could have gone together. What fun we must have had!

Thank you a million times for the gloves; they match my dress perfectly. I shall cut quite a dash at Lady Tarleton's dance tomorrow! I wish I had your eye for color, but try as I may, I *cannot* manage to match anything except muddy browns. Which is exceedingly odd, as even Aunt Elizabeth admits that I have an instinct for which colors look best on people. Speaking of which, I do hope you have not allowed Aunt Charlotte to have all your new dresses made up in insipid blues. She thinks that because something looks well on Georgina it must be becoming to everyone. Last year she tried to persuade me to let her buy me a lilac pelisse just because it was stunning on Georgy, and you know I look awful in lilac.

The house in Berkeley Square sounds perfectly *sumptuous;* I do wish I could see it. Have you been receiving many callers? Reverend Fitzwilliam says (with evident disapproval) that all people do in London is shop and receive callers and go to teas and parties. And does your bed truly have lion's paws, or are you bamming me?

I thought the Elgin Marbles sounded very interesting, but Oliver says it is a great deal of fuss to be made over a lot of broken statues. He is still wandering gloomily about the house like a bad imitation of Lord Byron. (And I do not understand why someone as proper as Oliver wishes to copy such a rackety character.) He plans to leave for London the day after tomorrow, as he is promised to be at Lady Tarleton's. I shall save this letter to finish after the dance, so that I can tell you all about it.

I'm sure it would be entirely proper for you to attend Sir Hilary's installation; after all, we have known him forever. Honesty compels me to add that Aunt Elizabeth would certainly disagree with me, but that is only because she disapproves of magic and magicians. Patience Everslee thinks it is because she suffered a Grave Disappointment in her Youth, but I simply cannot picture Aunt Elizabeth in such a situation.

Lady Tarleton's dance was last night, and, oh, Kate, what a lot I have to tell you!

We left Rushton Manor at about eight. I wore my pomona green crape and your gloves, and the little gold locket that Mama left me. Papa looked very well, though a little rumpled as always. Oliver was surly but elegant in silk breeches, a dark green dress coat, and an enormous cravat, which he proudly informed me was knotted in a style called the Mathematical. And you would not have recognized Aunt Elizabeth! She wore a stunning gown in gold silk and a necklace of amber beads, and looked most elegant.

We are not, of course, such great friends of the Tarletons as to have been invited to the dinner beforehand. When we arrived at Tarleton Hall, the dinner things had already been cleared. Lady Tarleton and Dorothea were greeting their guests, and Tarleton Hall was already beginning to fill up. Simply everyone was there; quite a number of persons appear to have left off going to London until later, so as to attend the party.

The dining room at Tarleton Hall is enormous; it's easily four times the size of the sitting room at home. The ceiling is painted with wreaths and medallions, and there must have been a hundred candles in tall, four-armed stands all around the room! I know that by now you must have seen far grander things in London, but it was quite the loveliest sight I have ever beheld.

And Patience was right—there was waltzing! At first Aunt Elizabeth would only allow me to dance the country dances, but then Lady Tarleton came to my rescue. She persuaded Aunt Elizabeth that it would be unexceptionable for me to waltz at a private party, and even got her son James to stand up with me. He is as dark-haired as I am and quite good-looking, and he dresses with great elegance. (Just before we left, I heard Oliver ask him about his style of tying his cravat, which is apparently something quite out of the common way. Mr. Tarleton gave him a set-down, of course, and I must say I think Oliver deserved it.)

I minded my steps most carefully, and only trod on Mr. Tarleton's toes once, which was *not* my fault. For when I asked whether he would be returning to London for the rest of the Season (just making conversation, which I have always been told is *essential* when one is dancing with a gentleman), he looked so very black that I could not help stumbling a little. He apologized very nicely and said that he would be staying at Tarleton Hall and not going back to London. On thinking it over later, I find it very strange, for you remember that Robert Penwood told us that since his return from the army, Mr. Tarleton considers the country entirely flat, which is why he has seldom visited Tarleton Hall in the past. Though now that I think of it, I do not know how Robert could be sure of such a thing.

Mr. Tarleton is an excellent dancer, much better than Robert or Jack, and I was disappointed when the music ended and he escorted me back to Aunt Elizabeth and Papa. To my surprise, he stayed to speak with Papa—some question of a difficult line in a Greek manuscript he was translating, on which Mr. Tarleton wanted an opinion. Naturally, Papa was perfectly willing to go off with him then and there. Aunt Elizabeth was very nearly as miffed as I, for she had told Papa most particularly before we ever left Rushton Manor that he was not to vanish into Lord Tarleton's library. I must add, however, that Papa and Mr. Tarleton were not gone above a quarter of an hour, which makes me think that Mr. Tarleton must have a great deal of address. I have never known *anyone* who could persuade Papa to abandon an interesting manuscript. And I could tell he found it interesting from the manner of questions he put to Mr. Tarleton. Nonetheless, Aunt Elizabeth maintains that they both behaved disgracefully.

Dorothea was perfectly lovely. All the men were quite smitten with her, and I must tell you, Kate, that Oliver was among them. He behaved quite foolishly, even after Aunt Elizabeth reminded him most sharply that it is not at all the thing to dance more than twice with the same lady. She made him escort me in to supper at the end of the evening, which put both of us out of temper—Oliver, because he had hoped to claim Dorothea's hand, and me, because there is nothing quite so lowering as having one's brother take one in to supper as though there was no one else who wanted to. Even the excellence of the refreshments (lobster patties, savory pastries, and those wonderful little lemon tartlets, among other things) was not enough to soothe my feelings.

Oliver still intends to leave for London today (really, he must do so, because the arrangements have all been made and he has several commissions from Papa to execute), but now he speaks of cutting his visit short, and I know it is only because Dorothea is staying on with Lady Tarleton for another month. Do not show this letter to Georgina; there is no point in *your* having to cope with Georgy's reaction to this news when it is all *Oliver's* fault. Besides, I hope that seeing Georgy again will bring Oliver to his senses. Unfortunately, one cannot depend upon such things, however much one would like to.

And it is not Dorothea's fault in the least, for I promise you, Kate, she did *not* encourage him in the slightest. She did not encourage *anyone* in the slightest, that I could see; they all just buzzed around her like so many bees. She and I are to go riding together tomorrow, which I think unexceptionable, as Oliver will be well on his way to London by then. But what on earth am I to do when he returns? For you know Oliver; he will make a great push to join us in everything, just as he used to do with the two of us and Georgina. And I *will not* be a party to it. Georgy may be a selfish peagoose, but she does not deserve such treatment. I must simply hope that you will have good news of Oliver to send me, so that I shall not have to fret over this impossible situation.

Yours in haste,
Cecy

20 April 1817
11 Berkeley Square, London

Dear Cecy,

It is the outside of enough for you to say I am bamming you just because London hasn't changed Aunt Charlotte a jot, nor Georgina, save to make her more of a watering pot than ever, and if I am to be accused by you, in addition to everyone else, of telling tales when I explain to you what happened to me at Sir Hilary's investiture, I shall go straight into a decline.

The past several days were spent putting the final touches on Georgy's and my gowns, assembling gloves, fans, bonnets, slippers, and stockings in such quantities that it sometimes seemed to me we were preparing for a voyage to the Indies instead of for the Season.

Once we were equipped to Aunt Charlotte's satisfaction, we were presented to Society for the first time at Lady Jersey's Venetian breakfast. (For Lady Jersey is indeed an acquaintance of Aunt Charlotte's, and appears willing to oblige us with any number of vouchers and introductions.) This involved rising early and waiting fully prepared for two hours while Aunt Charlotte made certain that the carriage was properly clean so that we could not possibly soil our gowns en route. We were then tucked inside and conveyed to Lady Jersey's breakfast as though we were made of bone china. Descending from the carriage, I snagged my stocking on the buckle of my slipper, but Georgy arrived intact. Her introduction to the assembled guests could not possibly have been more satisfactory. With perfect serenity she triumphed over the entire guest list. Not only was she the loveliest girl there by far, she displayed a very becoming reserve. Not even the attentions of the elderly Duke of Hexham troubled her. She sailed through it all calmly while the mamas of her rivals glared at her perfection.

If the Venetian breakfast was the opening shot of a war, the next few days featured a perfect volley of entertainments. Routs, drums, suppers, luncheons—we received invitations to them all.

Oliver arrived on Friday. At first he seemed as glad to see Georgina as she to see him, but he was very quickly dismayed by her steady stream of admirers and annoyed by their demands on her time. (Yes, Cecy, we have callers here in Berkeley Square. Indeed, Aunt Charlotte says the knocker, which is never still, gives her the headache.) Among the new acquaintances we have made are the Grenvilles: Alice,

George, and Andrew. George and Andrew are twins, though not the sort of twins who dress alike or finish each other's sentences. They are both impressed with Georgy's beauty, although I think it puts them off a little when she pretends she cannot tell them apart. Alice is their younger sister. She shares what the twins call the Grenville coloring, chestnut hair and fair skin that tends to freckle, with her twin brothers. Alice is very delicate in appearance but very brisk and lively in spirit and orders the twins about mercilessly. Her father, Lord Grenville, will give a great ball later in the Season, and Alice has already asked us to attend. Michael Aubrey, who is some sort of relation of the Grenvilles and a constant companion of the twins, has already tried to get Georgy to agree to give him a dance. Georgy knew just how to deny him without discouraging him. It's the sort of thing she's been getting a great deal of practice in lately.

You and I expected this, but I think it came as a bit of a surprise to Oliver. At first he was delighted to meet our new friends, but by Saturday morning, Oliver said he was already tired of London and longing to be back in Essex. No entertainment we suggested pleased him. What he wanted was to be alone with Georgy. Barring that, he wanted to be where he did not have to make polite conversation with any of Georgy's admirers. Thus, I was able to persuade him to desert Georgy's outing to see the bears at the Tower and walk me to the hall to see Sir Hilary's investiture. As usual,

Oliver was a rather taxing companion. He complained the whole way that the drizzle took the curl from his hair, and said he thought the Royal College of Wizards ought to at least arrange to have pleasant weather for their investitures.

Once inside, we encountered a great press of people, almost all of them dressed in their best and many in the lordly robes of the college. I have never seen such embroidery in my life, nor ever heard of the brocades, silks, and cloths of gold and silver that were there.

The investiture itself is a brief and simple ceremony, a matter of presenting the honored newcomers to the college with a blue sash, a silver medallion, and a daub of scented oil between the eyebrows. That, repeated twelve times in rapid succession, would hardly provide entertainment enough for an entire afternoon, so the college expanded the ceremony with a choir of boys from the abbey school and a detachment of Royal Guardsmen to arch their sabers over the wizards as they approached the dais for investiture.

I think the ceremony was all that could be wished. Even Oliver was not bored. He pushed ahead, squeezing forward to see better, but because I am so short, it did me no good to try. Instead, I skirted the back of the crowd and walked along the north aisle, gazing about me at the hall. There are many banners, very threadbare and tattered, and many stone slabs underfoot, well worn by centuries of steps, all worked with symbols and signs to identify the wizards who placed them there. I walked along happily, admiring the splendid clothes of the onlookers and the general air of faded elegance and chilly, damp, historical glory, until I encountered a little door in the north hall, only latched, not locked, its pointed arch scarcely higher than my head.

I only meant to glance in to satisfy my curiosity, but beyond the door I found a cloistered garden, planted with daffodils and hyacinths, as tranquil and remote as if it were in Essex or some more distant place. I couldn't resist stepping through the door. It swung shut behind me and as I took a few steps forward, I saw I was not alone. In the center of the garden was a tea table and two chairs. In one chair sat a little woman with hair so white it was almost blue in the sunlight—which was odd, for the day outside was a gray and drizzly one (at least, it had been as we walked to the hall). I took the vacant chair at the little woman's gracious gesture. The instant I sat, my legs and feet went first pins and needles, then quite numb. The little woman watched me very hard and when she saw my puzzlement she beamed with pleasure. At first I thought she was old, because of her hair, but when I looked closely I saw she had only powdered her hair white, as was the custom in our grandparents' day. Her skin was smooth and carefully painted, her eyes were dark and very hard. She smiled kindly at me and asked if I would take chocolate with her.

You and I often played at dolls' tea party together, Cecy. I will never again remember such games with pleasure. The very thought chills me, for now I know how the dolls felt when we poured out tea for them. For the life of me all I could do was nod and smile inanely and hold out my cup. She took this for acceptance, and poured me a cup of chocolate from the most beautiful chocolate pot I have ever seen. It was blue porcelain, a blue that made me think of the sky in September, or the lake at Rushton, or Georgina's eyes. I could scarcely look away from it.

"I was sure you couldn't resist one last attempt to recover it," she said. "Sir Hilary mocked me, but I knew you could not stay away. So I set a trap, as you see, and you have fallen in. But I suppose you deserve credit for confounding my expectations so completely. You've always seemed so exceptionally masculine to me, Thomas, it never occurred to me to think what kind of woman you would make. Really, who would expect you to disguise yourself as your utter opposite?"

Understandably, I found her words as puzzling as they were insulting, but it was difficult to spare enough attention from the chocolate pot to be properly vexed with her.

"Do drink your chocolate, Thomas," she went on, a chill amusement behind her gentle words. "It won't hurt you a bit—and think how appropriate it will be for you to go this way. Almost by your own hand."

I was very confused and very frightened. With all my heart I wanted to get up and run away. But all I could do was say, "That is a very singular chocolate pot."

"You have the most sardonic sense of humor, Thomas," she said, "really, almost morbid. It's a fake, of course. I thought you'd realize it at once. Hilary couldn't deny me my chance at a trap for you, but he wouldn't risk using real bait. No, you've ventured your last stake, my darling Marquis, and all for a cheap copy of your own magic. I find that most amusing, don't you?"

"Not really," I said, and spilt my chocolate on her.

She dropped the chocolate pot, which instantly became the drabbest earthenware bowl imaginable, and overset her chair as she leapt to her feet, slapping at the dark stain on her dress, which rapidly spread to her hands. It seemed to burn her, for she kept jumping and slapping. The pins and needles vanished. I swept my skirts up and found I was able to get to my feet and run, stumbling and gasping, for the little door. It was latched but not locked, thank goodness, and I slammed it to behind me, then leaned against it to catch my breath. And realized every onlooker in the hall was staring, for I had slammed the door at the very height of the smallest choirboy's solo.

I don't need to tell you the rest, do I? How Oliver collected me, as red as a lobster with his shame at owning my acquaintance. How Aunt Charlotte scolded me for a liar when I tried to explain, forbade me to use the spinet, and set me to learn an entire chapter of the prayer book by heart as a punishment, or how Georgina shook her head as I tried to convince her by showing her the tiny spot on the hem of my gown where the chocolate splashed and ate clear through the fabric, leaving only a little hole edged with black.

So, my dearest Cecelia, I depend on you to understand that if I meant to lie, or even jest, I could do a much better job than this (remember the goat, after all!). Never, *never* have I wished so to have you here with me, and it seems sheer cruelty of fate to decree that your Season is to be next year, when I am making such a mull of it alone. Oh, Cecy, *yes* my bed has lion's feet, and *yes*—*all* my gowns are blue muslin, and if you were only here, surely you would manage some way to coax Aunt Charlotte into mercy, or at least help me drill the prayer book so I might get my punishment over more quickly.

Your miserable cousin,
Kate

25 April 1817
Rushton Manor, Essex

Dearest Kate,

Sir Hilary's investiture seems to have been a true adventure. I do wish I'd been there (though I quite see that it must have been excessively alarming while it was happening). I am *appalled* by Aunt Charlotte's reaction, but it is *just* like her to disbelieve you, when anyone with an ounce of sensibility would realize how foolish it would be to make up such a tale. And you have *never* been foolish, Kate. Aunt Charlotte should know better. After all, she was at Rushton when Oliver's dog bit that horrid Hollydean boy, and you did not cry or faint like Georgy, but called Canniba to heel and then made Frederick hold still while you bandaged his hand. I am also reminded of the way you kept your head and came up with perfectly splendid explanations of where we had been whenever Aunt Elizabeth got wind of one of our expeditions and began asking awkward questions. (On second thought, perhaps it is better not to mention that to Aunt Charlotte.) It should have been quite obvious that you had sustained a severe shock, for otherwise I am sure you would have come up with something else to tell Aunt Charlotte, and so avoided memorizing prayers.

I have read most carefully the account of Sir Hilary's investiture in the London papers (which arrived here several days late, as usual), but I could not find anyone named Thomas among the list of guests. I thought he must have been there, for it is obvious that Thomas is a magician (else how could the white-haired lady in the garden have mistaken you for him? Unless, of course, she is impossibly nearsighted, but I am sure you would have noticed that). It seems, however, that Thomas did *not* go to Sir Hilary's investiture, which I think shows a great deal of good sense, given what happened to you.

I mention this because it seems to me that if the white-haired lady is indeed trying to make away with someone named Thomas, it would be only right to warn him. And it does appear that this is exactly what she was attempting to do. (For, of course, even the strongest and hottest chocolate does not makes holes in one's gown. Stains, certainly; I am still trying to get the brown splotches out of my second-best gloves.) I do so wish I were there to help, for Aunt Charlotte and Georgina are bound to be a great handicap. However, I have the greatest faith in you.

I am much reassured by your news of Oliver. He appears to be as caper-witted as ever, but at least he is not infatuated with Dorothea anymore. It does seem rather odd, however, for though Oliver is nearly as much of a peagoose as Georgy, he has never been *fickle*. I think I shall discuss it with Dorothea the next time I see her (I shall be *most* discreet, I promise you!). In the meantime, do try to keep Oliver in London, just in case. For I must tell you, nearly every eligible (and ineligible!) bachelor for miles around has been at Dorothea's feet ever since the night of the ball. Every time I visit her, I trip over Robert Penwood, or Jack Everslee, or Martin De Lacey.

The only man who does not appear to be completely smitten is James Tarleton, and even he shows occasional signs of being as besotted as the rest. The other day, Dorothea and I went riding in the fields by Tarleton Hall. I had a good gallop on the way over, which was fortunate, for Dorothea prefers to keep to a far slower pace when she rides. We had just turned to go back when I thought I saw a flash of white among the trees that line the avenue, and I caught a brief glimpse of someone on a black horse.

"Who is that?" I said.

"Where?" Dorothea said, turning her head. "I don't see anyone."

"I thought I saw someone on the avenue," I said. Whoever it was had disappeared—ridden on, perhaps, or hidden. "But I must have been wrong," I added, when I saw that Dorothea looked a little distressed.

I thought no more of the incident until we returned to Tarleton Hall. Dorothea thought her mare had strained one of her forelegs (how a horse could strain a muscle when it has not been ridden above a walk, and for less than an hour, is beyond me). We stayed by the stables after we dismounted, so Dorothea could explain the difficulty to the grooms and be properly reassured. As we crossed to Tarleton Hall, James Tarleton came riding in on a magnificent black gelding—far better even than Oliver's Thunder. When he saw us, he pulled up short, frowning, and greeted us with the barest modicum of civility.

"That is a truly splendid horse, Mr. Tarleton," I said, for Aunt Elizabeth is forever reminding me that one is not allowed to be uncivil simply because someone else has been so.

"Thank you," he said curtly. Then, apparently feeling that this was too abrupt, he added, "I hope you found the South Meadow pleasant."

Dorothea murmured something that was almost completely inaudible, so I said that it had indeed been a pleasant ride, and we went on into the house. It did not occur to me until later to wonder how he knew where we had been riding. I supposed it might have been a lucky guess, but it seems to me just as likely that he had been the rider I had seen in the avenue. As there is nothing I can think of that would have drawn him in that direction on an errand, I thought he must have been following us to watch Dorothea. (It is not unprecedented; Martin De Lacey did as much last Tuesday, in order to meet us "by accident" and so have a chance to see Dorothea.) I suggested as much to Dorothea, but she shook her head at once.

"James would never do such a thing," she said quite positively. "He does not like me, you see."

"You must be wrong," I said, taken aback.

"Oh, no, I am quite sure of it," she replied in a soft voice. "He avoids me most of the time, and when he cannot, he ignores me. I do not even know what I have done to give him a dislike of me."

I would have responded indignantly, but I could see that the subject was distressing for Dorothea, so I did not continue it. James Tarleton seems to me to be treating his cousin quite shamefully. And if he *was* watching us from the avenue, then his behavior is worse than she supposes. I do not see, however, that there is anything I can do about it for the moment, especially as I am not at all certain that Dorothea has read the situation aright.

Apart from a little riding, and a few morning calls on Dorothea, nothing else has happened that is at all noteworthy. There are a few amusements planned for the immediate future—Patience Everslee has proposed a picnic by the lake (I am quite sure her brother Jack talked her into it as an excuse to see Dorothea, for you know how Patience hates the water). Not to be outdone, Robert Penwood has arranged an outing to see the maze at Bedrick Hall. I find that I am to be included in both parties, as Dorothea and I have become such excellent friends, so perhaps I shall have more to say that is interesting (or at least amusing—Robert and Jack are making *such* cakes of themselves!) in my next letter. Give my love to Aunt Charlotte and Georgina, and tell Oliver that Papa and I are both well. And do *try* to talk Aunt Charlotte into buying you at least *one* gown in a decent color!

Enviously,
Cecy

30 April 1817
11 Berkeley Square, London

Dear Cecy,

Your optimism is justified. What a wonderful time we shall have next Season when you can be here to manage things firsthand!

Be sure I shall tell you every detail, but I mean to set it all down in an orderly fashion, for I have learned something of *great* importance.

Tonight we went to Almack's Assembly. I dreaded it, you know I did, and at first it was just as bad as I feared. We were introduced mercilessly for the first twenty minutes and then Georgy vanished into a swarm of young men. After a while a young man detached himself from the swarm and asked me to make up part of a set for a country dance. He had beautiful manners, save for the way his head kept swiveling on his neck in an effort to keep Georgy in view. When the set had ended he made a beeline back to her and claimed the next dance, plainly his reward for the sacrifice of dancing with me.

You know me well enough to know what I did then— retire to the sidelines with a stiff back and an "I don't care a jot" expression concealing the fact I felt a complete antidote. Just as I found a good spot to fade into the other wallflowers, I found myself intercepted by Lady Jersey, who began with a great deal of fudge about her respect for Aunt Charlotte and ended by introducing me to the man at her side.

Cecy, I promised you, if I could faint, I'd have fainted then. The man, very dark, not too young, not too tall, with a sardonic expression of pained civility was the Marquis of Schofield. And Sally Jersey thought it would be perfectly plausible for me to dance with him. And the next dance a waltz! I stammered something completely idiotic. He took my hand and said, at least, I *think* he said, "Yes, I know," and we waltzed.

Cecy, if this is what a London Season can be like, I don't wonder people like Sally Jersey enjoy themselves year in and year out. It's better than a play. Of course you know how *well* I waltz. For the first few bars I was utterly certain I would cannon into someone and fall down, or step on him, or trip over my hem, so I staggered after his lead, rigid with discomfort. But he danced very simply, with none of the panache of the other couples, and I was able to follow him well enough to relax a little. (Do you ever wonder if driving a team is like dancing? Being where you're wanted when you're wanted, with no words, just hints? I never thought of it from the horse's point of view, but perhaps it is, and perhaps that is why good dancers and good drivers are both rare and highly thought of.)

When he was able to believe I would not topple over or froth at the mouth, the Marquis spoke, softly enough that I could only just hear him over the music.

"I owe you my thanks," he said. I must have looked completely mystified, for he smiled and said, as though reminding me of a joke we'd shared, "I'm Thomas."

We danced in silence for a complete circuit of the room while I digested this. Then, when he judged I was ready for more, he said, "You sprang a trap intended for me and I'm grateful. Miranda can be very obtuse sometimes, but I trust that seeing us together will disabuse her of the notion that you are me in disguise."

I promise you, by this time, my head was spinning.

"I do have methods of going unnoticed," he continued, "but I have never assumed a lady's identity. Miranda's imagination can sometimes reach more lurid heights than even Mr. Lewis and his Monk."

I finally found my voice, but not, unfortunately, much to say. "She doesn't like you."

"I don't like her, either," he replied. "And she won't like you after this dance convinces her you know me. So don't go into any gardens by yourself, will you? In fact, stay in well-lit ballrooms as much as possible."

"That's all the explanation I get?" I demanded. "Who is Miranda? Why does she wish to poison you with chocolate?"

"That's all the explanation you get," he replied. "For the rest, forget it. It's no concern of yours. Just mind your own affairs. Practice your dancing. With enough study you might attain a degree of proficiency."

"What a rude thing to say!" I replied. "I would practice, but practice requires a partner."

He smiled with such a degree of cynicism I almost expected his teeth to glint metallic. "You won't lack for partners now. I've made Sally Jersey give me a waltz with you. Everyone will be agog to find out why."

"Don't you want to know what I'm going to tell them?" I asked.

"Oh, they won't ask, don't think it. No, they'll dance with you and then say I am justly called mysterious," he said.

"You are odious."

"Quite so, but admit you've never danced better than these last few moments when you were too angry to think about it."

The music ended and he had returned me to Aunt Charlotte before I could think of a suitable answer. For, of course, he was right. Infuriating. I did not sit out a single dance. In fact, I danced until I got a stitch in my side. Aunt Charlotte told me my face was red, but I didn't care. I had a wonderful time, and if I could only have thought of something truly cutting to say to the Mysterious Marquis, my evening would have been quite perfect.

Now, tell me, I beg you, all about the picnic at the lake and Robert's pranks in the maze. (For you can never convince me he could resist such a perfect chance to get Dorothea as much to himself as propriety permits.) My love to you all.

Your footsore cousin,
Kate

P.S. Before you ask, no, no sign of the white-haired lady (who must be the Miranda Thomas mentioned). Perhaps she disguised herself as someone else?

Dearest Kate,

I am positively eaten up with envy. Dancing *every* dance at Almack's! What did Aunt Charlotte say? Oh, I *wish* I were there to see! The Mysterious Marquis sounds quite intriguing, which I suppose is what he wants. I feel compelled to point out that he *did* find out who you are in order to say thank you, and I cannot think of any ulterior motive for him to have done so. I quite agree, however, that he should have given you more of an explanation. After all, this Miranda person very nearly poisoned you instead of him; the least he could do is tell you why. Particularly as he seems to think she will be interested in you now that you have danced with him. Personally, I do not see that this follows at all logically, but I suppose the Marquis expects you to take his word for it. Men are like that; they think all females are like Georgy and Dorothea—sweet, biddable creatures who aren't worth explaining things to because they won't understand above one word in seven.

I may be doing Dorothea an injustice in saying that; she is certainly not so goose-witted as Georgy. She lacks a certain spirit, however—*she* would never suggest slipping out after midnight to kidnap a goat from Squire Bryant! I am quite out of patience with her today. You remember I said in my last letter that I would ask her about Oliver's infatuation? Well, Wednesday, when we were quite private, I broached the subject as delicately as I could, and Dorothea immediately burst into tears! She refused to explain this extraordinary behavior, much less discuss her attraction for the male population of the county. The only bit of information I could gather was that she does not have a *tendresse* for Oliver, which is just as well, under the circumstances.

Perhaps I am growing restless. The stirring tales of your adventures in London simply do not compare with my quiet life at Rushton Manor. I have consoled myself with concocting a plan to force Aunt Charlotte to get you a gown in a becoming color. It came about in the most fortunate manner! You see, yesterday it rained and Aunt Elizabeth decided that we should sort through some of the trunks in the attic. I was quite prepared to be bored silly. It is one thing to go through dusty old clothes and faded ribbons when one has someone to laugh with about how curious they look; it is another thing entirely to spend an afternoon cooped up in an attic with Aunt Elizabeth.

Just as we were preparing to go up, however, Mrs. Fitzwilliam called. Aunt Elizabeth sent me off to begin alone, while she had a cup of tea and a good gossip with Mrs. Fitz. (She did not say that was what she wanted, of course.) So I poked about in the trunks without interference for nearly an hour, and in doing so I found the most *stunning* silk shawl! (I believe it was Mama's.) It is rose-pink, with the most delicate embroidery and—but you will see for yourself soon enough.

For I am sending it to you, with a letter to Aunt Charlotte saying that Mama most *particularly* desired you to wear it for your first Season. Aunt Charlotte will not wonder at it, since she thinks I am caper-witted enough to have forgotten the shawl in the excitement of your leaving. And since a rose-pink shawl would look exceedingly odd with a blue dress, Aunt Charlotte will *have* to have a dress made for you in rose! I am sure you will be able to handle things from there.

Jack's picnic is tomorrow; I will write you all about it then.

⇾ 3 May

Well, it has been a day! I am inclined to think that it must match even the excitement of a day in London, though I do not currently have a basis for comparison. You will have to judge for yourself.

It began with Mary, the little upstairs maid who is so good about slipping me tea when Aunt Elizabeth has decided my character will be improved by an evening's fasting. I was trying to decide what to wear to Jack's picnic when she knocked at the door. She came in, looking upset, so of course I asked what was wrong.

"It's Mr. Oliver, Miss," she said. "That is, it's his room. Mrs. Gordon said I was to give it a proper clean, seeing as he's gone, and I found this under his mattress."

She handed me a little drawstring bag about half the size of my fist. It was made of leather, with a gold "O" embroidered on it in rather large stitches (the kind I use when I am trying to finish something quickly, that Aunt Elizabeth always makes me pick out and do over). I opened it and nearly gagged on the strong scent of herbs. I shook a little into my hand, but the leaves were so dried and crumbled I couldn't tell what any of them were. I could, however, see snippets of wavy brown hair mixed in with the herbs.

"I didn't mean to snoop, Miss," Mary went on. "But Miss Rushton's that strict, I didn't rightly know what she'd do if I said I'd found a charm-bag in Mr. Oliver's room. I was afraid I'd be turned off, Miss. So I come to you."

"You did quite right," I said. I shook the bits of herbs and hair carefully back into the bag and pulled the drawstring shut. "You don't happen to know what *kind* of charm-bag this is, do you?"

"No, Miss," Mary said, looking surprised.

"Then there's no need for you to be involved any further," I said briskly, hiding my disappointment. I wished very much that she *had* known what kind of charm-bag it was, for I haven't the slightest notion how one tells the differences among love charms, curses, protections, or blessings! The only thing I was reasonably sure of is that it wasn't the sort of charm-bag used by barren women who want a child—there would be no sense at all in anyone putting something like that in Oliver's room! "I will take care of this," I told her. "Don't speak of it to anyone else."

"Yes, Miss Cecy," Mary said, and went away looking somewhat relieved. I sat down on the bed with a plop, wondering how on earth a charm-bag had gotten into Oliver's room and what, if anything, I ought to do about it. It wouldn't be the least use to tell Papa; he would just look at it and nod and say that the Sumerians had a very similar sort of thing, only made of goatskin stuffed with clay and feathers, and isn't it interesting how such things change over the years. Aunt Elizabeth would probably have strong hysterics and insist on calling Oliver back from Town—you know how she feels about anything that smacks of magic, however faintly. And I am persuaded that calling Oliver home would be the worst possible thing to do. After all, whoever put the charm-bag in his room is *here*, not in Town. Unless, of course, Oliver did it himself, but I think this exceedingly unlikely. If the bag were his, he'd have taken it with him. Oliver may be nearly as hen-witted as Georgy, but he is not absentminded the way Papa is!

Which led me to the question of who *had* left the charm-bag in Oliver's room. At that point a rather frightening thought occurred to me, and I jumped up and tugged at my own bed. There was nothing under the mattress, however, and I am not sure whether I felt more relieved or disappointed. I shoved the bed back together (rather the worse for my exertions, I fear) and sat down on it again to think.

Who put the charm-bag in Oliver's bed? Papa wouldn't have bothered. Aunt Elizabeth—well, given her dislike of all things magical, I simply cannot picture it. *I* certainly didn't do it. As for the servants—Mary couldn't have, or she'd just have cleaned the room and left. Mrs. Gordon has been our housekeeper for years and enters into Aunt Elizabeth's sensibilities on everything, including magic, so she's unlikely. And no one else would have had the opportunity to go into Oliver's room.

I had just reached this point in my deliberations when Aunt Elizabeth knocked at the door to remind me to hurry, as it was almost time to leave. I jumped up and threw on the first thing that came to hand (my figured muslin walking dress, fortunately), shoved the charm-bag into my reticule, and dashed off to the picnic.

By the time our carriage reached Tarleton Hall, I had resolved to put the matter of the charm-bag out of my mind and enjoy the picnic. Lady Tarleton and Dorothea joined us (the disagreeable James, I was relieved to see, did not), and we went on to the lakeside. Patience was already there, firmly seated as far from the water's edge as she could manage. Her brother Jack was down by the lake with Robert Penwood and Martin De Lacey, messing about with the boats. All three of them abandoned their work as soon as we (or, rather, Dorothea) arrived, and came to greet us.

Jack had apparently decided that a picnic was not impressive enough (and, I suspect, that he would not be able to get Dorothea much to himself). He had therefore come up with the boats. Patience wasn't at all pleased, but she really couldn't do anything about it except refuse to ride in one. Robert offered to stay behind with her (and Aunt Elizabeth and Lady Tarleton), which left me with Martin. (Jack, of course, had Dorothea as a partner.)

The boat ride was quite pleasant, though it was rather disconcerting to have a partner whose head was constantly turned sideways. You would have thought that it was Martin's duty to chaperone Dorothea and Jack! This made our progress around the lake erratic, to say the least. I gave up trying to make conversation after the first few "Oh! Quite so" and "Umm, yes of course" responses, and concentrated on not being splashed by Martin's rowing.

We made it around the lake at last, and started back. As we neared the shore, I saw something moving in the bushes. "What's that?" I said without thinking.

"Umm, what?" said Martin, who had been watching Dorothea again.

"I thought I saw something in the bushes," I said.

"Probably a dog," Martin said without interest.

I could see it was no use talking to him, so I let him go back to Dorothea-gazing while I watched the bushes. Just before we landed, I distinctly saw a dark head pull back out of sight. I was stunned, Kate, for I was quite certain that the head belonged to none other than James Tarleton!

I did not say anything more to Martin, but as soon as I was safely out of the boat I announced that I intended to go for a walk. Martin offered (rather halfheartedly) to accompany me, but I told him I preferred to go alone. That brought Aunt Elizabeth down on me with a lecture about propriety, but as everyone else was staying by the lake with Dorothea, she eventually let me go.

As soon as I was out of sight, I circled around toward the bushes where I thought I had seen James Tarleton. (All of those years of sneaking about after Oliver and Robert came in very useful.) Sure enough, there he was, peering through a screen of bushes at the picnic. I was thinking so hard about an appropriate opening remark that I neglected to watch my feet, and trod on a twig.

James Tarleton whirled, and one hand went to his pocket. Then he recognized me, and his startled expression turned to a wary civility. "Miss Rushton," he said. "I fear you startled me."

All of the things I had been planning to say flew right out of my head. "What are you doing skulking about in these bushes and spying on us?" I demanded.

"I might ask you the same question," he replied with a smile. He pulled a little blue snuffbox from his pocket and opened it as he spoke. I blinked, for I have never seen such a brilliant blue as that box was. It positively hurt my eyes, Kate. I was the more surprised because Mr. Tarleton had not previously struck me as the sort of person to carry around oddities in vulgar colors. Upon reflection, however, I have concluded that someone who sneaks about in bushes in order to spy on his cousin is quite likely to have poorer taste than I had at first assumed.

"You aren't very good at skulking; I saw you from the boat," I said. "And I came to find out what you mean by it."

"I am sure your curiosity is very natural," he said. "But I'm afraid I am not at liberty to explain."

"I suppose you think I ought to consider it the most natural thing in the world to discover someone sneaking about in the bushes at a picnic," I said with some asperity.

Mr. Tarleton's lips twitched. "I don't believe I would go so far as that."

"Then tell me why you are spying on Dorothea!" I demanded.

All of the expression washed out of his face at once, and he shut the snuffbox with a sharp click. "What makes you sure it was Dorothea I was watching?" he said in a flat voice.

"Because it isn't the first time I've seen you watching her," I said. "And I think it is the outside of enough for you to ignore her at home and then turn around and spy on her behind her back." I am afraid I was not very clear, but by this time I was quite annoyed.

"So you have appointed yourself her champion," Mr.

Tarleton said. There was a bitter, mocking undercurrent to his voice, and his eyes were very cold and suspicious. "Out of the noblest of motives, I am sure. Or could it be that you hope for some of her leavings?" He glanced pointedly back at the picnic, where all the men clustered around Dorothea like flies around a honey pot.

"I *like* Dorothea," I said hotly. "She's just like Georgy."

His eyes narrowed. "And who is Georgy?"

"My cousin, Georgina Talgarth. She's beautiful, too, and all the boys fall in love with her and all the girls dislike her because of it, and it isn't her fault at all."

Mr. Tarleton blinked, and looked thoughtfully back toward the picnic. "It hadn't occurred to me that it might be unconscious," he said, half to himself. "But if that is the case . . ." His voice trailed off and he stood frowning, deep in thought, as though he had quite forgotten I was there. He was still holding the snuffbox, and he stroked the lid with one finger in an absentminded manner. There was a peacock enameled on the lid of the box, in bright blues and greens, which I thought was quite appropriate.

"I think you had better leave now, Mr. Tarleton," I said with as much firmness as I could manage. "I am sure you have a great deal to do at Tarleton Hall."

"Undoubtedly," Mr. Tarleton said. "However, I am in no hurry to return home."

"Go away, or I shall tell Lady Tarleton that you are spying on Dorothea," I snapped.

"Then I'll tell her that you arranged to meet me out here in the woods," he replied with maddening calm. "Assignations are not at all the thing for a young lady of quality."

"Oh!" I said, too furious to make sense. "You are—you are the most *unprincipled* man I have ever met!"

"Quite so," he said cordially. "Now, I suggest you return to your companions."

"And leave you here to spy on us?"

"Why not? You aren't planning to do anything . . . indiscreet, now, are you?"

I turned on my heel and stalked away, refusing to dignify that comment with a response. I spent the entire walk back to the picnic trying to think of something dreadful enough to be suitable for him, like frogs in his bed, and coming up with all the cutting remarks I ought to have used on him in the first place. When I got back, Aunt Elizabeth told me with approval that the walk had put some color in my cheeks.

You can imagine my consternation, therefore, when the discussion turned to Robert Penwood's planned excursion to Bedrick Hall and I learned that Robert had invited James Tarleton to accompany us! "Oh, no!" I said involuntarily.

"I beg your pardon?" said Lady Tarleton.

"I mean, I am persuaded that there must be some mistake," I said hastily. "It hardly seems that Mr. Tarleton would care for such an outing."

"I shall speak to him about it," Lady Tarleton said, and I

was forced to let the matter drop. After thinking about it for some time, however, I have decided that James Tarleton will probably find some excuse to avoid being a member of the party. I find this thought very comforting; I only wish I could be more certain of it.

The rest of the picnic passed without incident. Patience and I had a comfortable chat while Robert and Jack and Martin danced attendance on Dorothea. I found myself watching her (Dorothea, I mean) more closely than usual, and I must tell you that I do not think she enjoyed the attention she was receiving. You know how Georgy accepts it sweetly whenever people pay her compliments? Dorothea would just nod and turn the subject, or say an uncomfortable "Thank you."

We finished the picnic at last, and Aunt Elizabeth and I took Lady Tarleton and Dorothea back to Tarleton Hall. When we arrived, Lady Tarleton asked us to stop in for a moment, and Aunt Elizabeth accepted. Just inside, a footman handed Dorothea an express letter, with an apologetic look at Lady Tarleton. Dorothea opened it, and no sooner had she finished reading it than she burst into tears.

Lady Tarleton whisked us into the morning room, but not before the commotion brought a great many people into the hall. We were so taken up with soothing Dorothea that we did not at first perceive that the morning room was already occupied—by none other than James Tarleton. He, of course, did not announce his presence, but waited until Lady

Tarleton led Dorothea to a seat. *Then* he stood up. Lady Tarleton, of course, took no notice; she was busy with Dorothea in any case. I glared at him, but it was hardly the time or place for any of the cutting comments I wanted to make, so I said nothing at all.

"There, now, child, it's all right," Lady Tarleton told Dorothea. "Now, what is it?"

"It's . . . it's . . . it's Mama!" Dorothea said. She waved the crumpled letter, which was still clutched tightly in her hand. "She's coming here!"

"Well, there's no need to make such a piece of work of it," Lady Tarleton said. "Goodness knows, we can manage a guest or two on short notice."

"She's going to make me go to London," Dorothea said tragically.

Lady Tarleton pressed her lips together. "Miranda never did have any sense," she muttered, then in a louder voice she said, "Time enough to discuss that when she arrives. Did she say when that would be?"

Just then Aunt Elizabeth poked me and we said our adieus, it being clearly *not* the time to stay for tea. As I left, I noticed Mr. Tarleton watching me with *such* an expression—partly thoughtful, partly suspicious, and altogether annoyed. I would have given my best gloves to know just what he was thinking of then.

So that is my tale. I am altogether exhausted; fortunately, it will be a few days before Robert's expedition to

Bedrick Hall, so I shall have time to recover. I shall also have time to consider what I ought to do about Oliver, the charm-bag, and James Tarleton's spying.

Do send news of how Oliver is faring; I find I am growing quite nervous about him. And if you have any advice, or any idea how I can discover what *sort* of charm-bag was hidden in Oliver's bed, pray tell me at once! I am positively distracted.

Your busy cousin,
Cecy

5 May 1817
11 Berkeley Square, London

Dearest Cecy,

Your letter and parcel arrived this morning as Georgina and I were sitting at breakfast with Aunt Charlotte, drinking cold stewed tea and wishing our toast was not always cold before it reached the table. (This is only one of the ways in which London does *not* surpass Rushton in terms of comfort.) The post arrived as Georgy was coaxing for the dozenth time to be allowed to have a domino and to go to Vauxhall in it. Aunt Charlotte is violently opposed to both these ambitions. (Indeed, I find it hard to tell which she objects to more.)

Mere words cannot express my gratitude for the shawl.

It is quite a brilliant scheme, and one which Georgy entered into with enthusiasm. In fact, with her help, I'm sure I shall have quite a presentable dress in time for Lady Haseltine's drum. She has given me a pair of pearl eardrops to wear with it as a sign of encouragement. I think the dancing at Almack's took a great weight off her mind. She is a shatter-wit, but it must be tiresome to be going everywhere with a sister who is one's complete opposite.

I have been practicing the accompaniment for two Italian songs that Georgina has been learning. She finds the melody simple enough but cannot seem to remember the proper order of the lines. One more good thing about Essex is that no one notices such things there. Here in London the audiences are more exacting. Not that the *Haut Ton* displays any particular appreciation for music—or the Italian language—but the young ladies are very competitive and delight in finding fault with one another's accomplishments.

I have encountered the Marquis of Schofield twice in the past few days. First, in St. James's Park, where Oliver and I went walking so that Oliver could observe what other young men are wearing. We met on the footbridge across the long duck pond. The footbridge is a pleasing structure, Oriental in design, very delicate and fanciful, and too narrow for three people to walk abreast. Thus, when the Marquis reached the center of the span as Oliver and I walked from the opposite direction, he paused and greeted me, then stepped civilly aside to let me pass. I returned his greeting and introduced Oliver. The Marquis listened politely to my commonplaces about the weather, but I thought I detected some amusement in his reserve. At first I assumed the wind had done something to my hair. Then I realized Oliver was not merely standing, mute as a block, at my elbow, but was staring—positively gaping—at the Marquis.

The Marquis glanced from me to Oliver and said, almost too solicitously, "Are you feeling quite well, Mr. Rushton?"

"Oh—quite well, thank you," replied Oliver, coloring up. "Only—I was admiring the way you tie your cravat. What do you call that fashion?"

The Marquis regarded Oliver with bland composure. "I call it 'the way I tie my cravat.'"

Already blushing fiercely, Oliver began a soft, incoherent gobble of apology.

The Marquis took his leave of us with automatic civility and crossed the bridge, leaving me with divided emotions. On the one hand, he was shockingly rude to Oliver. On the other, I have often been shockingly rude to Oliver myself, and I understand the impulse. Certainly I have been bored time out of mind by his discourses on hair *à la Brutus, à la Sappho,* and *à la Penthesilee,* and on neckcloths twisted in styles called the Waterfall, the Corinthian, and the Nonsuch. Often he has corrected me with great severity when I got the names wrong. But pleased as I am that the Marquis seems to have no more patience for such fripperies than I, it was wrong of him to make his feelings so plain. Still, I imagine that when a man is born to a title, it is only to be expected that he assumes lesser folks' feelings to be of little importance in comparison to his own.

Then, two nights ago, I went in to dinner at Lady Muker's with Michael Aubrey and George and Alice Grenville. When we were seated, I glanced up to see that the Marquis was across the table from me. He saw me see him and gave me a brilliant smile, which caused Lady Muker to nudge Lady Grenville and lift her eyebrows. I gave the Marquis an awkward little nod of recognition and fixed my attention on the lobster bisque and George Grenville's conversation.

George was telling me about a particularly interesting horse race he happened to see in Derbyshire once. During the final furlongs my mind wandered and I glanced up. The Marquis was attending to the conversation of Mrs. Talbot, the lady to his right, and so presented only his profile to me. As George crossed the finish line, I allowed myself to study that profile.

It is curious how the least amiable people are sometimes the most interesting in appearance. The odious Marquis has regular enough features, but his appearance is set quite out of the common way by two things. First, his nose, which is not disfiguringly large, but aquiline, giving him the look of an Italian despot on one of the Renaissance coins your Papa showed us last year. Second, his eyes, which are dark and bright and altogether too knowing. But don't think I was staring at him. I promise you I was taking my soup in a perfectly unexceptionable way when he glanced up at me and gave me another brilliant smile. I nodded again, even more awkwardly, and devoted myself to soup and steeplechasing until the soup plates were removed.

I think his thanks to me were in the nature of a warning, but I would give a great deal to know how he learned so precisely what passed in that very odd garden and whether, should I go back to the hall, I would find that little door again.

James Tarleton's behavior is wretched, of course, but I'm sure you'll keep a close watch on him at the maze. There is something particularly infuriating about seeing a man behave rudely out of spite and a desire to amuse himself.

Please tell me if Dorothea's mother can possibly be the white-haired lady the Marquis referred to as Miranda. If I had her for a mother, I would burst into tears, too. Despite the hair, which she could not wear powdered without attracting a great deal of remark, she ought to be recognizable, if only for those eyes, the blackest, coldest, hardest eyes I've ever beheld. And if it should be the same Miranda, Cecelia, *beware*. More than ever, I find I wish you were here in London, if only to prevent you from meeting that woman. Or that I were home in Rushton, where things never used to be so lively unless we made them so ourselves.

It is curious you should have remembered that Hollydean boy. He is seventeen now and just as horrid as ever. We met him at tea at Lady Haseltine's. He's been sent down from university already (something to do with gaming debts), and now he and his dreadful tutor, Mr. Strangle, are on the Town, at least to the extent of coming to tea at the most unlikely houses. I was seated between them and had to listen to them in counterpoint, prosing on in a very boastful manner about the Grand Tour of the continent they mean to make one day when they find a ship fine enough to meet their exacting standards. Mr. Strangle is as tall as the Reverend Fitzwilliam and about half as wide. He kept leaning across me to see what sandwiches were left on the plate, and pressing his bony knee against my skirt. Really, he is just the sort of tutor one would expect Frederick Hollydean to have. (And if Frederick construes one more Latin tag for me, breathing crumbs into my ear as he does so, I shall bite him myself. *Dear* Canniba.)

As ever,
Kate

P.S. I've just remembered. Didn't Mrs. Foley (the game-keeper's wife) sew a charm-bag for Martin De Lacey when he was afraid he had yellow fever and wouldn't be able to ride in his first hunt? Of course, it turned out to be chicken pox instead, but maybe she'd know about things???

P.P.S. Who do you suppose was leaving Lady Haseltine's just as we arrived? Sir Hilary Bedrick, who sends his best regards to Aunt Elizabeth and your Papa. Investiture in the Royal College of Wizards is attended by a mighty social schedule, so his time in London is much taken up. But he was perfectly charming to us and regretted he had not time to pay a call upon "such near neighbors" as we have been. Sometimes London has the feel of a very small town indeed.

8 May 1817
Rushton Manor, Essex

Dearest Kate,

If you found *my* letter disturbing, only think how I felt about yours! I had not considered that your Miranda and Dorothea's mother might be the same woman—your Miranda does not sound at all like a Mrs. Griscomb, or even like a Lady Griscomb. But then, I suppose people do not have to look like their names. Also, I *cannot* be easy in my mind about Oliver, despite the fact that, from his behavior with the odious Marquis, I conclude that the charm-bag I found in his bed has not had the slightest effect on him.

I did manage to talk to Mrs. Foley about charm-bags, in a very general sort of way. She was not much help, as she seems to have the impression that I was interested in making up a love charm to retrieve one of the boys who has fallen under Dorothea's spell. (As if I would! Robert Penwood is the only one who is worth a farthing, and frankly I think he would be far better suited with Dorothea than with me. If, of course, he were thinking of being suited, which I doubt.) Anyway, she gave me a good deal of advice on making up a love charm, and even mentioned that some of the "great folk" have written books about such things. That gave me a perfectly splendid idea, so I thanked her very kindly indeed and went home to cogitate.

By yesterday morning, I had worked out all the necessary details, for you must know, Kate, that yesterday was Robert Penwood's excursion to Bedrick Hall. The weather was quite perfect, sunny and a little cool, which gave me the excuse to wear the shawl Aunt Charlotte gave me for my last birthday, the one with the pockets on the inside. It is, of course, blue, and so I had to wear one of the walking-dresses of Georgy's that Aunt Elizabeth had made over for me when she was having that fit of economy last fall. I did not look anything like my best, but it was in a good cause, and besides, I was quite sure that all eyes would be on Dorothea rather than me.

Imagine my chagrin, therefore, when we arrived at Bedrick Hall to discover that James Tarleton had accepted Robert's invitation after all, and was to make up one of the party! I suppose he felt that it would be easier to spy on us from inside the group, so to speak. It was the outside of enough! Not only was I going to have to deal with a thoroughly unprincipled, spying man, but I was going to have to do so knowing that I looked a complete dowd.

To make matters worse, it was Mr. Tarleton who handed me down from the carriage. He studied me the way Cook studies the joints the butcher sends, and I was quite sure that he could tell that my gown was made-over (and last season's style into the bargain!). I found it most uncomfortable, and I did not even have the consolation of a properly cutting remark, for as I had not expected to see him, I had not thought anything out in advance. Next time, I promise you, Kate, I will not be so caught out.

I moved away from him as quickly as I could and paid my respects to Lady Tarleton. Then I went over to Dorothea, who did not look at all happy. I asked her what the matter was, and she whispered, "Mama is coming for me tomorrow! And, oh, Cecy, I do not want to go to London!"

"Not want to go to London!" I said in astonishment. "But I thought you told Lady Tarleton that you were anxious for your Season!"

"That was when Lady Tarleton was to bring me out, and I thought you would go with me," Dorothea said sadly. "But now I shall be in London all alone."

"Don't be a peagoose," I said. "The whole point of a Season in London is that one *cannot* be all alone."

"You know what I mean!" Dorothea said. She was practically in tears. "I don't know anyone in London!"

"You'll meet people soon enough," I said, and I forebore to add that with her looks she could hardly help it.

"You don't understand about Mama," Dorothea said.

We had walked a little away from the others, so I whisked her around the corner of the main house and found a bench. "All right, then, sit down and explain to me," I said.

"Oh, I couldn't!" Dorothea said, and turned quite white. "She'd find out."

"How?" I said. "*I* certainly won't tell her."

But all Dorothea would say was that her Mama is horrid and hateful. Apparently she is determined that Dorothea will marry some specific but unnamed peer (whom Dorothea paints as a cold-blooded ogre). Dorothea appears to think that there is some sinister scheme behind this determination and that her Mama will call on a variety of unprincipled friends to assist in achieving her ends. I suspect that she thinks this solely because she has formed a *tendre* for someone else, but the whole conversation was so dreadfully confused that I could not be sure of anything. Finally, I told her to call on you when she reaches London (assuming, of course, that her Mama really will carry her off without any notice at all, as Dorothea appears to fear).

We were interrupted by Robert Penwood, come to collect us to begin the tour, and for the next hour or so we all made polite comments about the beauty of the gardens, the wonderful views, etc. James Tarleton behaved with excruciating correctness in spite of the insipid conversation, which I am sure must have bored him to tears. I think boredom only his due for foisting himself on us as he did.

Finally we reached the part of the tour I had been waiting for—the maze. Aunt Elizabeth and Lady Tarleton begged off, but the rest of us went cheerfully in, and in a very short time we were all lost among the hedges. I let the others get ahead of me, and as soon as they were out of sight I headed straight for the shortcut. (You remember, the little gap in the far corner that we always used to use to beat Jack Everslee to the center of the maze.) It was still there, and I used it to get out of the maze instead of going farther in.

So in no time at all I was standing at the far side of Sir Hilary's maze, free to do as I pleased for at least an hour before anyone would come looking for me. I went up to the house at once (being careful to keep the hedges between me and the place where we had left Aunt Elizabeth and Lady Tarleton), and blushingly explained to the footman who answered the door that I would like to use the necessary. He was quite taken aback, poor man (I don't think it had ever occurred to him that Young Ladies of Quality ever needed such plebeian artifacts). He called the housekeeper, a Mrs. Porter, who conducted me to the proper place. She was a motherly type who was quite receptive to my suggestion that a glass of lemonade would be more than welcome, after running about the gardens in the heat all day.

The point of this whole charade was, of course, to be left alone in Sir Hilary's library. Mrs. Porter eventually did so, whereupon I made a rapid survey of Sir Hilary's books, looking for something that appeared to have information on charm-bags. At first, I was a bit daunted by the sheer number of volumes; I had no notion that a wizard was required to do so very much reading! I soon realized, however, that most of the books were the ordinary sort that one would find in any well-kept library, and after a brief search I discovered the section I wanted. I was quite prepared to take several, if need be (the pockets in that shawl are quite spacious), but I discovered a slim red book titled *The Theory and Practice of Charms: Being an Inquiry into the Making of Bags, Boxes, and the Like by Country Witches and Their Ilk.* I tucked it into my shawl and was about to take the book beside it when I heard someone at the door. I straightened hastily, thinking it was Mrs. Porter with my lemonade, and turned to say something innocuous about the number of books Sir Hilary has.

It was, of course, not Mrs. Porter at all, but James Tarleton, who ought to have been safely lost in the maze with Robert, Dorothea, Patience, and Jack. "What are you doing here?" I demanded.

"I believe I am the one who should ask you that," Mr. Tarleton said. His eyes were very hard and suspicious, and he looked exceedingly angry.

"That is none of your affair," I said.

"Indeed." He strolled over to the bookcase and began studying the section I had been looking at. I backed away as he came forward, not wanting to stand at all close to him. I was very glad I had done so, for he took one look at the books and turned to me, looking more thunderous than ever. "Just what is your game, young woman?"

"I do not have the slightest idea what you are talking about," I said with dignity.

"No? You take up with Dorothea Griscomb the moment she arrives, aid and abet her in all her schemes, and you expect me to believe you do it simply because she reminds you of some cousin of yours?"

"It is quite true," I told him.

He gave a bark of laughter that was not at all pleasant. "Too late, Miss Rushton. I'm not so gullible that I can be caught twice with a smoothly told tale. I might have believed you once, but not after I saw your reaction to the news that Miranda Griscomb is coming to Tarleton Hall, and not now that I find you poking through Sir Hilary's magic books. I'm afraid you're out of luck there; he keeps the really important ones in his laboratory, like most good wizards."

"I was simply admiring Sir Hilary's collection," I said, retreating around the end of a low couch. I felt better with something between me and that angry expression.

Mr. Tarleton snorted. "It won't wash, my girl. Miranda and Hilary have had a falling-out, I suppose, and she's taking advantage of all this to have you snoop through his things."

By this time I was quite outraged. "I was *not* snooping," I said. "How dare you accuse me of any such thing? If anyone is snooping, it is you, and I very much wish Squire Bryant had *another* goat, for I think you deserve it!"

Mr. Tarleton ignored this completely. "What is Miranda up to?" he demanded.

He was starting toward me, and in quite a menacing manner, when a knock at the library door announced the housekeeper, at long last bringing my lemonade. I took it gratefully and downed it with far more speed than was strictly ladylike (to keep her in the room; I did *not* want to be alone with James Tarleton again!). Mr. Tarleton took snuff while I drank; it is a habit he seems to resort to when under stress. (And I must say that I am still amazed that someone as well turned out in other ways as Mr. Tarleton would use such a vulgarly ostentatious snuffbox as that green-and-blue enameled one he carries. I suppose he must be sentimentally attached to it for some reason.)

When Mr. Tarleton and I were quite finished snubbing each other with magnificent unconcern, Mrs. Porter escorted us to the side door. This let out onto the veranda where Aunt Elizabeth and Lady Tarleton were sitting. Aunt Elizabeth was quite surprised to see us together, and coming from the house instead of the maze, but Mr. Tarleton passed it off with a remark about my having been overcome with the heat. Aunt Elizabeth looked at me suspiciously, for she knows I never swoon and am quite fond of warm weather, but she did not say anything, and the rest of the day passed off without further incident.

I was relieved to reach home with my pilfered book safe (do not scold, Kate; I shall return it to Sir Hilary anonymously, by post, as soon as I am finished with it, and how else was I to find out anything about charm-bags?). I spent the evening reading it, and was quite impressed with how complex a charm-bag really is. Unfortunately, it is very hard to identify the type of charm unless one knows what herbs were used. I shall spend part of tomorrow trying to sort out the herbs in the bag Mary found in Oliver's room, but one dried bit of leaf looks very much like another, so I have little hope of success. The whole matter makes me dreadfully uneasy; I have taken to cleaning out my hairbrush every morning and burning the residue. I hope to finish Sir Hilary's book tomorrow evening; in the afternoon, I intend to pay a call on Dorothea and see whether I can get a peek at her Mama.

Yours ever,
Cecy

10 May 1817
11 Berkeley Square, London

My dearest Cecy,

I'm afraid I've made a dreadful mull of it this time. I've told Aunt Charlotte that Oliver's gone back to Rushton for a few days, just on business for Uncle. And, of course, he may have, and oh, *dear,* how I wish he might have, but really it is just another bouncer of mine. But I had to think of something, because he's gone missing.

I do hope you can read my handwriting. I skinned my palm and even though it is much better this morning it makes it hard to hold the pen quite steady.

It was in Vauxhall Gardens I last saw him, and that was my dear sister's fault entirely. We had gone to dinner at the Grenvilles' and were meant to go from there to the opera with Alice Grenville and her twin brothers. But no sooner was the meal over than Alice Grenville and Georgina swept me upstairs, where they had dominoes for the three of us— and George and Andrew escorted us not to the opera but to Vauxhall, without paying the slightest attention to a word I said. (I wanted to see that opera particularly. It was the last performance of *I Dilletanti*.)

Because I knew perfectly well that I would get the blame for the entire expedition, I was in no mood to be pleased, but I admit Vauxhall is pretty enough. I doubt you'll have the chance to see it for yourself next Season, since it is *nearly* as vulgar as Aunt Charlotte said, so I'll just describe the place as best I can.

Vauxhall is a large garden with carefully arranged thickets and sandy paths. In the heart of the garden are boxes with flimsy chairs where one may sit to watch other people promenade about by the light of paper lanterns, or dance to a little orchestra playing popular airs (ever so slightly flat). As we entered the lantern-lit clearing, Alice Grenville declared there were nightingales in the thickets. So no sooner were we in the box George and Andrew procured for us than Georgina went off with Andrew to search for one, leaving me with Alice and George. George insisted on ordering rack punch and slivered ham, despite the perfectly enormous meal we had just consumed at Grenville House.

Well, of course, after a quarter of an hour, I expected to catch a glimpse of Georgina among the crowd walking past. I was a bit concerned for her, alone with her twin. By the greatest misfortune, Oliver chose that moment to arrive in pursuit of Georgy. He pounced on me and demanded to know what I was thinking of to let life in the Ton go so dreadfully to Georgina's head. I was taken aback for a moment but replied at once in a calm voice that I've almost grown to hate (for I seldom know what I'm going to say in it, and sometimes it comes out with the most dreadful lies, always in the same plausible tone) that Georgy and I had made a wager that she masked could dance with more men than I unmasked. My voice went on quite pleasantly to say that if he couldn't keep from interfering in a simple sportin' wager, he should go home and get Aunt Charlotte to make him a posset. Otherwise, he'd best sit down and join us.

"A simple sportin' wager," he huffed at me. "I should think you would know better than to jest about such things with a member of the family. And if you're not jesting, you must be mad."

"I suppose I must be," I agreed, "but at least I am not

bacon-brained enough to preach a sermon in Vauxhall Gardens."

You may imagine Oliver's response. It was a masterpiece of priggish indignation that, reduced to its bare essentials, amounted to an accusation that we were having fun without him. When he was quite finished, he called me a rag-mannered chit and marched off to find Georgina, which, I own, I was hoping he would do for quite some time.

I apologized to Alice and George and went back to craning my neck to look for Georgy.

An hour went by, Cecy, and a worse hour I have yet to pass, in London or out of it. I saw Oliver in the distance twice, but there wasn't a sign of Georgy. As you may imagine, I grew worried and then more worried, until finally Alice and the twin agreed to stroll with me in the direction of the illuminations. After all, Alice told me bracingly, it was possible Oliver simply didn't recognize Georgy in her domino.

We walked down a winding path and reached a little Greek temple lit with paper lanterns. It seemed a good idea to separate and search the shrubbery round about. I took a wrong step somehow, and found myself in a thicket with no temple in sight and no reply to my call. After a moment of uneasiness, it struck me what seemed wrong. The shadowy coppice was altogether silent. No nightingale sang, nor could I hear any faint strain of the orchestra.

Puzzled and a little alarmed, I stood in the dark, the flat

of my hand resting on the trunk of the tree before me. I was struck with a sudden sense of unreasonable apprehension (in addition to my perfectly reasonable apprehension, common to any girl foolish enough to lose herself at night in the woods of Vauxhall). You may therefore imagine my reaction when a hand covered mine and held me there, palm against the smooth bark.

"I thought I told you to stay in well-lit ballrooms," said Thomas Schofield in my ear.

I managed to stop my scream before it got to my lips. After a moment I said quite evenly, "Ill met by moonlight, my dear Marquis." I admit this was not exactly brilliant, but I think that under the circumstances I did fairly well.

"On the contrary, my dear half-wit," he replied, "for your sake, we are very well met. But a very little longer and you'd not have left this wood for quite some time." Right hand over my right hand, he moved to stand behind me. "Hold out your left hand," he said.

"Stop that," I said. "What on earth are you doing?"

"Rescuing you, silly," he said. "Hold out your left hand."

Cautiously, I did so. He took it in his and stood so close behind me that I have no doubt that but for the hood of the silken domino I wore, I could have felt his breath stir my hair. The fingers of his left hand laced with mine and he drew our clasped hands forward until our fingertips rested very lightly against my forehead, as though to shield my eyes.

I stood straight and still, trying to ignore his proximity, as he held me circled in his arms. For the Marquis's part, he seemed to ignore me in return. In addition to the oddity of our stance, he began to mutter. His voice was a very soft steady repetition of words I could not catch, a droning chant that almost had a tune. After about four bars of this, I realized I could hear the orchestra again, a faint distant music through the trees.

"There," said the Marquis. "Nothing elegant, but it ought to do the trick." His right hand still on mine, he clasped hard and pried it off the bark of the tree. And indeed, when it did come free, it felt to me as though I left every bit of skin on my palm stuck to the bark. It hurt like blazes and I would have liked very much to exclaim aloud, but I did not wish to do so before the odious Marquis. He kept my hand clasped firmly in his right while he fumbled in his pocket with his left. After a moment he produced a silk handkerchief and did a fairly clumsy job of bandaging my hand with it, muttering under his breath the while.

Perhaps it was the muttering or perhaps the silk handkerchief, but in a few minutes the pain eased and I was able to say, "I can't think how you knew I was here."

"Luckily for you," he said, "you shed hairpins the way Hansel and Gretel shed crumbs. I followed your trail." He pressed a half dozen hairpins into the palm of my left hand. "Now let us return to light, safety, and society."

He led me out of the thicket back to the little temple, and we found ourselves in the ring of lamplight. In the center of the ring were both Grenville twins, Alice Grenville, Frederick Hollydean, and Georgina, who had her head on Alice's shoulder, sobbing lustily.

I glanced back at Thomas Schofield to find him gazing down his nose at me in a most annoying way. "What's happened?" I demanded. "Is she hurt?"

"I suggest you ask her," he replied. "I do so hate to intrude in a family squabble."

"Truly," Georgina was saying, between sniffs and sobs that made the Grenville twins look thunderously upon Frederick Hollydean, "I never meant to flirt with all of you. I never meant to flirt with *any* of you. I only meant to make Oliver angry. And now it's all gone wrong, for I sent him a note telling him I would be here and he didn't even bother to come rescue me from the consequences of my folly."

"But Oliver is here," I said briskly. "I sent him after you. I can't imagine what's keeping him. He was quite angry enough to suit even you, Georgina."

Georgy lifted her head and regarded me with reproach. "Kate, where have you *been?*"

I looked back at Thomas but the wretch was gone, melted back into the shrubbery. If he guessed what the rest of that particular squabble would be like, I can't blame him. If I'd known, I'd have gone slinking off myself. At the end of Georgina's tirade I was finally able to distract her (for she seemed strangely eager to forget her behavior by complaining of mine) by asking, "Yes, but where's Oliver?"

And no one knew. We searched the gardens until the lamplighters came to put out the lanterns, without success. The Grenvilles brought us home so late Aunt Charlotte had dozed off in her chair beside the door, so we were able to avoid her first wrath. But now we are no better off, for I am confined to my room and we cannot send anyone to search for Oliver without giving the entire business away.

It's all the most dreadful muddle, and I'm sure I have quite a thousand other things to tell you but I can't think of a thing but poor Oliver. I'm so worried I could scream, and I can't betray more than faint concern lest I set Georgina off into tears again.

I can't help but wonder if Aunt Charlotte allowed me to have a bedroom all to myself expressly so she could lock me up when I was disobedient. Only think how difficult it would be for her to confine me to my room if I still shared with Georgy.

Believe me, I shall write the instant I have any news. Meanwhile, do try not to go mad with concern. It would be quite foolish for all three of us to fuss ourselves into fits when none of us can do anything.

Love,
Kate

Dearest Kate,

Miranda Griscomb is *just* as dreadful as Dorothea says she is, and though I am not *perfectly* certain she is your Miranda, I do not have the least difficulty in believing that she would try to poison people with chocolate.

She arrived yesterday while I was taking tea with Dorothea and Lady Tarleton. They were awaiting her arrival, of course; in fact, she was two days later than her letter had led them to expect. When we heard the carriage drive up, Dorothea turned quite white. A few minutes later, the footman threw open the sitting room door and announced Mrs. Griscomb.

She *swept* into the room, Kate, looking for all the world as if she were returning to her own house after a morning's shopping instead of arriving at Tarleton Hall after goodness knows how long in a traveling coach. I do not know how she achieved such an effect, for she is quite short and, considering matters dispassionately, not at all imposing. When she is present, however, it is not possible to consider matters dispassionately. I believe it is because she has what Aunt Elizabeth refers to as a *forceful* personality. It does not hurt in the least that she is so prodigious elegant that she makes even Lady Tarleton seem a dowd. I cannot picture her with her hair powdered, but her eyes certainly fit your description—hard and cold and very dark.

In any case, there she was, looking down her nose at all of us. Lady Tarleton presented me, then asked if Mrs. Griscomb would like a cup of tea, in the sort of polite tone that means one would really rather she didn't. Mrs. Griscomb, of course, accepted. I was strongly tempted to ask whether she wouldn't prefer chocolate instead, but I restrained myself. Under the circumstances, it would have been an entirely goose-witted thing to do.

"Rushton," murmured Mrs. Griscomb as she seated herself on the sofa, where she could watch all of us at once. "Surely I have heard that name before. Did we meet in London?"

"I'm afraid that isn't possible," I said politely. "I have never been to London. Perhaps you are thinking of Papa; his histories are very well thought of in certain circles."

"I daresay." Mrs. Griscomb turned to look at Dorothea, apparently dismissing me from her mind as unworthy of notice. (I must own, Kate, that I felt unreasonably relieved.) "Are your trunks ready, my dear?" she asked Dorothea.

"N-no, Mama," Dorothea said in a scared little voice.

"Miranda, you can't mean to carry the child off at once!" Lady Tarleton said, sounding shocked. "It is quite impossible."

"Nonsense," Mrs. Griscomb said coolly. "Go up and finish your packing, Dorothea, and don't dawdle. We will not reach Brentwood tonight as it is."

"My dear Miranda, you cannot be serious," Lady Tarleton said sharply. "You must stay the night, at least."

"Are you concerned with what the local gossips will say?" Mrs. Griscomb asked. "I assure you, it does not concern me in the least. And Dorothea will be in London, making her curtsey to Society, so it cannot matter to her what opinions are in Rushton."

"But you cannot mean to present Dorothea now!" Lady Tarleton said. "The Season is half over! Have you no regard for Dorothea's prospects?"

"I am quite capable of taking care of Dorothea's prospects," Mrs. Griscomb said. She favored Lady Tarleton with an extremely cold smile. "More so than you may think. Dorothea comes to London with me, this very day."

"I—I would rather stay here, Mama," Dorothea put in. "At Tarleton Hall, I mean."

Everyone looked at her in surprise. "You are being ridiculous, Dorothea," Mrs. Griscomb said sharply. "Anyone would think you did not wish to be presented."

"I don't wish it!" Dorothea said, and burst into tears. I set my teacup down at once and did my best to soothe her, but she was quite overset. Miranda Griscomb just sat watching us with a stiff smile and a tiny frown line between her eyebrows.

"Really, Miranda," Lady Tarleton said, and stopped. She looked at me as though she had just realized I was still there. Which was probably exactly what had happened, for I very much doubt that she would have argued so openly with Mrs. Griscomb had she remembered my presence. I took the opportunity to suggest that Dorothea and I retire until Dorothea was more composed and, perhaps, packed. This found favor with both ladies, so the two of us departed with great relief on all sides.

I accompanied Dorothea up to her room, where she gradually became calmer. To be quite accurate, she stopped crying and simply sniffed dolefully into a handkerchief. Though I certainly sympathized with Dorothea (and, after all, Kate, my own hopes to join her for a Season next year were quite as cut up as hers), I could not see that anything was being gained by continued weeping.

"Dorothea, do try to control yourself," I said. "It is too bad, but perhaps Lady Tarleton will be able to persuade your Mama to see reason."

"She is not my Mama!" Dorothea said passionately.

"Not your Mama?" I said. "But—"

"She is my Stepmama, but she pretends to be my Mama and makes me call her so," Dorothea said. "And, oh, how I wish Papa had not made his fortune in India, for I am sure that is the only reason she married him, and if she hadn't we could be comfortable!"

"I quite agree that she is an odious woman and you would be better off without her," I said, "but I cannot think that you would be at all comfortable if your Papa had not got a fortune. At least, rented lodgings with leaky roofs and no servants and having to make over your gowns has never sounded comfortable to me, and that is the sort of thing that happens to people with no fortune. Unless, of course, you became a housemaid or a governess, but that's not much better."

"Anything would be better than Miranda!" Dorothea said.

I had a strong inclination to agree with her, but I saw that it would only send her back into the mopes, so instead I said, "Well, but one must be practical, after all. Do *try* to stop crying, Dorothea, and let us try to think of something."

"It will not be the least use," Dorothea said gloomily. "She is going to force me to go to London and marry that horrid Marquis, and I shall be miserable for the rest of my life!"

I was struck by a sudden horrid suspicion. "What Marquis?" I said.

"The Marquis of Schofield," Dorothea sniffed, confirming my worst fears.

I sat very quietly for a few moments, while Dorothea reiterated her passionate desire for an early death and her equally passionate certainty that she was doomed to a long and miserable life. I cannot see why, if Miranda Griscomb dislikes the Marquis of Schofield enough to poison him with chocolate, she would be willing to have her stepdaughter married to him, but Dorothea was quite positive on this point. Dorothea, of course, has no desire whatever to be married to the Marquis.

"But do consider, Dorothea," I said at last. "If you marry the Marquis, Miranda will not be able to order you about any longer. And you will have a great position as well, which Aunt Elizabeth says is most important in spite of being Vain and Worldly."

"I don't want to marry the Marquis! I want to marry Robert!" And Dorothea burst into tears again.

"Robert? You mean, Robert *Penwood*?" I said numbly. Dorothea immediately gave me to understand that it was indeed so, and embarked on a list of his excellent qualities that made Mrs. Radcliffe's heroes seem insipid by comparison. I let her talk, as it seemed to do her good and it gave me time to think. Robert is nice enough, certainly, but I find it difficult to see how he could engender such depth of feeling in Dorothea. Still, there is no accounting for tastes.

"Does Robert reciprocate your affection?" I asked, cutting off her panegyric.

"I believe so—that is, he has always been most truly a gentleman," Dorothea said, blushing.

"In that case, we must clearly do something," I told her.

"There is nothing to be done," Dorothea said, reverting

to gloom. "Mama will force me to marry the Marquis, and I will never see Robert again!"

"That is a great piece of nonsense," I said impatiently. "For one thing, your Stepmama cannot possibly make the Marquis of Schofield offer for you if he does not wish to. And from what I have heard of him, I cannot think he would wish to."

It occurred to me as I said this that my sentiment was not as tactfully expressed as it might have been, but Dorothea did not appear to notice. "Oh, do you really think so?" she said, and her face brightened momentarily. Then she frowned again. "But Miranda will make him offer for me somehow, I know it."

"Miranda cannot bully everyone into doing as she likes," I said in exasperation. "The thing to do is for us to make sure that whatever plans she makes go astray."

Dorothea showed signs of weeping again and insisted that Miranda's plans are impossible to overset. It took me a deal of time to persuade her otherwise, but at last I got her calmed down enough to discuss matters more intelligently. I thought at first of manufacturing some excuse to keep her at Tarleton Hall, but I quickly saw that it would not do. It must appear far too convenient, for one thing, and I do not wish to make the mistake of underestimating Miranda's intellect. That would be *fatal*! So we settled that Dorothea would agree to go to London, and pretend to be eager for the balls and parties, but she is to avoid the Marquis of Schofield as much as possible and never, ever, to be alone with him. And I have told her again to visit you as soon as she reaches London (but without letting her Stepmama know), for I know I can depend upon you to sympathize with her about the Marquis, and to perhaps instill her with a little spirit. I am to speak to Robert Penwood, and between us we will devise some plan.

This seemed to me to be a rather slender hope, but it cheered Dorothea wonderfully, and in a little while she was composed enough that we could return to the tea table. I remembered to have Dorothea summon her maid to pack before we left the room, for I did not think it wise to further irritate Miranda by ignoring her express commands. Then we went downstairs to inform Miranda that Dorothea would be ready to leave within the hour.

You may, therefore, imagine my surprise when we entered the sitting room and Miranda announced that she and Dorothea would not be leaving for at least another day. I was even more astonished to learn that they were remaining at the behest of James Tarleton, who had come in and joined Lady Tarleton and Mrs. Griscomb while Dorothea and I were upstairs. And he had brought in a bouquet for Dorothea, which he said he had picked himself!

Mr. Tarleton's behavior continued to be quite unaccountable. He leapt to his feet as soon as Dorothea entered the room, and held her chair (for which there was not the *least* need), and paid her a great many compliments, which were positively *fulsome*. I would have said something, I am sure, if I had not noticed Miranda Griscomb watching him closely with her hard little eyes. Upon reflection, I think she found his behavior quite as suspicious as I, though she cannot have known that he has not previously been among Dorothea's admirers. I can only wonder if that is why she decided to remain at Tarleton Hall. In any case, I am glad I did not express my surprise. For no matter how bad James Tarleton may be, Miranda Griscomb is clearly *much worse,* and I should not like to be of any assistance whatever to her. Also, it seems to me quite likely that if I had said anything about James Tarleton's peculiar behavior, he would certainly have taken it as added evidence that I am in league with Miranda.

I was so absorbed in these considerations that I did not realize my teacup was empty until Mrs. Griscomb leaned over to me and said, "Will you take some more tea, Miss Rushton?"

"No, thank you," I said quickly. James Tarleton gave me a sharp look, and Miranda stared at me in an odd, speculative way, so I added, "I really must be going. Aunt Elizabeth will be expecting me."

Mrs. Griscomb accepted that and turned back to her conversation with Lady T., but Mr. Tarleton's eyes narrowed. I could *feel* him watching me as I took my leave of Lady Tarleton and Dorothea; it was very uncomfortable.

After I returned home, I thought about that tea for a considerable while. The only conclusions I came to are that

I do *not* like Miranda Griscomb, and that it is positively *odious* of James Tarleton to think that I am in league with her. And, of course, that something will have to be done for poor Dorothea.

I told Aunt Elizabeth that I had the headache, and went upstairs to finish that book on charm-bags that I took from Sir Hilary's library. It is far more complicated than I had suspected, and I have quite given up on discovering what sort of charm-bag it was that Mary found in Oliver's room. I have, however, hit upon the idea of making up a charm-bag or two of my own (do not fret, Kate, for I intend to experiment only with the protective spells, and I will test everything on Canniba first). With Miranda Griscomb about, I feel the need for some protection.

14 May

Your letter regarding Oliver just arrived. I can only hope that you have had news of him by now, because he is certainly not at Rushton! I came very near to telling Papa the whole, for it seems to me that Oliver's disappearance is far too serious to hide, but as it turned out I did not have to say anything. Aunt Charlotte wrote Aunt Elizabeth a letter, which arrived at the same time as yours, desiring her to have Oliver bring her white work to Town when he returns. Aunt Elizabeth, of course, went straight to Papa, demanding to know where Oliver was and what she was to tell Aunt Charlotte. Papa, when he finally understood, simply laughed and said that Oliver has probably gone to see a cockfight or some such thing, and that he is old enough not to be hovered over by a pair of aunts.

This put Aunt Elizabeth quite out of countenance, and she went off in a huff to write to Aunt Charlotte. Under the circumstances, I decided not to add anything, for once Papa gets an idea in his head it is impossible to dislodge it. If he has decided that Oliver has gone to some disreputable sporting event, nothing will persuade him that it is more serious than that, unless Oliver remains missing. But if you do not have word of him in your next letter, I must tell Papa everything. Write soon and tell me he is safe! He may be the most provoking, tedious, goose-witted brother in the world, but he is the only one I have, and I should hate for anything dreadful to happen to him.

Miranda and Dorothea left for London yesterday. I rode over to Tarleton Hall to see Dorothea off, and I very nearly did not make it in time. My mare stumbled badly at the bottom of the hill where the Tarleton lands begin; if I had been galloping, as I usually do, I would certainly have been thrown. I stopped and checked to make sure my horse had taken no injury, and then I went back to see what had made her stumble. I half expected a poacher's snare. I saw no sign of one, but there was a strip of grass half an inch wide that had been burned away right down to the ground.

When I got to Tarleton Hall, Miranda and Dorothea were just stepping into their coach. Miranda seemed surprised (and not at all pleased!) to see me; I don't think she approves of my friendship with Dorothea. James Tarleton was there as well, still playing the flirt in the most *odious* fashion. I thought his expression was a bit strained, and I noticed that he was taking snuff more frequently than usual. (He has a new snuffbox in silver filigree, which I consider a great improvement over that garish blue enameled one he used to carry everywhere.) Once he glanced from Miranda to me in a puzzled fashion when he thought neither of us was looking. Dorothea was most grateful for my presence, though with her Stepmama standing beside her she could do no more than give me a speaking look. I feel for her, Kate, I truly do.

My experiments with Canniba and the charm-bags have been quite successful (you may imagine how careful I have had to be, to keep it all from Aunt Elizabeth!). Last night I made up one for myself (the incident with my mare has made me rather nervous), and this morning I made up one for Oliver. I had almost finished it when I was interrupted by the arrival of the post and the subsequent argument between Papa and Aunt Elizabeth. I went to Oliver's room at once, hoping to find a bit of his hair in his hairbrush, but there was none. So I am forced to enclose two incomplete charm-bags—one for you and one for Oliver. You can tell which is which by the embroidered initials. I am sorry they came out crooked, but I was in a great hurry. Put a lock of hair into each one, close them up, and put yours under your pillow or carry it in your reticule. (Oliver's had better go into his mattress, I suppose.) And once you've closed them, don't open them again; that breaks the protective spell.

I haven't the least notion whether this will do any good, but I have to do *something*! Write me as soon as you have word of Oliver, and take the greatest care of yourself, and do be kind to Dorothea. She does not deserve her Stepmama in the least.

Your worried,
Cecy

15 May 1817
11 Berkeley Square, London

Dear Cecelia,
Still no news of Oliver.

Aunt Charlotte has decreed that I am to remain in my room until further notice. After the night we spent beating the shrubbery for Oliver some rest was welcome, but solitary confinement soon grew tiresome. I have reread your letters and racked my brains and can come up with nothing new regarding this muddle, except to suggest that if charm-bags are useful to those who wish to have children and Mrs.

Fitzwilliam is increasing at last, there may possibly be more households than Rushton Hall with interesting additions to the bedclothes.

I am sorry to tell you that I haven't found your silk yet. There was a lovely green watered moire but it seemed a bit dark to me. When we visit the modiste again (if Aunt Charlotte ever relents), I will ask for a snippet to send you to judge by.

I have given up hope of getting my blood out of the Marquis's silk handkerchief. Such a pity, for it is a lovely bit of silk and in one corner, where some people put their initials, there is a peacock embroidered with the finest stitches, complete down to the shading from green to blue on the peacock's breast. I soaked it in cool water and rubbed the stains until my fingers were numb. (No need to tell me I must not rub silk too roughly; I remember Aunt Elizabeth's instruction in these matters.) I even tried her trick of using spirits of hartshorn in the rinse water. All I could think of as I scrubbed was the odious Marquis: his droning chant, his soft mutter as he bandaged my hand, his shameless flight at the sound of Georgy's vapors, and his probable complacency at my incompetence if I couldn't get the stains out.

But I didn't get them out. The blood has set—the spirits of hartshorn did no good at all, unless that is what caused the stains to turn violet when dry instead of brown. It is a far more attractive color, but I would still like to be rid of the stain entirely.

I completed the charm-bag you sent for Oliver, by dint of shaking Georgy's lock of his hair out of her prayer book and closing up the bag as you instructed. Georgy won't notice the lock of hair is missing. She never used her prayer book much anyway, and since she has adjusted to the delights of Town, she has little time to be homesick.

I have mended every article of clothing in my sewing basket, including the stocking I ripped at Lady Haseltine's, and have experimented with new ways of doing my hair. At the moment it is screwed up into a knob at the top of my head, which is not at all becoming but keeps it out of my eyes. And it does stay up for a change, with only two combs to hold it. It is still raining. Georgina is at the Grenvilles and Aunt Charlotte is home guarding the house lest I venture out of my room. I always wanted my own bedroom. I never guessed how dreary it could be to be shut up all alone.

 Later

Cecelia, Oliver is safe. I don't know where, but I believe Schofield even when he's being provoking.

Just now Aunt Charlotte sent to tell me I was wanted in the blue saloon. I went down just as I was, wearing the oldest muslin gown you let me pack and a sash of Georgy's that Canniba once played with. At the foot of the stairs Aunt Charlotte met me and opened the door to the blue saloon. I entered and she closed the door on me before I knew what she was about. Astonished, I turned and tried the knob, just as I heard her latch it from outside.

"Remarkable woman, your aunt," said a familiar voice behind me. "Thinks on her feet."

I whirled about to stand with my back to the door, hands pressed against the panels.

Across the room Thomas, Marquis of Schofield, rose from his chair, smiling at me in a decidedly sardonic way.

I turned back to the door and pounded my fist upon it. "Aunt Charlotte!"

"Do you really dislike me so much?" asked Thomas. There was a rising tone under his words, a slight unsteadiness that made me turn back to face him. Once I did, I could see the unsteadiness must be laughter, for he was having difficulty in restraining a grin.

I drew myself up with as much dignity as the knowledge that I looked an utter fright allowed me to muster and said, "I am completely indifferent to you, my lord. Only I forgot something in my room."

"Oh, I see," said Thomas. "Something important?"

"Your handkerchief," I replied. "Though I'm afraid I was not able to get the stains out of the silk."

"Keep it," said Thomas. "In fact, I wish you would accept it as the first of many things I wish to give you."

I looked at him very hard. "Are you foxed?" I demanded.

Thomas grinned broadly. "I ought to be, but I'm not. I came here today for two reasons. The first was to tell you that your cousin is safe."

I put my hands over my mouth but not in time to catch the sound of surprise I made. "Oliver? You've found him? Where is he?"

"Miles from here, in a place where no one will think to look for him," Thomas replied. "You understand I dare not tell you his whereabouts. In any case, I doubt the name would be familiar."

"Where did you find him?" I demanded.

"Oh, in Vauxhall Gardens," Thomas replied airily. "Remember your tree? I ought to have done something about it when I found you, but I left it as it was and Oliver stumbled on it. He was eavesdropping in the shrubbery, it seems, and so he may have deserved some slight misfortune. Still, I think turning him into a beech tree was a little excessive. I changed him back and I've sent him somewhere safe. No one has anything against him, of course. It was intended for you."

You may imagine how I gaped at him.

"You've made them curious," he continued. "They don't know what your part in all this is and they wanted to ask you."

"Well, I'm sure I don't know, either," I snapped.

"Oh, that's of no importance," he assured me. "That's part of the second reason I came here. You will agree you owe me some slight favor for rescuing you and your cod's head of a cousin? I wish to make you an offer."

I nodded as intelligently as I could and said, "Very well, I am very grateful to you for recovering dear, stupid Oliver. What sort of an offer?"

Thomas regarded me with an air of disbelief. "An offer of marriage, my dear half-wit. What other sort of offer did you expect?"

Cecy, I do think it is unfair. People in novels are fainting all the time, and I never can, no matter how badly I need to. Instead, I stared at him for what seemed like years, with the stupidest expression on my face, I'm sure, because I felt stupid. For I couldn't imagine why he should say such an extraordinary thing. Finally I realized he was waiting for me to say something.

I said, "I can't imagine why you should say such an extraordinary thing."

"Well, that's simple enough," Thomas replied. "In the first place, it may soothe them to know what your part in all this is, though I doubt it. And in the second place, I need a fiancée rather urgently."

"London is full of girls on the catch for husbands," I reminded him. "Why pick me?"

"Oh, I'll think of something," Thomas assured me. He grinned again. "I'm sure you have many sterling qualities."

How I longed to slap him. "There's more than a touch of

brass about *you*, my lord," I said. "Sterling qualities!" I snorted.

"Don't do that," he said. "It reminds me of someone. You'll be perfectly free to cry off when the Season is over, you know. But I need a good reason not to fall at someone's feet until then. And you're the only woman I could possibly ask, since anyone else would take it all far too seriously. Oh, come now, Kate, think what fun you'll have jilting me."

"What a singular notion of fun you must have," I said. "Still, it might be amusing at that. But what if we should set a fashion? Soon every betrothed couple in the Ton could be jilting one another for the fun of it."

"I'll risk it," he said, "but you will agree, won't you? Your aunt will certainly have some strong words for you if you refuse, for I'm afraid I discussed this with her before you arrived."

"That's why she locked me in," I said. "Oh, you odious man, I wish Miranda *had* lured you to her garden and I wish you'd drunk up every drop of her horrible chocolate."

"No, you don't, really you don't," Thomas assured me. "It would have been so unpleasant, you have no idea."

"That's so," I agreed coldly. "But I don't get an explanation, do I? No, all I get is roundaboutation and arrogance!" My voice rose alarmingly.

"Softly, softly," he said. "I had no idea you felt so

strongly about it. Well, perhaps it isn't exactly cricket to propose to you without giving you an idea of what you'd be getting into. How's this, then—you accept and I'll explain, hmm?"

"First you explain, and then I'll tell you whether I accept or not," I countered.

"Do you take me for a flat?" he asked. "No, either you agree to marry me and I explain things to you—or you don't and I don't."

"But you just said that wasn't cricket—," I protested.

"Well, I'm not playing cricket," Thomas answered. "More like a foxhunt, really."

"Oh, very well," I said crossly. "I agree. Now, out with it."

"You already know Miranda doesn't like me," Thomas began. "I have another enemy as well—but right now Miranda is my chief concern. She's sending someone to London expressly for me to fall in love with and marry. I'm not quite sure how powerful she is at the moment—it depends upon the degree of cooperation she's received from my other adversary. But I can't take the chance that they are working together. I need to make quite certain she can't trap me into proposing to the girl. So, Kate, our betrothal."

"Names, Thomas," I said, "I demand names."

"Miranda, I told you," he answered. "Miranda Tanistry."

I felt a sinking sensation in the pit of my stomach. "Tanistry? Not Griscomb?"

"Oh, I suppose," he replied. "She married some nabob or other, they say. But she was Miranda Tanistry when I first crossed her path. Why, do you know Griscomb?"

"Never heard of him," I declared. "What about your other adversary?"

"Sir Hilary Bedrick, if you must know."

You may imagine my reaction, Cecelia. After a moment I mastered that sinking sensation enough to say, "But that's impossible! We have known the Bedricks forever."

"Yes, very likely," he said, "dear Sir Hilary has every social grace. Nevertheless, he stole something rather important from me, and he and Miranda have been working individually and in unison to get me from under their feet permanently ever since."

"And to do that, they've decided to turn Oliver into a tree and burned a hole in my dress with hot chocolate—" I began to list recent events quite clearly but after a few words I was sputtering.

Thomas nodded. "Yes, quite so."

"All that—because Sir Hilary stole something from you. Something like a chocolate pot, for example?" I demanded.

I had the satisfaction of watching his face redden slightly. "Something like that," he agreed. "Any more questions?"

"Yes, thousands," I said.

At that moment Aunt Charlotte began to unlock the saloon door. Thomas reached out and took my hand, turned it palm up, and said, "I believe that's healing very nicely."

Aunt Charlotte opened the door just as he turned my hand over again and brushed a kiss across my knuckles. I experienced a nearly overpowering desire to hit him in the eye. Only the thought of Aunt Charlotte's reaction prevented me. Instead, I stood mute while he informed her that I had accepted his proposal of marriage, and took his leave of us with an oiled ease that suggested he has had years of experience slithering into betrothals and out again. When he had gone, I turned to Aunt Charlotte.

"I hope you are quite satisfied," I said as levelly as I could, and left the room.

Evidently the Marquis of Schofield's offer for my hand in marriage came as a considerable surprise to Aunt Charlotte. While it is true he has not displayed the slightest interest in Georgy, and no other gentleman has displayed any particular interest in me, Aunt Charlotte was not expecting an offer for anyone but Georgy. That I have received the first proposal, and that it should be a brilliant match—well! Aunt Charlotte's temperament has never been precisely sunny, and this turn of events has made her moodier than ever. On one hand, it affords her an opportunity to gloat over rival ladies bringing out eligible daughters. But on the other, I think she feels that Georgy has been slighted.

So here I am again, locked in my room, this time from the inside. I am in such a state of indignation that the first person who wishes me happy is likely to get her ears boxed.

Please don't tell me you are delighted—help me rather to contrive the best possible way to jilt the odious Marquis!

Yours,
Kate

⟨ 17 May

I shall add this scrawl to my letter to let you know I received your most recent letter. Thank heaven it arrived before Dorothea did, for I promise you that if she thinks Robert is "always most truly a gentleman" I shall need to school my features not to betray myself by laughing.

Of course, I shall do my utmost to help her—and I can certainly sympathize with her reluctance to marry that odious man Schofield.

What a muddle it all is—and how I wish you were with me so I could be encouraged by the confidence and courage you put into those familiar words, "We must clearly *do something.*" Indeed we must—but what?

And thank heaven again that you weren't riding in your usual neck-or-nothing fashion when you encountered that mysterious barrier in the grass. I smell Miranda behind that, plain as plain, and am very grateful for your charm-bags. Mind you keep your own close by you.

—K

Dearest Kate,

Your letter arrived this morning and I pounced on it at once. I was relieved by your news of Oliver, though it is not exactly specific. Thomas certainly does seem to delight in being enigmatic. It would not surprise me in the least to learn that he had invented the name "the Mysterious Marquis" himself. However, I must say that I admire Thomas's thoroughness. Papa received a note from Oliver yesterday, saying that he had gone off to stay for a few days with some friends he had met in London and, of course, neglecting to give their direction. (It is quite obvious to me that the Marquis arranged for Oliver to write the note; Oliver would never have thought of such a thing on his own.)

I find your description of the change in the bloodstains on Thomas's handkerchief very worrying. I haven't the least notion what it means, but I'm quite sure it means *something*. Washing does not normally turn bloodstains violet, however strong the hartshorn, and after all, the Marquis *is* a wizard. I think you should keep it very safe, but I do not know what else to recommend. I *wish* I knew more about magic; then perhaps I might advise you better.

I should also mention that I saw the announcement of

your engagement to Thomas, Marquis of Schofield, in last Friday's *Gazette,* which arrived with today's post. Fortunately, there were also letters from Aunt Charlotte to Papa and Aunt Elizabeth, so they cannot truthfully say that they learned of the engagement from the newspaper. Not that Papa would mind in the least, but Aunt Elizabeth is a different matter. She is not in transports over your engagement, by the way. She keeps her reservations to herself in company and says all that is proper, but my long experience with her allows me to detect a certain lack of enthusiasm. I suppose it is because Thomas is a wizard. She is taking me to visit the Reverend Fitzwilliam this afternoon, which is a sure sign she is upset.

Regarding the Marquis—I sympathize with your position, but I am very much afraid that you have let your justifiable annoyance run off with your sense. We have several months in which to arrange a way for you to jilt Thomas; I doubt that Miranda Griscomb will wait so long. I must own that your Marquis has been very clever. No matter what Miranda intended, she will never be able to force him to become engaged to Dorothea now. Though, really, it is most inconsiderate of him. For how can you find and encourage an eligible connection while you are engaged, however spuriously, to the Marquis?

I am afraid I find your Thomas's "explanation" very inadequate, but at least he has confirmed some of our suspicions regarding Miranda. I wonder how he knew what she was planning? I must tell you that the reaction of most of the local bachelors to Dorothea's departure has not been at all what I expected. None of them seems the least bit cast down. In fact, with the exception of Robert Penwood, they seem to have forgotten her almost completely. At church yesterday, I heard Jack Everslee refer to Dorothea as a "taking little chit, but bird-witted"—this after he was ready to call Martin out two weeks ago for (he claimed) slighting Dorothea's eyebrows!

I find this very disturbing, particularly knowing what little we do about Miranda Tanistry Griscomb. It seems to me very likely that she has put some sort of spell on Dorothea to make her irresistible as long as she is about. For, you remember, the same thing happened to Oliver—he was very taken with Dorothea, but as soon as he went up to London, he forgot all about her. This makes it all the more urgent that *something* be done to overset Miranda's schemes and rescue Dorothea. For it is quite obvious to me that Dorothea is an innocent pawn in her Stepmama's game; she is so terrified of Miranda that I doubt if she could cooperate even if she wished.

I was also shocked and disturbed by the Marquis's accusation about Sir Hilary. Upon reflection, however, I find it quite plausible to think that Sir Hilary stole a chocolate pot from Thomas, and even that he conspired with Miranda to poison the Marquis. This shocked me even more; it is a perfect example of what Aunt Elizabeth and the Reverend

Fitzwilliam are always saying about the Shallowness of Society's Judgments and the True Worth of Men being more than mere address. It is very lowering to discover that the Reverend Fitz is right about *anything*. However, it has given me an Idea.

If Miranda Griscomb and Sir Hilary Bedrick are working together, would it not be a good thing to make them suspicious of each other? And as we have known Sir Hilary for ages, do you not think that Miranda would find it quite plausible that you were in league with him to foil her plans for Dorothea and the Marquis? I don't mean, of course, that you should tell her any such thing, but if you were to see her at a ball or some such and mention Sir Hilary's name, and then look confused, she might very well jump to conclusions without any further effort on your part. And if Miranda were to think that Sir Hilary were trying to foil her plans, she might very well try to poison *him* with chocolate, and stop bothering you and Oliver and the Marquis.

I should point out that this plan has an element of risk, for it will bring you to Miranda's attention again in quite a different way. I do not like to think that this might put you in danger. On the other hand, you have already been nearly poisoned and come close to being turned into a tree, even without pretending to be working with Sir Hilary. I trust you realize that this plan will probably annoy the Marquis as well. He sounds like the sort of person who wants to think of everything himself.

In the meantime, I will go up to Bedrick Hall and look about. (I had already determined to do so, for I must get that book of Sir Hilary's back *somehow*, and I have discovered that it is quite impossible to post something anonymously in a town as small as Rushton, particularly a parcel.) It will have to wait a day or two, as I must think up some tale for Aunt Elizabeth.

 Later

I have just returned from visiting the Reverend Fitzwilliam with Aunt Elizabeth. Mrs. Fitz was not in evidence, which is unusual; she is apparently not in the best of health due to her Interesting Condition. Aunt Elizabeth and Reverend Fitz discussed it at some length, and with much hyperbole out of respect for my tender sensibilities. (Though I cannot imagine how Aunt Elizabeth can believe that I *have* any sensibilities; she has certainly lived with us long enough to know better!)

In any case, we had not been at the house for very long when an additional visitor arrived, a Mr. Wrexton. He stood stock-still in the doorway for the longest time after he had been announced, just staring over at Aunt Elizabeth and me. Aunt Elizabeth took one look at him and stiffened in her most absolutely starched-up manner. I could not see any reason for her to take Mr. Wrexton in dislike, for I observed him closely. (He is a moderately tall man of about forty-five, I should guess, and dressed with great elegance. I must hasten to add that I do not mean the exaggerated sort of elegance that Oliver affects; Mr. Wrexton is more like James Tarleton—positively understated.) This was a mistake, for it meant that both Aunt Elizabeth and I were all but staring at him. As soon as she noticed, she gave me one of her looks, and I knew I would be forced to endure a lecture on manners for the better part of the way home.

In any case, Reverend Fitzwilliam performed the necessary introductions and Mr. Wrexton joined us. He says he is staying with friends in the area and has always made it a practice to call on the vicar when he does so. I thought this a little odd, but Reverend Fitz was flattered to have his profession so highly thought of. Aunt Elizabeth was quite cool for the remainder of our visit, which was much shorter than usual. Mr. Wrexton took her hand and bowed very low over it as we left, and said something about coming to call on Papa. Aunt Elizabeth was not encouraging.

Just outside we met Robert Penwood, driving his gig into town on some errand. I could not say much, due to Aunt Elizabeth's presence, so I exercised *all* my powers of persuasion and managed to get Aunt Elizabeth to agree that I might drive with him, and Robert to agree to take me up. So I climbed into the gig and Aunt Elizabeth continued on home.

"Robert," I said as soon as we were off, "I must talk to you about Dorothea."

He looked at me with dislike. "I suppose she told you everything."

"Well, I think so, but she was in the greatest distress!" I replied. "You did not meet Miranda—Mrs. Griscomb—but I did, and Dorothea has every reason to be terrified of her."

Robert stared down at his reins. "I know. If there were only something I could do!"

"There is a great deal you can do!" I said impatiently. "It only wants a little *resolution*, Robert!"

"Don't be ridiculous, Cecy!" Robert said. "What do you expect me to do? Ride off with Dorothea across my saddle-bow, like the hero of one of those novels you read? Elope to Gretna Green? Have a little sense!"

"From what Dorothea said, I don't think she would have minded either one," I told him. "Though riding flung across someone's saddlebow sounds excessively uncomfortable to me. But *something* must be done to rescue Dorothea from Mir—from Mrs. Griscomb."

"Don't talk fustian!" Robert said. "Mrs. Griscomb is Dorothea's Mother; she has every right to—"

"No, she is not," I interrupted. "She is Dorothea's Step-mama, which is an entirely different thing."

"It doesn't matter," Robert said gloomily. "She is responsible for Dorothea's welfare."

"You think forcing Dorothea to marry the Marquis of Schofield is looking out for Dorothea's welfare?" I demanded. "Really, Robert!"

"And how can I compete with a marquis?" he said roughly. "I'm neither rich nor titled, and as for prospects . . ." He snorted.

"Dorothea loves you," I pointed out. "And she can't marry the Marquis of Schofield, because Kate has just become engaged to him."

If I had thought Robert would be pleased by this intelligence, I was quite out, for he pulled at the reins so hard that the horse jobbed and we were very nearly overturned. He looked positively fierce. "Cecy! Is this another one of your queer starts? Because if it is, you and Kate can just stop your interfering right now."

"Oh, stuff!" I said. "*I* didn't have anything to do with Kate's betrothal to the Marquis, and she's never even met Dorothea. All I meant was that we can turn it to our advantage."

"How?" Robert said suspiciously.

"You can become engaged to Dorothea before her Stepmama has time to find another man to offer for her," I said.

"Don't be a fool, Cecy," Robert said, but he sounded a trifle more hopeful. "Mrs. Griscomb would never consent to her daughter's—her stepdaughter's marrying a nobody."

"You are not a nobody," I said firmly. "Why, your grandfather was the son of a duke! And it is Dorothea's Papa who must consent to her marriage, not her Stepmama."

Robert stopped the gig and looked at me with an arrested expression. "You're right. Cecy, I never thought of that!" After a moment, he slumped again. "But I cannot think that Mr. Griscomb will favor my suit any more than his wife does."

"You won't know unless you try," I said. "And you simply cannot leave Dorothea at the mercy of that woman without any hope whatever!"

"I'll do it!" Robert said. He paused, then went on diffidently, "I don't suppose—would you write to Dorothea and tell her? I know it isn't the thing to be asking, but . . ."

"I'll see," I said noncommittally, for it occurred to me just in time that Miranda may well read Dorothea's letters (it would be just like her). And in any case, I do not think Dorothea would be very good at dissembling. It would never do for Miranda to become suspicious because Dorothea was happy! So I am writing you with this news instead, and when you meet Dorothea and have a chance to judge, you may tell her as much as you think wise.

Robert was quite congenial for the remainder of my ride with him, if you can consider someone who is in ecstatic raptures over another lady to be congenial. He let me down at the end of the drive and went off to Tarleton Hall to discover Mr. Griscomb's direction. I sincerely hope that Mr. Griscomb is not in some outlandish place weeks from Town. I would feel much reassured if Dorothea's future were safely settled.

When I arrived at the house, I was informed that I had had a caller while I was away. You will never guess who it was, Kate—James Tarleton! I cannot imagine what he wants of me, but whatever it is, he wants it rather badly, for he left a message that he will call again Thursday and hopes I will go driving with him. I am strongly tempted to have the headache.

Your cousin,
Cecy

25 May 1817
11 Berkeley Square, London

Dear Cecy,

Aunt Charlotte says I must go to bed and stay there until she tells me I may get up. I shall do so as soon as I finish this letter to you, and then, if possible, go into a decline of the most spectacular sort.

I apologize for not having written sooner, but, indeed, things have been happening so rapidly there was not time to pause and think it out. Now it appears I shall have all the time I need and more.

Dorothea arrived a week ago, Miranda apparently having no qualms about travel on the Sabbath. Dorothea wasted not a moment in calling here, for I returned from the modiste's on Monday to discover she had left her card. She paid another call on Tuesday, and I was able to offer her what comfort tea and sympathy could provide. The poor child has the most touching faith in you, Cecy. Every sentence she speaks has a "Cecy says" sprinkled in it somewhere. Evidently she has the notion that you have a sort of Grand Plan to reunite her with Robert. I tried to clarify matters a little, but could not really tell her much without contradicting her apparently unshakable faith in you. She seems to have been able to conceal much of her fear of Schofield since learning of my betrothal. Indeed, she wished me happy in a very affecting way, and then spent a merry quarter hour cutting up his character with me.

My betrothal to the Marquis has had unexpected benefits, new gowns among them. The modiste required me for nearly the whole of Wednesday, but I own that judging by the dress I wore to Lady Melbourne's ball Thursday evening, all the fittings and consultings will be well worthwhile. Georgy helped me with my hair and I really do think I looked quite well. Isn't it funny, Cecy—I only came to London because Georgina could not come out before me, and I never thought I'd really find a suitable *parti* in Town— but the instant it became known that Schofield had offered for me, many eligible young men and a great many more ineligible old ones were suddenly able to perceive my charms for the first time. I had a splendid time, for the first half hour.

On our arrival, the room was almost full of the Ton, but neither Dorothea nor Miranda was in evidence. Thomas appeared and led me out in a country dance, selected according to some private strategy of his. He seems to have worked out a little timetable so we can appear together for the briefest possible time before the greatest possible number of people. Georgina was surrounded by her usual throng of beaux. Even Aunt Charlotte appeared to be having a nice fencing match with some of the mamas, who were inquiring pointedly about the suddenness of my betrothal.

Dorothea and Miranda arrived in a little stir of attention, which grew until the entire room was murmuring like the wind in a grove of trees. When Dorothea was presented to Lady Melbourne, a hush fell upon the room. It lasted only a moment, but for that single moment there was not a sound from the guests and the music seemed loud and just a touch flat. Dorothea glanced shyly about once, then dropped her gaze to the fan she held and kept it there. As one, every man young enough to walk without a stick surged toward her. A great sigh ran through the room, and then the murmuring began again, like the wind rising.

The dances continued, but this time Georgina lacked her beaux, and I was one of the many in the chairs along the wall. A throng of young men surrounded Dorothea, and first among them was that odious man, Thomas.

Miranda stood watching it all with an expression of serene amusement, until she caught sight of me, seated across the room and attempting to look as though I didn't care two pins for anything. She gave me a graceful little inclination of her head as a nod of recognition and then smiled at me—quite the most unpleasant smile I've ever seen in my life.

I spent the remainder of the evening paying no attention whatever to Dorothea and Thomas. (He stood up with her for three waltzes, that monster. And Dorothea would never have consented to a single one, had she not had a childlike faith in me and my ability to rescue her from him.) I was far too concerned with Georgina in any case. She took her sudden fall from grace with great composure, but the gossip that rose in whispers all around her required many brilliant smiles from both of us to deflect.

The next day, I was startled to receive an invitation to tea with Miranda and Dorothea Griscomb. Georgina went with me, on the theory that it would do Georgy's reputation nothing but good to be seen to be friendly with the beauty who had so recently taken the shine clean out of her. The pair of them hit it off at once, and departed in short order to examine the Griscombs' collection of India curiosities, leaving Miranda and me alone over the teacups.

"Will you have more bread and butter?" Miranda inquired.

I accepted, though it was rather stale, since the alternatives were marzipan bonbons shaped like little clenched fists and meringues tinted a distinctly peculiar shade of green. I took a cautious sip of tea.

"Your sister is truly lovely," said Miranda.

I regarded her with suspicion. It seemed most out of character for her to praise anyone, still less a stranger. "Dorothea is as beautiful or more so," I replied carefully.

"Thomas certainly appeared to think so," agreed Miranda. "It must be very galling for you to be treated so. Yet perhaps it is wise for you to be used to such behavior from the very start, for I'm sure he'll be just the same once you're married."

"That's of little importance to me," I said in as indifferent a tone as I could muster. I took another sip of tea and added, "I hardly think our marriage will last long enough to inconvenience either of us."

Miranda gave me the full benefit of those cold dark eyes. "Your romance was a whirlwind affair."

I smiled. It was hardly more than a baring of teeth, but I managed it. "My romance was timed precisely according to my instructions."

Miranda's expression did not change but I could sense the focus of her attention as it sharpened. "Instructions?" she purred.

I put my teacup down on my saucer and gave my best snort of exasperation. "Don't play the innocent with me."

Miranda's eyes widened at my words. If she has spent any time at all in Sir Hilary's company, she could hardly fail to recognize both the snort and the sentiment. Remember how you and Robert chopped your hole in the hedge of the maze? Those were Sir Hilary's exact words when he questioned me. I flatter myself I even came close to the cadence of his voice.

Miranda's eyebrows crept up her forehead as she peered at me searchingly. I wanted very badly to take another sip of tea but was afraid that if I tried the cup would rattle in the saucer and betray my nervousness.

At that moment, very fortunately I think, Dorothea and Georgina returned. We took our leave with much affection on Georgina's and Dorothea's behalf and much insincerity on Miranda's part and mine. I think the seed of a suspicion has been planted. I hope it turns out to be suspicion of Sir Hilary and not entirely suspicion of me. If Sir Hilary and Miranda are conspiring to rid themselves of Thomas, surely they wouldn't let him marry Dorothea and live happily ever after, when with a little resolution they could kill him and gain control of his estates through Dorothea. And if that is so, surely Miranda could believe that I should find the prospect of wealthy widowhood an appealing one. I preferred to try for a light touch in my reference to Sir Hilary. If she questions him, he may admit to a long-standing acquaintance between our families. Is that the sort of suspicion you had in mind?

Despite Schofield's behavior at Lady Melbourne's ball, I agreed to drive out with him on Friday. Again, obedient to some schedule of his own, he selected a spot in which the most people would observe us in the briefest period of time, St. James's Park. We spoke scarcely at all, so industriously were we nodding and smiling at our respective acquaintances, but I knew immediately when he saw Dorothea, for he stiffened beside me like a hunting dog coming on point. She was strolling with Michael Aubrey and Alice Grenville, looking perfectly fetching in a lilac walking dress and pelisse. Really, she reminds me terribly of Georgy, that perfect profile and the elegant line of her throat. It made it worse, in a way, that she did resemble Georgina, for it has happened to me before, that chill sensation when I feel my companion's attention drawn from me to her. Not that I cared for his attention, mind, only it was disagreeable to have it happen *again*.

Schofield pulled up and we chatted, and in a matter of moments, I was walking beside Alice Grenville and Dorothea was up in the carriage. It seemed the most natural thing in the world, and I'm sure no one could have remarked upon it. Only, of course, Michael Aubrey stayed to speak with Dorothea as Alice and I strolled on along the way alone.

I have mentioned, I believe, the Oriental footbridge over the long duck pond. Alice and I were at the center of the bridge, discussing the ducks and swans that paddled nearby, hopeful of crumbs, when Alice spied the Grenville twins strolling past. She greeted them with enthusiasm and walked forward to meet them. George and Andrew met her before she was off the bridge. Andrew and Alice stepped onto the footpath, debating the merits of a visit to Gunther's. George passed them, intending to join me. Briefly, I was alone at the highest point of the bridge, perhaps seven feet above the surface of the water. At that moment, I felt the structure tremble; then, as the bridge shivered itself into splinters, I fell into the duck pond.

My first thought was "Earthquake!" My second, "I will never be able to wear this bonnet again." Then I was able to get my feet under me and rise, cascading green water, shocking the ducks, and offending the swans. When I stood, the water only reached my waist, so I was able to clamber out of the pond unassisted.

Judging from the needlelike bits of wood that had once been the footbridge, which now bobbed and floated on the surface of the pond, nothing natural caused the bridge to collapse. It was a sensational event and attracted much attention on every hand. Most of it, however, was directed toward George Grenville, poor man, who managed somehow to fall off the bridge as it went down and break his arm. While he was being attended to, Frederick Hollydean and Mr. Strangle drew up in their landau and insisted I allow them to escort me home. I was wet to the skin, chilled to the bone, and torn between embarrassment and fury (not a sign of the Marquis, of course), but I was otherwise unharmed, so I accepted. I did some damage to the upholstery, since I was covered in mud and streaming with water. I'm afraid neither of them got much sense out of me, though both of them cross-questioned me the entire way home, since all I could do was clutch my reticule to my chest and sniff back silly tears.

Aunt Charlotte was very severe with me, calling for a mustard plaster to be applied to my chest, and explaining to me that if I had not so improperly abandoned my escort for another, this would never have happened. It seemed a good idea to let her work off her rage by allowing her to minister to me, so I submitted to a day of scrubbing and scolding and being tucked up in bed with a stocking around my neck to keep off the cold.

Next morning I was permitted to go down to the blue saloon when Alice called to say that George was going to be fine. We condoled together over the catastrophe and speculated on the probable effect it would have on the ducks. Shortly after her departure, Thomas, Marquis of Schofield, called. I received him in the blue saloon, this time taking pains to seat myself in the chair he had claimed on his earlier visit. I was a little piqued to receive him once again looking less than my best, but at least this time I was decently dressed and groomed, and only the redness of my eyes and nose betrayed the cold I had contracted.

"You're looking very earnest this morning," I said when he had accepted a chair across the room from me and stared at me without speaking for a full minute.

"I have come to ask you to cry off, Kate," he said. His voice was very even but his expression was gloomy.

I regarded him with astonishment. "I thought you needed a fiancée rather urgently."

"Circumstances are not what I expected they would be," he said.

I regarded him with gravity equal to his own. "I will release you from your promise on the condition you give me your word that you will not offer for Dorothea," I said. "You may think only of yourself, but she has given her heart elsewhere and I have promised her she shall not be forced to marry you."

He sneered slightly. "Do you really think force need enter into it?"

"Let us at least be honest with one another," I said. "I won't let you tangle me up with your sardonic remarks. I won't try to pretend I don't know what's really happening. That girl is an innocent tool in Miranda's hands. You can't use her against her own Stepmother just to protect yourself. I won't let you."

"My dear half-wit, Dorothea Griscomb has nothing to fear from me," Schofield replied. "If she is innocent, as you say she is, it is Miranda she must battle."

"Then you promise you won't offer for her," I persisted.

"I can't," Thomas said. "Please don't make me put out the rumors myself, Kate. Release me."

"I won't," I told him. "I won't let Miranda win. If I cry off and let you offer for her, it means the spell on Dorothea is too powerful for you to resist. And if Miranda wins,

Thomas, it isn't just you who loses. Dorothea loses and Robert loses, too—"

I put my head down, only for a moment, only because I had to blow my nose. My eyes were streaming, but it was merely my cold. I looked up when I heard the door close. He was gone.

And now I have sneezed seven times in the past hour and Aunt Charlotte will give me only barley water instead of dinner. At any moment I expect to hear the first rumors that my betrothal is at an end. I only hope that Schofield has the decency to let it seem I was the one to cry off. I will write again when I have better news to report.

Your loving cousin,
Kate

27 May 1817
Rushton Manor, Essex

Dearest Kate,

The Marquis of Schofield is behaving in the most singularly cockle-headed manner imaginable. Perhaps he will realize it when James Tarleton writes to tell him what happened on our ride Thursday, but I place no dependence on it. Anyone who believes that Dorothea could stand up to Miranda must be even more goose-witted than Oliver, and I had not believed that was possible. And what, pray, is to happen to Oliver if Thomas falls into Miranda's clutches? I cannot think that Miranda would like it known that she had turned Oliver into a beech tree, however inadvertently, and your precious Marquis is the only one who knows where Oliver is. Nor has Thomas considered what the effect on your own reputation will be if you become engaged and then un-engaged in less than a month! There are also poor Dorothea and Robert, to whom he does not appear to have given a thought. He is clearly not even thinking of himself.

For you are quite right, Kate; Miranda is *not* the type to let him live happily ever after with Dorothea (even if one assumes they would be happy, which is clearly absurd). Miranda has some sinister plan for Thomas, and he is so befuddled by her spells that he doesn't care. Or perhaps she has fooled him into thinking he can handle everything alone. In short, if we wish to see anything sensible done about the situation we will clearly have to do it ourselves.

It is extremely fortunate that men are not allowed to cry off from an engagement. Under no circumstances must you allow Thomas to persuade you to do the crying off! I expect it will be unpleasant, with all the whispering about his attentions to Dorothea, but perhaps you can give the gossips the impression that you are determined to be a marchioness no matter how your future husband behaves. In any case, Thomas has made it quite clear that he will offer for poor Dorothea as soon as he is free to do so, and that cannot be permitted until Robert has had a chance to find

Mr. Griscomb and speak with him. The Marquis has obviously been caught by whatever spell Miranda has put on Dorothea to make her so impossibly attractive. (Which just shows you what an unprincipled woman Miranda is. I'm sure she could have done something so that the spell wouldn't affect men who are married or betrothed, but I'll wager she never even thought of it. She probably enjoys cutting up everyone's happiness. Not to mention cutting up other parts of people; given her penchant for poisoning people and turning them into beech trees, I fail to see how she has reached thirty without leaving a trail of bodies behind her.)

I am enclosing another charm-bag for you to make up for Thomas. It may lessen the effect of Miranda's spell; if so, it will give him a chance to think clearly about his idiotic notion of jilting you to offer for Dorothea. I've doubled the mixture to make the charm stronger. Sir Hilary's book (which has been truly useful; if you happen into a bookshop, do see if you can find a copy. I should like to have one, if I can keep it hidden from Aunt Elizabeth) says that a charm-bag, properly prepared, can work from a distance, though it is better if one keeps the bag near one. So even if you cannot get Thomas to carry it, it may help. I don't know how you are going to get the hair for it; perhaps you should just ask him.

It would probably also help if you could think of some way to get Thomas out of London. All of the boys here (except Robert) completely forgot about Dorothea the day after she left Tarleton Hall, so it is only when she is about that Miranda's spell has any effect. On second thought, it may not be wise to persuade Thomas to remove from London. Miranda would certainly drag Dorothea off to follow him, no matter how odd it would look.

It seems to me that your conversation with Miranda went *very* well. If she does not now believe that you are working for Sir Hilary, she must be a complete idiot, and we both know that that is not so. I wish I could think of a way to plant some similar suspicion in Sir Hilary's mind, but I cannot think of a way that is not much too risky. Sir Hilary, after all, has known us both for a good many years, and I fear he would be exceedingly suspicious of any tale either of us brought him.

I am truly glad you were not seriously hurt when the footbridge collapsed, and it is just like Aunt Charlotte to go into one of her grand fusses over a ducking. I had to tell Aunt Elizabeth about it and the cold (she is beginning to wonder what we can be corresponding on at such length when I never have any gossip to report to her). So Aunt Elizabeth is sending you some of her Special Cough Mixture, the one made with blackberries. I trust you will not find it *too* nasty. She also gave me a long lecture on the Proper Deportment of Girls Who Are Engaged to Be Married, which she wished me to pass on to you. I deduce from this that she, too, does not approve of your chatting with George Grenville when you are engaged to the odious Marquis.

And now I must tell you about my drive with James

Tarleton last Thursday. He arrived most punctually in a curricle, looking wonderfully elegant in an olive coat, tan pantaloons, and Hessians polished bright enough to see your face in. I saw him from the window, and all I could think was that Oliver would kill to be able to dress like that. Of course, I had not intended to drive with him, but I had forgotten to tell Aunt Elizabeth that I had the headache. She told Mr. Tarleton that I would be down directly, and I was forced to go.

Mr. Tarleton was very quiet until we reached the end of the drive, which gave me the opportunity to study his team. They were the most perfectly matched pair of grays I have ever seen, and all my annoyance at Mr. Tarleton disappeared in a ridiculous longing to drive them. I was so absorbed in admiration that I was quite startled when Mr. Tarleton finally addressed me.

"I believe I owe you an apology, Miss Rushton," he said.

Kate, you could have tipped me off the seat with the end of your little finger. I stared at him with what I am sure must have been an expression of thoroughgoing stupidity and finally managed to say, "I beg your pardon?"

He flushed under his tan and said stiffly, "I suppose I deserved that. I can only say again, I apologize for misjudging you, Miss Rushton."

I opened my mouth and shut it without saying anything. (I have never been more thankful for Aunt Elizabeth's constant adjurations to think before I speak. Had I not stopped to consider, I would certainly have said something dreadfully insulting and had to walk all the way back to Rushton.) "Does this mean that you have decided I am not in league with Mrs. Griscomb?" I said at last, in as careful and neutral a voice as I could manage.

He looked at me with a somewhat surprised expression, but said readily, "Yes, that is what I mean."

"Good," I said. "Then you won't mind explaining why you were spying on Dorothea."

"I'm afraid I can't do that," he said. His voice was much less friendly, and his eyes narrowed. "And just why do you want to know?"

"Dorothea is my friend," I told him firmly. "And she has enough problems already."

"I suppose that is what you were doing in Sir Hilary's library," he said in a cold, considering tone. "Helping Dorothea with her 'problems.'"

"That was nothing to do with Dorothea, and it's nothing to do with you, either," I snapped. "And if you brought me out driving just so you could insult me—"

"Oh, not *just* to insult you," he said in the most maddening way. "I think perhaps— Ah, there's the lake."

The curricle swept around a bend in the road and I saw that he was quite right. I was surprised at how quickly we had reached it; really, Mr. Tarleton's grays are a perfectly splendid team. (And no matter how annoying he is, I must allow that he drives to an inch.)

"What are you planning to do, drown me?" I said.

His lips twitched. "I believe I can resist the temptation," he said. "Though, I admit, it will be difficult." His expression changed and he studied me the way Aunt Elizabeth studies a difficult pattern before she begins to embroider. "I don't know what to make of you," he said, half to himself.

"You needn't make anything of me," I said coldly. My temper was rising; in spite of his apology, he was apparently still in doubt as to my motives. I was determined not to quarrel with him, however, as I was sure that quarreling would only make Mr. Tarleton more positive that I had some ulterior motive for coming out riding with him. (I could hardly tell him, after all, that I was only there because I had not had sufficient forethought to establish that I had the headache before he arrived.) So I said, "I would like to get down and walk a little."

"I can't leave the grays," he said shortly.

"You don't need to," I said from between clenched teeth. "I'm perfectly capable of walking on my own. I've been doing it since I was two."

He laughed and reined in the grays. "Very well, then. We will both let our tempers cool."

He had seemed more amused than angry to me, but I was too glad to be getting away from him to correct him. I jumped down before the curricle had quite stopped and began walking briskly toward the spot where Jack had arranged his picnic. I was halfway there, and just climbing over a rather large rock, when I heard Mr. Tarleton call out.

I turned, one foot still on the rock, and stood stock-still, staring. Now I know what all those novels mean when they talk about being too stunned to move, which I have always thought a great piece of nonsense, because unless one has been struck over the head or ensorcelled or some such, one is perfectly capable of moving. But it is not so, Kate. For I *was* too stunned to move.

The air between the curricle and me was *rippling*, and it smelled like something burning, though I could not see any flames. James Tarleton was standing in the curricle, his mouth moving as if he were shouting, but I could not hear anything at all. The rippling grew rapidly worse, and so did the burning smell. It was like looking in a very old, distorted mirror, or through a very badly made windowpane. James leapt down from the curricle and ran toward me, still shouting soundlessly. He had something in his left hand that he was waving back and forth in front of himself, as if he were trying to clear a path.

Suddenly he tripped and fell, and did not rise again. I shook off my paralysis and ran forward. (Perhaps I ought not to have done so, with the air behaving so oddly, but I was not thinking too clearly at the time.) I do not have a perfect recollection of the next few minutes, though I have a vague impression of suffocating heat. Then I plunked to my knees beside James Tarleton.

He was barely conscious, and he seemed to be having trouble breathing. I ripped off his cravat in a manner that would surely have drawn a protest from Oliver, had he been present, and stopped short. A length of ribbon was twisted around his neck, of the same lavender shade that Miranda Griscomb was wearing the day she and Dorothea left for London.

I pulled at the ribbon, but though it was not knotted, it would not come free. In fact, it grew tighter, and James Tarleton's breathing became even more labored. In desperation I upended my reticule, hoping that I might have a forgotten pair of scissors in it. My charm-bag fell out. I grabbed it at once, jerked it open, and dumped all of the crumbled herbs over James's neck, muttering as I did as much of the protective spell that goes with the charm-bag as I could remember.

The effects were immediate. The ribbon loosened, and I snatched it away and crumpled it up in my fist. James's breathing eased at once, and he began to come back to consciousness. I watched him with the greatest anxiety, as I was not at all certain of my ability to come up with a reasonable explanation of what had happened should he be permanently damaged in some way. And so I heard him mumble, "Cecelia! No!" and then, "Thomas will murder me."

I sat bolt upright and stared down at him, noticing for the first time that his left hand was still clenched around that ostentatious enamel snuffbox I thought he had disposed of. I had no time to wonder why he was clutching such a peculiar object, for just then his eyes opened and he started to struggle upright. "Cecelia!"

I shoved him down again, and not gently. "Lie down until you've got your breath back," I said.

He froze, staring at me as if he could not believe his eyes. "Cecelia? Miss Rushton? You're all right?"

"Yes, I'm all right," I said. "You're the one who almost got killed. Don't you have *any* sense?"

"More than you seem to," James said grimly. He sat up and looked around. The rippling and the burning smell and the heat were all gone as if they had never existed. "How did you get out of—" He broke off as his eyes fell on the little velvet bag with my initial on it, which was lying empty on the ground next to my reticule. "Where did you get that?" he demanded.

"I made it," I said. "And you ought to be glad I did, for it saved your life. Have you got a pair of scissors?"

"Scissors?" He stared at me with an irritated expression. "What would I be doing with a pair of scissors?"

"A knife, then," I said impatiently. "I don't want to have to hang on to this silly ribbon until I get home, and I have a decided aversion to letting it lie around loose where it can find someone else to strangle. I don't know much about magic, but if we cut it up into very small pieces I don't see how it could possibly do any more harm."

"Ribbon?" His irritated expression changed to worry, and he said in a gentle, humoring tone, "Cecelia, please, explain what you are talking about."

"This," I said, opening my fingers far enough to show him a corner of the ribbon. "When I came up to you, after you fell, it was wrapped around your neck, choking you. I could see it getting tighter." I shivered slightly, due, I am sure, to the contrast between the recent strange heat and the wind that was now coming off the lake. "I dumped the herbs from the charm-bag over it, and it loosened up enough for me to get it off, but I don't know whether it's safe to let go of it or not." (I was remembering the letter in which you said that Thomas had told you that Oliver fell afoul of the same tree in Vauxhall Gardens that had almost caught you. I was not about to make the same mistake and leave a spell lying about for someone else to trip over.) "I believe," I added, "that it's Miranda's."

James's expression had been changing slowly from worry to thoughtful consideration, but as soon as I mentioned Miranda's name he looked at me sharply. "What do you know of Miranda? And no more games, Miss Rushton."

"What do you know of Thomas?" I countered.

I had the satisfaction of seeing him change color, then he said, not very convincingly, "Thomas who?"

"You know quite well," I said severely, "and you need not pretend otherwise. You muttered his name as you were coming around a moment ago."

He stared at me again, then shook his head. "I don't think I should tell you."

"Perhaps you have forgotten that my cousin is engaged to him," I said sweetly, for I was quite certain that the Thomas James had been mumbling about was your odious Marquis. After all, it is exceedingly unlikely that there would be *two* Thomases mixed up in Miranda's business.

"Just how much do you know?" James said in a detached voice.

"I know that Miranda Griscomb is a magician," I said cautiously. "And she's put a spell on Dorothea to make every man she meets fall in love with her, and taken her to London to try to trap the Marquis of Schofield. And I know that Miranda and Sir Hilary Bedrick have an, er, uneasy alliance." I glanced at James and added, "And I know that you are a friend of the Marquis's, and—That's why you were spying on Dorothea!" I said suddenly, then bit my lip in chagrin.

"You are too clever by half," James said grimly.

I glared at him. "I suppose that's why you changed your mind about me so suddenly, too. Thomas Schofield wrote you about Kate and Georgy and Oliver, didn't he?"

"He sent me a message, yes," Mr. Tarleton said. "I'd very nearly come to the same conclusion myself, however."

"How nice," I said coldly. "Does that mean you will leave off spying on me? You aren't very good at it. I told you that the first time I found you skulking in the bushes, and you haven't improved any since. That act you put on for Miranda's benefit, pretending to be enamoured of Dorothea, wouldn't have fooled a ten-year-old child."

"That's none of your concern," James said stiffly.

"It is when you take me out driving and one of Miranda's spells nearly strangles you," I pointed out. "How *did* you keep from falling under Dorothea's spell? I mean, under the spell Miranda put on Dorothea?"

"Thomas has seen Miranda use that spell before," James said. "He gave me something to keep it from affecting me." And he held out that bright blue enameled snuffbox with the peacock on the lid! I stared at it and finally understood why James always seemed to be using it whenever Dorothea was around. I felt rather silly, too, for you told me that Thomas's handkerchief had a peacock embroidered in the corner, and I really should have connected it much sooner with the peacock on James's snuffbox.

"I should have sent it back to him when Dorothea left," James went on, frowning worriedly. "But there wasn't any way of getting it to London ahead of Miranda, and he did tell me to keep it until he could collect it personally."

"You should have sent it anyway," I said, thinking of the description of Thomas's infatuation with Dorothea you gave in your last letter. It seems that even if one knows perfectly well what is going on, one cannot resist Miranda's spell.

Mr. Tarleton shook his head stubbornly. "Last time I ignored Thomas's instructions about one of his magical things, it caused a great deal of trouble for both of us. I'm not going to do it again."

"I think that being half strangled by a lavender ribbon

could certainly be described as 'a great deal of trouble,'" I pointed out.

"If it comes to that, you're the one who started it. You could have been killed; I think you would have, if it hadn't been for that charm-bag of yours. Where did you get it?"

"I told you, I made it myself," I said. I picked up the velvet bag and smoothed it, frowning. "I think I had better make another as soon as I get home. Drat! I wanted to—" I remembered who I was talking to just in time and stopped short, for I had planned to spend the evening plotting some way to get inside Bedrick Hall to return Sir Hilary's book.

"I had no idea you were a wizard," James said affably.

"I'm not," I said crossly. "Aunt Elizabeth doesn't approve of magic. And if there are very many wizards like Miranda Griscomb, I can understand why."

"Then how . . . ?" He gestured toward the charm-bag.

"I taught myself out of a book," I said. "It seemed as if it would be a good idea to have *some* kind of protection. Besides Canniba, of course."

"Canniba?"

"My brother Oliver's dog. He would be very good protection against a poacher, I think, but I doubt that he could do anything about ribbons that strangle people. Which reminds me, you never said whether you've got a knife or not. My fingers are getting tired."

Tarleton's shoulders were shaking, but he pulled a small

clasp knife from his waistcoat and gave it to me. "My dear . . . Miss Rushton," he said as he watched me saw the ribbon into inch-long pieces, "it seems to me that other people are more likely to need protection from you than you are to need protection from them."

"Don't be ridiculous," I said. "I've thought and thought, but I can't come up with anything that is likely to discomfit Miranda Griscomb in the least."

James laughed outright, but sobered quickly. "It's just as well that that's true," he said seriously. "Cecelia, don't tangle with Miranda. She's dangerous to cross."

"It doesn't seem like it to me," I said without thinking. "She's tried twice to do something to me, and failed both times."

"Twice?" James said sharply.

I sighed, but there was no help for it. I told him about the almost-accident to my mare the day Dorothea left for London, making as light of it as I could under the circumstances. He looked very worried, but all he said was, "May I take your charm-bag? I want to show it to someone."

"If you like," I said, surprised. "I'll have to make another anyway. The protective spell breaks when you open the bag."

"I know." James was looking grim again. "Be very careful, Miss Rushton, even after you've made yourself a new charm. Who knows how many more of these pleasant little traps Miranda may have left behind her?"

There was nothing I could say to that, so I allowed him to raise me to my feet and assist me back into the curricle. The grays had not moved, being exceptionally well trained, and we drove back to Rushton in silence. When he let me off at the door I said all that was proper, and to my surprise he requested the pleasure of my company this coming Wednesday for a similar outing. I was so astonished that I accepted without thinking.

Mr. Wrexton called on Papa last Friday. I believe I mentioned Mr. Wrexton before; he is the gentleman Aunt E. took such a dislike to when we were visiting the Reverend Fitz last week. He and Papa spent a considerable time in the study discussing some of Papa's work. Then Mr. Wrexton visited with Aunt Elizabeth and me, which I thought very civil of him, though Aunt Elizabeth remained quite stiff the whole time. Papa even joined us after a while, and you know how uncommon that is! Usually it takes three calls before he will come to dinner, and then Aunt Elizabeth has to go and pry him away from his books.

My last news is that Robert Penwood left on Friday in search of Mr. Griscomb. Lady Tarleton was able, after some searching, to give Robert his direction. Somewhere in Yorkshire, I believe, so it will be an unfortunately long time before we will have any news of the outcome. Still, it may serve to cheer Dorothea if she is moped.

Your cousin,
Cecy

29 May 1817
11 Berkeley Square, London

Dearest Cecy,

The one benefit of being confined to my bed by Aunt Charlotte is the breakfast tray she sends up every morning. Today it was poached eggs and streaky bacon, porridge with a pat of butter on top, strawberries and some proper toast, and a pot of tea. Georgy came in to sit on the end of my bed and steal strawberries while she told me the latest *on-dit* she heard last night at Almack's:

The odious Marquis has been pursuing Dorothea as scandalously as every other young man of the Ton. He has justified his behavior by spreading the rumor that I am suffering from an inflammation of the lungs contracted after my accident and may never rise from my bed again, in short (as Georgy puts it), that I am about to cut my stick! I suppose it is preferable to the alternative, that is, of jilting or being jilted, but not much.

I should have thought that Aunt Charlotte would try to squelch such an obvious falsehood, but she is more interested in coddling me past all possible dangers to my health. For the first few days, indeed, I was very glad to be bullied into staying in bed. But now I feel much better and am a little astonished at the sheer numbers of the handkerchiefs I have got through, the cups of beef tea, the glasses of barley water, even the hot bricks to my feet. Indeed, Aunt Charlotte appears to best advantage as a nurse, and she dealt briskly with the callers who came to inquire after my health this week, sending even Mr. Strangle to the right-about. She conceals all this kindness with threats and stern doses of Aunt Elizabeth's Special Cough Mixture, which I have never found all that horrible. I grimace and shudder to make Aunt Charlotte feel better, but really, it is no worse than ratafia, and far better than barley water.

I hope you are not driven distracted with stitching at charm-bags. You have always been very deedy with a needle, but even you must be hard-pressed to meet the sudden demand for them. Mine, despite its wetting (for I carry it in my reticule as you advised), seems to still be good—it dried quickly and still has a pleasant aroma of herbs. I would like to scalp the odious Marquis, but I doubt he would permit me, even if it was for his own protection, so his bag remains in among my gloves and fans.

Georgina seems to have taken it into her head that Oliver overheard her in Vauxhall Gardens and has gone off to the country as a sort of punishment for her scheming. She took it as a penance at first, but in the past day or two has begun to pout when his name enters the conversation and to say gruffly that she supposes it is only to be expected that he should find cockfighting and boxing superior diversions to spending time with her. I'm afraid that is quite true, but I know better than to agree with her.

Miranda has been quite benign these past few days. Georgy tells me she was at Almack's, looking as though she owned the place, and that she (G.) overheard Lady Jersey tell Lady Grenville that it didn't surprise her at all that Dorothea was such a success, for Miranda Tanistry had made her debut in much the same style. I would cheerfully give my pearl eardrops (if I could only find them) to have heard the rest of their conversation, but, of course, Georgy was not able to remain beside them long. Even though every man in London may wish to partner Dorothea, she can only dance with one at a time, and so Georgina is in almost as much demand as before.

For gossip, I know I can trust the fertility of your imagination to produce suitable material to amuse Aunt Elizabeth. To leaven your accounts, you may wish to use a few of the following details: The notorious poetess Lady Caroline Lamb continues to scandalize society with her exploits. Lord Byron continues to scandalize Lady Caro with his uninhibited attempts to rekindle their affair. (Forgive me if my blunt language puts you to the blush. That's what gossip is *for*.) Young men of temperament (like Oliver) continue to dress as Lord Byron does, in the hope that, since Lady Caro modeled her famous *Corsair* on her friend in happier times, stylish dishevelment will give them Corsair-like appeal to young ladies of temperament.

Lady Haseltine paints her toenails silver. Sally Jersey told Aunt Charlotte that she has only seen three girls more beautiful than Georgina and two of them married dukes. Lady Grenville thinks that one can reduce one's figure by eating only grapes. Lord Grenville drinks even more claret than most gentlemen and is far fatter. (Evidently one must eat the grapes and not drink them.) Mr. Strangle *says* he was at Brasenose with the Reverend Mr. Fitzwilliam. I can't help feeling very dubious of almost everything Mr. Strangle tells me.

I can't think of anything else just now, except receipts for cold remedies, which is all I've discussed with anyone lately. Dorothea very kindly sent a basket of glazed fruit and her wishes for my good health and swift recovery. I refused to touch the fruit on the chance that Miranda had been at them, but Aunt Charlotte ate several pieces and pronounced them very good indeed. It is such a shame that Miranda has meddled so with Dorothea's natural charm. She is such a dear creature. Of course, men would call her bird-witted, but if she were at all clever, they would doubtless call her blue and turn up their noses on that account. Men can be such provoking creatures. One would think the entire world and everything in it were made only for their enjoyment and approval. I do hope Robert shows a little backbone and perseveres in his search for Mr. Griscomb, for he could not find himself a girl of more tractable nature.

I am very concerned about your mischance during the curricle ride with James Tarleton. There seems to be no end to Miranda's ingenuity—perhaps there *has* been a trail of dead bodies strewn in her wake. She certainly displays a fine disregard for the consequences of her acts. Fortunately, James Tarleton seems to have the wit to see he has been grievously mistaken in your character and motivations, and enough strength of character to admit the fact. I am glad you saved his life. Nothing could give him a clearer picture of your courage and resource. But I hope you will not be quite so suddenly put on your mettle in the future.

How odd of Aunt Elizabeth to be so stiff with Mr. Wrexton, for you know she usually finds Mr. Fitzwilliam's callers to be completely charming—even though you or I can only see that they are sadly fusty, stuffed-up bores.

Do thank Aunt Elizabeth most particularly for the cough mixture and tell her I found it very soothing. Indeed, my cough is nearly gone and I look forward to the day when Aunt Charlotte will let me get up. While I was ill most of the dresses came from the modiste, including one of very fine white tiffany shot with gold thread. It would look better still on Georgy, of course, but it looks very well on me and I love it far better than Georgy ever could. I can scarcely wait to wear it, and will tell you every particular of the next squeeze I attend, in detail even Aunt Elizabeth would find wearisome.

Love,
Kate

28 May 1817
Rushton Manor, Essex

Dearest Kate,

Aunt Elizabeth is going to wonder at my diligence in writing, but I must get all this down before I begin forgetting the details.

James Tarleton appeared promptly this morning to take me on the drive he had arranged. I was ready, but it had occurred to me that it was just the excuse I needed to get into Bedrick Hall without Aunt Elizabeth's knowledge. Fortunately, the book I took from Sir Hilary's library is not large, and I was able to conceal it inside my reticule. It made the reticule bulge most awkwardly, but I was careful to hold it on the opposite side of myself from Aunt Elizabeth, and she did not notice anything amiss in the few moments it took for me to descend the stairs and be handed up into Mr. Tarleton's curricle. Mr. Tarleton exchanged a few words with Aunt Elizabeth, then sprang into the other seat and we drove away.

"What were you saying to my aunt?" I asked as soon as we were away from the house.

"Only that my mother has invited you to tea," Tarleton replied. "I did not want your aunt to worry if we were a little longer than seemed reasonable."

"Why? What have you planned?" I demanded. I had been so busy with my plans for returning Sir Hilary's book that it had not occurred to me that James Tarleton must have some purpose of his own for our ride, and I was most annoyed with myself.

"Nothing you will object to," James replied in a soothing tone. I cannot think how he came to imagine that he would know what I might or might not object to. "Do you remember my telling you I wanted to show your charm-bag to someone?" he went on. "I did, and he is anxious to meet you. He is waiting at Tarleton Hall."

"And if I would rather not meet him?" I said.

A worried frown crossed Mr. Tarleton's face, but he said, "In that case you need not."

"Well, I have no objection to meeting your friend," I said, and paused. "Provided you let me run a little errand on the way."

James looked at me with a wary expression. "What sort of errand? Where?"

"Bedrick Hall."

"No," he said at once. "Good God, have you *no* sense? Miranda's malice will be nothing compared to what you'll face if Sir Hilary finds out you've been poking around there."

"I have no intention of poking around," I said, trying to sound as if I meant it. "I have business at Bedrick Hall."

"What sort of business?"

"I wish to retrieve the fan I dropped in the library, that day everyone else was lost in the maze."

"You weren't carrying a fan that day," James said positively. He looked at me with a grim expression. "The truth, Cecy."

It is most annoying to be faced with someone who refuses to accept even the most plausible subterfuge. I sighed. "I have to get into Sir Hilary's library to return a book I took," I said.

"You stole a book from Sir Hilary's library?" Mr. Tarleton looked positively aghast.

"I most certainly did not," I said. "If I had stolen it, I would not now be looking for a way to put it back. And before you make any foolish objections, you should remember that if Sir Hilary returns and discovers one of his wizardry books is missing, I will be in just as much trouble as if Mrs. Porter tells him I have been poking about. She won't, though. My excuse is a perfectly unexceptionable one."

James argued a bit longer, but eventually he was forced to admit the good sense of my proposal. For, as I pointed out, it would look very odd for me to ride all the way over to Bedrick Hall simply to retrieve a fan, but it is quite reasonable that I would ask him to stop if we happened to be driving by. I did not add that Mrs. Porter, like many housekeepers, is of a romantic turn of mind, and will certainly conclude that I persuaded Mr. Tarleton to take me to Bedrick Hall out of a desire to be longer in his company. Somehow I did not think he would appreciate the fact that this erroneous conclusion would make Mrs. Porter even more willing to believe my tale.

To my surprise, when we reached Bedrick Hall Mr. Tarleton handed his horses over to one of the footmen and requested that he walk them for a few moments. Then he accompanied me into the house. I told Mrs. Porter my fiction about the fan, and she looked at me doubtfully and said that she rather thought the room had been turned out since then, but I was welcome to look. She looked a little taken aback when Mr. Tarleton said very blandly that he would accompany me.

"What are you doing?" I hissed at him as we followed Mrs. Porter down the hall.

"Making sure you won't go looking for a new way of getting into trouble," he replied.

I was forced to swallow the furious retort that rose in my throat in answer to this outrageous behavior, for we had reached the library. I made a great show of looking behind several chairs, then bent over as if to check behind the sofa. I had no difficulty in slipping Sir Hilary's book out of my reticule, but I did not think I could replace it on the bookshelf without Mrs. Porter's noticing. I therefore put my hand against the books and tipped a number of them onto the floor as I rose, trying to make it seem as though I were simply being clumsy. As they fell, I let go of the book on charm-bags (not without a pang, I promise you, for it has been not only interesting but exceedingly useful, as I know you will be the first to agree!).

"Oh!" I said in accents of dismay. "Oh, dear, I'm so *dreadfully* sorry! I can't imagine how I came to be so clumsy!"

Mrs. Porter made soothing noises. I bent over the books again and began putting them back onto the shelf, continuing to apologize the while. James joined me, amusement flickering in his eyes. "Very clever," he whispered as he returned a brown leather-bound volume to its place.

"Thank you, Mr. Tarleton," I said. I picked up the last book, a greenish gray volume. *Epicyclical Elaborations of Sorcery* was the title on the spine, and the author was Everard Tanistry. I hesitated, strongly tempted to take it away with me, for I remembered you writing that Thomas had said Miranda was a Tanistry before she married Mr. Griscomb, and I wondered if Everard might have been some relation.

I was not given the chance. Mr. Tarleton plucked the book from my hands and shoved it back into position on the shelf as though he were disposing of a live snake. "That's the last of them, I think," he said in a pleasant tone, and held out his hand to help me rise.

"I sincerely hope not," said a familiar, vaguely supercilious voice from the other side of the room.

I jumped, startled, and peered over the edge of the sofa to find Sir Hilary Bedrick standing in the doorway, just behind Mrs. Porter. He had obviously only just come in, for he had not stayed to put off his driving cape. Fortunately, Mrs. Porter was even more flustered than I; she curtseyed and began apologizing at once, which gave me time to collect myself. Sir Hilary dismissed her with a nod; then he turned and raised a quizzing glass to study James and me.

"Tarleton," he said, nodding a greeting. "No doubt the servants neglected to inform you that I was from home."

"He came with me, Sir Hilary," I said quickly.

"Indeed. Do come out from behind the sofa, Miss Rushton," he said. "I cannot imagine why I find your presence in my library surprising, but I must confess I do. Perhaps you would be good enough to explain?"

"Miss Rushton thought she had dropped her fan here," Mr. Tarleton said. "Your housekeeper was good enough to allow her to come in to look for it."

Sir Hilary looked at him and snorted. "Naturally, you believed every word of her story."

Mr. Tarleton raised both eyebrows. "I don't believe I thought much about it, one way or the other," he said.

Sir Hilary gave him a sharp glance and turned to me. "And have you found your fan?"

"No," I said with as much composure as I could manage. "I must have lost it in the maze. I do apologize for intruding like this, but I was very anxious to retrieve it. Oliver gave it to me for my last birthday, you see."

"Indeed." Sir Hilary snorted again. Then he gave me a rather thin smile. "And how is Oliver these days?"

"As caper-witted as ever," I said disgustedly. "He was in London for a few weeks, but he has now gone to visit friends, and though he wrote Papa not to expect him home soon, he neglected to furnish us with his direction."

"Ah." Sir Hilary looked closely at me, and smiled again. "Dear me, I have been so long on the road that I am forgetting my manners. Allow me to invite you to join me for some refreshment."

"I am afraid we must decline, Sir Hilary," Mr. Tarleton said. "My mother is expecting Miss Rushton to take tea with her, and we are already late."

"Then, of course, you must go," Sir Hilary said. He moved aside from the doorway, and I was surprised at the relief I felt at being allowed to leave. Sir Hilary accompanied us to the front of the house, and I gave him a completely spurious description of the nonexistent fan, in case one of his servants should run across it. He asked after Papa and Aunt Elizabeth, and I congratulated him on his recent election to the Royal College of Wizards. A peculiar expression crossed his face when I mentioned that, but it was gone so quickly that I may have been mistaken, and he handed me up into the curricle with unimpaired courtesy. As we drove away, I saw the servants unloading trunks from Sir Hilary's traveling carriage.

Neither James nor I said anything until we were well away from Bedrick Hall. I do not know about Mr. Tarleton, but I was thinking furiously. I know of no reason for Sir Hilary to return from London nearly a month before the end of the Season. I therefore have hopes that the ruse you played with Miranda has been successful, and he and she have had a strong difference of opinion, which has led to his departure. I do not wish to be overly confident in this opinion, however, for one can never tell with Sir Hilary.

I had just reached this point in my deliberations when Mr. Tarleton broke the silence to say, "Perhaps I had better take you home."

"I thought you wanted me to meet someone," I said, looking at him in surprise. His expression was one of concern, and I said without thinking, "Oh, you cannot think that I am overset by a mere encounter with Sir Hilary! It was startling, I must own, but—"

"Forgive me, Miss Rushton," James interrupted, "but Sir Hilary is precisely what is worrying me. I don't believe he has given me a second thought until now, because Thomas's dislike of Miranda extends to avoiding all her connections, however remote. After finding me crawling about on the floor of his library, however, he can hardly fail to become suspicious."

I considered this briefly, and decided that James was quite right. It is so provoking! For if Sir Hilary is going to be suspicious of me anyway, I could just as well have taken that book by Everard Tanistry, and perhaps learned something.

"Well, I am exceedingly sorry," I said at last, "but I do not think it fair for you to blame me. It was, after all, an accident."

"I am not blaming you," James said. "I'm trying to keep you from getting further involved."

I did not pretend that I did not understand. "My cousin, who is my dearest friend, is engaged to your friend—" (I almost said, "Your odious friend," but I stopped myself in time) "—Thomas; my brother Oliver has been turned into a beech tree and has now disappeared; Miranda has tried twice to have me killed or injured because I am fond of Dorothea. Pray tell me how much further it is possible for me to become involved."

He was silent for a time. "I don't like it," he said at last.

"You don't have to," I said, feeling quite cross. "But I *am* involved. And if Sir Hilary finds out that you took me straight home, instead of to tea at Tarleton Hall as you told him, he is bound to become even more suspicious than he already is."

"I suppose you are right," James said gloomily, and turned the horses toward Tarleton Hall. "How did you know your brother had been turned into a beech tree?" he said after a long pause.

"Kate wrote me," I said.

He looked at me sharply. "How much has she told you?"

"How should I know?" I retorted. "If one does not know the whole, it is impossible to say how large a part of it one *does* know. And in any case, what Kate tells me is none of your affair."

He relapsed into gloom, and we rode the remainder of the distance to Tarleton Hall in silence. In fact, he did not speak again until he escorted me into the pink saloon at Tarleton Hall. To my surprise, Mr. Wrexton was waiting in the saloon. (And he is not a "fusty, stuffed-up bore" in the slightest, Kate, even if I did meet him at the Reverend Fitz's.) He rose as I entered and bowed. "Miss Rushton! What a pleasant surprise."

"Why, Mr. Wrexton!" I said, looking uncertainly at James from the corner of my eyes. "I had not thought to meet you here."

"You know each other?" James said, frowning.

"Mr. Wrexton was kind enough to call on Papa last Friday," I said.

Mr. Wrexton was looking from me to Mr. Tarleton with a bemused expression. "My dear fellow! You can't mean that *this* is . . ."

"The person who made that extremely interesting charm-bag I brought you, yes," James said.

"Why on earth didn't you say so?" Mr. Wrexton asked mildly. "There would have been no need for this subterfuge; I could have called on Miss Rushton at home." He gave me a warm smile.

"I am afraid that would not have served," I said regretfully, returning his smile. "At least, not if you wish to talk about my charm-bag. Aunt Elizabeth would never allow me to do anything so improper as to receive a gentleman unchaperoned, and Aunt Elizabeth has a strong aversion to anything that smacks of magic, however slightly. She would have shown you to the door as soon as you brought the subject up."

"I see." Mr. Wrexton looked exceedingly thoughtful. "That does complicate matters. Well, now that you are here, won't you sit down and discuss it with me?"

He offered me a chair, then took the one beside me, leaving James to sit on the other side of the tea table. I took a cup of tea, and we began chatting about charm-bags. Or rather, Mr. Wrexton asked me a great many questions, and I answered as well as I could. Mr. Wrexton, it seems, is a magician of some note, and has even worked with the Duke of Wellington. I suppose that is why Aunt Elizabeth took him in dislike. He specializes in complex and powerful spells, and claims to have been most impressed by my charm-bag.

"Spells of that kind depend a great deal on the power and ability of the wizard," he told me. "Yours was quite remarkable; even after the bag had been opened, there was a significant magical residue. I wish I had had the chance to study it while it was intact."

"I've made another," I said, and pulled it from my reticule. Mr. Wrexton did not seem surprised, but bent over it at once, turning it this way and that in his hands.

"And the herbs?" he said at last.

I told him the mixture I had used, and found myself explaining about the book I had taken from Sir Hilary's library. He nodded thoughtfully. "You have a great deal of talent, my dear," he said when I had finished. "It would be a shame for you to waste it. We must find some way of teaching you."

"Now, wait a minute, Wrexton!" Mr. Tarleton said. "You can't—"

"I would like that very much, Mr. Wrexton," I said, smiling. "I have always been interested in magic."

Mr. Tarleton was plainly furious, but he could hardly quarrel with me in Mr. Wrexton's presence. To avoid being shouted at on the way home, I accepted Mr. Wrexton's offer to drive me back to Rushton himself. We had a marvelous time, and he gave me a number of hints about charm-bags and spell casting in general. When we reached Rushton, I invited him in, which did not seem to please Aunt Elizabeth, though she thawed a little when Mr. Wrexton said that he had the intention of continuing on toward town, to visit the Reverend Fitzwilliam. He offered to escort her, should she wish to see the Reverend Fitz herself. Aunt Elizabeth declined, but she was quite in charity with him by the time he left.

So I am to have magic lessons, at least I will if I can contrive a means of keeping it from Aunt Elizabeth. I also intend to return to Sir Hilary's library and get a better look at that book by Everard Tanistry, though that will have to wait a little. It would never do to arouse his suspicions (always assuming they are not *already* aroused) by being discovered a second time going through his library.

 I June

Your letter arrived yesterday, and I am glad to hear that you are feeling better. I am enclosing a spare charm-bag for you, just in case. (A wetting won't hurt it; the only thing that will break the spell is opening the bag.) Oh, and I have asked Mr. Wrexton, in as general a sort of way as possible and without being too specific about names, just what might have made the stains on the Marquis's handkerchief turn violet when you washed it. He said he couldn't tell without actually looking at it, but that the color violet usually indicates safety or defense when it turns up in this kind of way. So the handkerchief may actually be doing you, or the Marquis, some good. It is a great relief to me to think so; I hope you have it safe.

Aunt Elizabeth and I paid a call on the Reverend Fitzwilliam yesterday. The Reverend Fitz does not recall having been at school with anyone named Strangle, and, in fact, became almost distressed in his efforts to recall the name. I said that I must have been mistaken in my understanding of what you had written me, and very likely you had only meant that Mr. Strangle was at some other school at the same time, or at

Brasenose just after the Reverend Fitz. I do not, of course, think anything of the kind, but there are times when it is necessary to employ a polite fiction. Particularly with the Reverend Fitz. Whatever the explanation, I thought you should know about Mr. Strangle.

Mr. Wrexton arrived barely fifteen minutes after we did, bringing a bottle of wine he had apparently promised Reverend Fitzwilliam on Wednesday. We spent a pleasant half hour in innocuous discussion before Aunt Elizabeth insisted that we leave. I have begun to wonder whether she suspects that Mr. Wrexton is a wizard, though how she could have discovered that is beyond me. It would explain her apparent distaste for his company.

I have heard nothing from Robert, but I did not really expect to have any news from him this soon. I am, in fact, rather grateful. It has occurred to me that even if Robert does obtain Mr. Griscomb's consent to marry Dorothea, Miranda would have no compunction about feeding him poisoned chocolate or making one of his cravats strangle him. I am very sorry this did not occur to me before I sent him off looking for Mr. Griscomb; still, something must be done about Miranda in any case. We cannot allow her to continue wandering around enchanting marquises, turning people into beech trees, frightening horses, and leaving ribbons about to strangle people. This simply means that we must deal with her a little sooner.

I shall make up a charm-bag for Robert, in case he finds Mr. Griscomb and announces his engagement before Miranda has been dealt with, and one for Dorothea as well. I will send them with my next letter. It will take me a little while to get them finished, as I do not dare work on them in Aunt Elizabeth's presence. I will also ask Mr. Wrexton's opinion, in a very general sort of way, of what can be done about particularly unscrupulous and powerful wizards. In the meantime, perhaps you could tell Dorothea that Robert has been quite moped since she left. I am sure she will let this slip to Miranda, which will give Miranda the impression that Robert is still in Rushton.

Georgy is being a goose, as usual. Oliver would be far more likely to lecture her at great length on the impropriety of her conduct than to absent himself from Town as a punishment.

Word has got round that Sir Hilary is back in residence, by the way, and Aunt Elizabeth has reluctantly agreed that we must pay a formal call sometime this week. It is fortunate that she has so strong a sense of duty, for otherwise I am sure she would refuse to visit a practicing wizard. She was stiff enough with him before he was ever admitted to the Royal College.

Your new dresses sound wonderful; you will have to model them all for me when you return from London. Take the greatest care of yourself, and if any notion occurs to you of how to deal with Miranda or Sir Hilary, write me at once!

Your faithful,
Cecy

Dearest Cecy,

I have given Dorothea your message about Robert. Dorothea had a most singular message for me—but let me start with your news. Far better for Sir Hilary to have suspicions of you than to have certain knowledge you are in a conspiracy against him when he catches you absconding with another of his books. What can such a volume tell us to match the risk you would run? After all, the important thing is that its existence confirms the sorcerous background of the Tanistry family.

That Mr. Wrexton says you have an aptitude for magic surprises me very little—remember when Georgy and I tried to charm away her freckles with morning dew? Then you tried, with the very same dew, and they faded completely. To this day, Georgy has never had another. Which just shows you.

The Marquis's handkerchief is perfectly safe. I put it into the second charm-bag you sent for me, on the grounds that it could be anyone's handkerchief, but it is my blood.

Dorothea called this afternoon, and I gave her the carefully edited news you sent regarding Robert. She was delighted by the mere sound of his name, and we discussed his virtues at great length, I thought, considering how few of them he possesses. After perhaps half an hour spent listing his excellences, Dorothea gave a little start. Then she plumped her reticule down on the tea table and began rummaging about in it. After a moment, she very gingerly brought out a small parcel, about the size of a teacup, done up in a crumpled bit of striped paper and a quite ordinary bit of string.

"I almost forgot," she said, putting it into my hand. "This is for you. Thomas sent it."

She informed me that he'd given it to her that morning when he took her out driving in the park. "He knew I would call here this afternoon, for I told him so yesterday. We were talking about you and I said you would be at Countess Lieven's tonight. That was when he asked me to go driving with him."

"You were talking about me?" I said. "Why?"

"Well, it is only natural, isn't it?" replied Dorothea. "After all, he is betrothed to you."

I regarded Dorothea with wonder. I never thought anyone could be sillier than Georgina, but Dorothea shows every sign of it. "And he gave you this to give to me?" I asked. She nodded.

I scrutinized the little parcel cautiously, half suspecting it to be some piece of Miranda's handiwork. But the paper was the green and white striped sort that Gunther's uses to wrap up boxes of bonbons and the string displayed signs of much previous use. I felt quite certain Miranda would do things a bit more elaborately.

"Aren't you going to open it?" asked Dorothea.

I undid the string and opened the paper. Inside there was a seashell, quite a pretty one in its way, but nothing extraordinary. I examined the wrapper minutely. There was no sign of any message. I turned the seashell over and over, but it was precisely what it seemed—a seashell. Finally, with a little sigh, I handed the shell to Dorothea.

"How very provoking of him," she said. "He told me it was something of great importance." Idly, she put the shell to her ear. "I can't even hear the sea in it."

I took the shell from her and put it to my own ear. She was correct. For a long moment, I could hear nothing from the shell. Then, quite as plainly as if he were standing behind me, I heard Thomas speak.

"Kate," he said, "if you mean to go to Countess Lieven's tonight, I beg you, do not. With matters as they stand now, I can manage things by myself, but I cannot protect you and handle wizards, too. Please use your common sense for once and stay at home. I will tell you when it is safe to return to Society."

There was another moment of silence, then the hushing sound proper to seashells began.

"Why, how queer and white you look, Kate," said Dorothea. "Are you feeling ill again?"

"No, no," I said. "Here, listen to it now. What do you hear?"

"Why, the sea," she said. "I can't think why Thomas thought it was so important. It is quite an ordinary seashell."

"I shall have to ask him about it tonight at Countess Lieven's," I said, and poured us each another cup of tea.

So, Cecy, in a few minutes I must begin to dress. I am a little late because I wanted to write to you on receipt of your letter—I shall write again directly I am back this evening—and because I took the time, after Dorothea's departure, to use the heel of my slipper to reduce that seashell to small bits. This act of wanton destruction has made me feel a little better, and I am looking forward to this evening very much. Perhaps I will be able to use the same technique on my lord, the Marquis of Schofield's skull.

Later

I shall add a few lines to this letter before I send it off just to say what a satisfactory evening it was. There must be some fiery element in the air of London, for I never liked an atmosphere of discord at home. Yet, at Countess Lieven's tonight, there was discord aplenty and it merely sharpened my enjoyment. The guests were split in two groups—some were whispering about Dorothea and her string of admirers, some about Georgy. (Apparently, Georgy's friendship for Dorothea excites comment.) It added an element of enjoyment for me, when Georgy and I greeted Dorothea, to know our friendliness with her displeased so many onlookers.

When Frederick Hollydean sidled up to me after the first dance to ask me to join him in the Sir Roger de Coverley, I had little choice but to consent. But before the set was made up, he said softly to me, "I wonder, do you share your sister's talents at the tables?" I did not get his meaning and I told him so. He dropped his voice to an even more conspiratorial whisper and said, "*Gaming*. Do you like it?"

I dropped his hand and stepped back. "That is a very poor jest," I said. My voice was quiet but cold. I do not know what my expression was, but I have an idea I might have resembled Aunt Charlotte to some degree, for Frederick dropped his eyes and began to beg my pardon extensively. I left him in mid-apology. This is the first reference to Grandfather's tendency that I've heard in Society. I suppose it must be known, but only Frederick Hollydean would find it a suitable topic of conversation. Still, it afforded me an escape from the dance with him.

After a moment or two I was able to compose myself and gaze calmly about the ballroom. It was wonderful to be out of my bedroom and free to dance and laugh and receive complimentary remarks upon my appearance. Either flouting snobbish young ladies improves my looks, or everyone there expected me to be at death's door after listening to the odious Marquis spin tales of my ill health for a week, for I have never received so many compliments in my life.

The dress was everything I had hoped. Georgy helped me with my hair, which she dressed with a gilt ribbon in a mode she insisted on calling *à la Grecque*. She lent me a pair of sandals of gilded leather, and (though Aunt Charlotte would certainly have shot us both dead on the spot if she had noticed) painted my toenails gold as well. On the whole, I think I looked very well, though, of course, vastly *fast* for a young lady in her first Season, betrothed or not. Had Dorothea not been there, in fact, I should have repented of my rashness, for it might have given some of the gentlemen there a misleading idea of my personality. But I could have been wearing a jewel in my navel and gone unnoticed by every man in the room, so long as Dorothea was there for them to rest their eyes upon. So I enjoyed myself immensely until the evening was half over, despite Miranda's gimlet gaze upon me as I danced.

Midway through the evening, the Marquis of Schofield arrived, looking a little weary, I thought, but as impeccably dressed as ever. He sought out Dorothea at once, and she slighted Michael Aubrey to give him an allemande, which he accepted with every show of enthusiasm. I was dancing with Andrew Grenville (George still has his arm in a sling, but does not bear a grudge against me) when he spied me. The look in his eyes could have cracked glass. I suppose the look in my eyes might have done some damage, too, for when he noticed my expression, Andrew exclaimed, "Oh, I say, I'm frightfully sorry—have I stepped on you again?"

I reassured Andrew and we went on dancing. But though we were moving as the other couples moved, the odious Marquis began to dance in our direction. He came toward us with a kind of graceful determination, tacking like a ship through the sea of dancers. When the allemande ended, Andrew turned from me to Dorothea with a glad cry as the orchestra began a waltz. The odious Marquis snatched me before I could elude him.

"What are you doing here, you—hetaera?" Thomas demanded.

"It may interest you to know, my lord, that my uncle is an antiquary and I am perfectly well aware what a hetaera is," I informed him.

"You don't surprise me," he replied grimly. "Didn't you get my message?"

"Indeed, I did, my lord," I replied. "I disregarded it."

"Oh, did you?" he sneered. "Doubtless you knew better than I."

"Quite so," I said. "You were reasoning from incorrect information."

"Go on, Miss Talgarth," said Thomas. "Correct me."

"You said you could handle things by yourself," I said. "Plainly you are mistaken."

My lord the Marquis of Schofield made no reply to this

in words, but executed a waltz turn that would have given me convulsions a month ago. As I have had a good deal of practice dancing lately, I followed him without mishap, and when we had come forth to smooth water once again, I continued.

"I wonder if you have been in communication with James Tarleton of late?" I said in a tone of mild inquiry. "Does *he* believe that you can handle things by yourself?"

Thomas executed another sudden maneuver and I found myself dancing the waltz in the Russian room at Countess Lieven's. Only slightly discomfited by this piece of effrontery, I followed his lead as he danced over to a settee in the corner. With a good deal of violence, he helped me take a seat. I arranged my skirts becomingly and smiled up at him insincerely. Thomas seated himself beside me and took my hand in his. From a distance it might have appeared to an observer that we were gazing ardently into each other's eyes. Seen close to, the annoyance in Thomas's expression was forbidding.

"You realize, don't you, that you have just ruined the effect I have put better than a fortnight's time into achieving?" he demanded. His voice was soft but fierce. "There will be no point, after this, in pretending to Miranda that I have any interest whatever in Dorothea. Her plan has failed, and the moment she realizes that, my plan does, too. And it is all your fault."

"Perhaps if you had told me your plan——," I began.

He shook his head impatiently. "What's the point?" he demanded. "I expected Dorothea to exert, er, an appeal she manifestly lacks."

"You certainly haven't behaved as if she lacked a thing," I said.

"That's what I meant Miranda to think. But she nearly murdered you when she thought you were all that stood in the way of her plans for me. Then you wouldn't cry off and I had to make the best of things without provoking her into another attempt to kill you."

"Thoughtful behavior from a man who looks as though he'd like to kill me himself," I remarked.

"It might have worked if you had listened to me and been a little helpful, but that was too much to expect. What, after all, was my wish compared to your desire to make a cake of yourself in front of the entire Ton? Why didn't you damp your dress as the Cyprians do? Then no one would have to rely on imagination at all."

"Oh, stop being so absurd," I said. It is the oddest thing, Cecy, that I was not at all angry. If anyone else had said such things to me, I would have slapped him. But all I could think of was that Thomas had no interest whatever in Dorothea, and if the expression of fury on his face was anything to go by, he had a great deal of interest in me.

"We are in a great muddle, it is true," I told him, "but I haven't made it any worse. Or at least not much worse. What was I to do? Pretend to languish for months while you play cat and mouse with Miranda? I would like to help you, if I may, for I am grateful for what you have done for Oliver. But I cannot be of much use until you tell me more about your plan—and your problem, for all I know certainly is that it concerns a chocolate pot."

"Well, you will probably make mice feet of the entire business but you can do no worse than you did by coming here this evening," he snarled. His tone was harsh but his expression had softened a trifle. He stared into my eyes for a long moment, then said with great satisfaction, "I regret to inform you, my dear half-wit, that you have a headache."

"Don't be silly," I began—and then I did have a headache, quite abruptly. Not as severely as that awful day when he came to ask me to cry off, but definitely a headache. I put my hand to my temple.

"My dear Miss Talgarth," said the odious Marquis in a somewhat louder voice, "may I fetch you something? Ratafia? Spirits of hartshorn? Sal volatile? Your Aunt Charlotte?"

"No, no," I said, "it's nothing. It will pass in a moment."

"Take you home?" he replied, as if I had not spoken. "Of course, my dear, at once. You should not have risen from your sickbed so promptly. Doubtless you are having a relapse."

Before I could protest, he was gone to find Aunt Charlotte. In less time than I would have thought possible, he had arranged to drive me home himself—yes, without even a chaperone, for, of course, Aunt Charlotte could not leave Georgy. Oh, odious that man may be, but he has more address than I would have thought possible.

Scarcely was I out in the fresh night air than the headache began to fade. I took my hand away from my forehead and blinked at him. "You shouldn't do things like that," I told him.

"Don't you want an explanation?" he replied. "How could I speak in there?"

I did not answer. The brush of Thomas's sleeve against my arm distracted me from his words. He was so near to me I could catch the faint scent of him, an interesting combination of shaving soap and wood smoke. It occurred to me that I had never been alone in the dark with a gentleman before. I found it a novel sensation and I wished to give it my full consideration, but Thomas went on talking.

"I never meant it to be a chocolate pot," he said. "I had a pocket watch I meant to use. But when the ceremony took place, things were a trifle rushed. Sir Hilary desired me to wait until he felt I was ready for such a strenuous exercise of my magic—and the wait would have been a long one, for he found it useful to be able to draw upon my magic for the execution of his spells. He was seeking me—and at the moment of the ceremony, the spell he was using found me. I knew he was nearly on me and I acted with dispatch. My magic was safely focused, but not through the pocket watch." He broke off. "Are you listening?"

I collected my scattered thoughts and said, "Yes, quite so, the chocolate pot," as intelligently as I could.

Thomas sighed. "Yes. I don't know why. There were a dozen more suitable objects on my desk at the time. Somehow it found the chocolate pot a more congenial spot. And somehow a little of Sir Hilary's magic, just a whiff of it as the seeking spell hit, found its way into the chocolate pot, too."

"How distressing," I said. I don't think Thomas can be considered musical, but his voice is very pleasant to listen to. I found myself speaking almost at random, more attuned to the pitch and inflection of his words than to the sense.

"It took me a long time to find out about Sir Hilary's contribution," Thomas continued, "for I left for the Peninsula that night and took my chocolate set with me. And if you think an officer on Wizard Wellington's staff travels in sufficient state to warrant taking a chocolate set everywhere he goes, well, you're mistaken. But while we were on campaign, we were far enough that Sir Hilary's magic couldn't reach me. It wasn't until after Waterloo when we all mustered out of the service that I came back to settle down and discovered that England was as good as a wasps' nest to me while Sir Hilary thought I had his magic under some sort of control."

Thomas fell silent at last. I was able, with a little difficulty, to recollect my wandering thoughts. "How did you lose the chocolate pot?" I asked.

It seemed I was not alone in my distraction, for it took

Thomas a moment to reply, and then his words had an abstracted air. "Oh, a bit of a misunderstanding," he replied, then said more briskly, "Oh, the devil, we're here."

And we were in Berkeley Square.

We behaved very properly, of course, for I knew Aunt Charlotte would certainly cross-question the servants when she arrived home. I was turned over to the maid who had kindly waited up for me, who helped me to untangle my hair and exclaimed in horror when she saw the state of my toes. When she left me I began this letter, for Cecy, how can I sleep? He doesn't care two pins for Dorothea, and never did.

Love,
Kate

✴ 10 June 1817
Rushton Manor, Essex

Dearest Kate,

Of course your odious Marquis does not care two pins for Dorothea. I cannot think how you could ever have supposed otherwise, for one really cannot count the emotions aroused by that insidious spell of Miranda's. I am quite put out, however, to learn that he was simply counterfeiting the effect, especially after all the thought we have put into trying to rescue him from it. He might at least have told you what he was about, and saved us both the effort.

There are, in fact, a great many things he might have told you, and I am exceedingly sorry you did not think to have him take a turn around the park on your way back from Countess Lieven's. He seems to have been in a confiding mood, and you might have got the full tale out of him. However, there is no sense in regretting it now. I can only hope that his mood has lasted, and that you have been able to chivy him into providing a few more of the details. For I must tell you, Kate, that I am not likely to get anything out of James Tarleton. He has not been next nor nigh the house this past week, and it is quite impossible to question someone who is not present.

Fortunately, Mr. Wrexton has been more particular. He has called three times, once to take tea and chat with Aunt Elizabeth, and twice to take me driving (and give me the first of my magic lessons). Aunt Elizabeth does not know of the lessons, of course, but she still does not approve of my outings with him. She cannot do more than be rather stiff about it, though. Mr. Wrexton is, after all, a friend of the vicar's, and as she had already consented to my driving alone with James Tarleton, she could not object to the outings on grounds of propriety. I believe she is worried that he is growing particular in his attentions, and means to offer for me. This is quite absurd, but I can hardly explain to Aunt Elizabeth that Mr. Wrexton's only interest in me is as a sorcery student.

My lessons are going well, I think, and as a result I may be able to shed a little light on the extremely muddled explanation Thomas gave you regarding the chocolate pot. It seems there are a great many magicians who, in order to use their magic most effectively, must have an object through which to focus their power. This object must be kept nearby when casting spells. (I believe it works along the same lines as wearing spectacles—some people need them, others don't; every pair is different and it does no good to try to use someone else's; one can see without them, but not nearly so well; and they do one no good whatever if they are not in place when one requires them.)

I believe that what Thomas was trying to say is that the chocolate pot is the object he uses to focus his magic. If so, its absence is a very serious thing, for without it his magic cannot be nearly as strong as it ought to be. With both Miranda and Sir Hilary hounding him . . . well, I do not like the implications in the least. I do not know what effect the "whiff of Sir Hilary's magic" that got into the chocolate pot would have, but I doubt that it can be a good one.

Thomas must know all this, and I can only say that it was *exceedingly* careless of him to have let Sir Hilary get hold of that chocolate pot in the first place. He would have been much better off, I think, if he had broken the silly thing and made himself another focus. I suppose he was too proud. Thomas's good sense appears to come only in flashes. It was very silly of him to suggest, for example, that you damp your dresses when you have just got over a shocking cold. One would think he *wished* you to have an inflammation of the lungs. And he himself admits that dangling after Dorothea in that odious manner was a stupid thing to have done. He has, however, managed not to fall into any of Miranda's traps, which argues rather more intelligence than he has been evincing recently. (On rereading your letter, I see that Thomas was not, in fact, advocating that you damp your skirts, so perhaps I am doing him an injustice in that instance.)

Speaking of magic, I do appreciate your loyal remembrance of our attempts at clearing up Georgy's freckles, but I cannot in conscience take the credit. I think Aunt Elizabeth's Strawberry Complexion Lotion far more likely to have done the trick—that, and the fact that since that summer Georgy has followed Aunt Charlotte's advice and avoided sitting in the sun.

I have not had another chance to investigate Sir Hilary's library. And it is the outside of enough for you to be asking me what I may learn by doing so. If I knew that, I should not need to ransack the library at all. I had hoped to manage it yesterday, when Aunt Elizabeth and I paid our duty call at Bedrick Hall, but under the circumstances, perhaps it was as well I did not attempt it. When Sir Hilary's butler ushered us into the gray sitting room, Sir Hilary was already there, along with Mr. and Mrs. Everslee and the Reverend Fitzwilliam. They had all come to congratulate him on his appointment to the Royal College of Wizards and (in the case of Mrs. Everslee) to see if there was any chance of his holding a party in celebration. Not that Mrs. Everslee has become frivolous, you understand; it is just that now both Dorothea and Georgy are away and Patience will finally have a chance to shine. Provided, of course, that there is an event for her to shine at.

The conversation consisted of empty pleasantries, for the most part. Then the tea tray arrived, and I was hard put to keep my countenance. For there, right in the center of the tray, was a perfectly beautiful blue porcelain chocolate pot.

I could feel Sir Hilary watching me as the footman set the tray down, so I pretended to be absorbed in what the Reverend Fitz was saying. (Something about the drains in the parsonage, I believe.) Then Sir Hilary asked Mrs. Everslee if she would be good enough to pour, and I turned my attention to the tea along with the rest of the group.

Mrs. Everslee gave Aunt Elizabeth a cup of tea, then turned to me. "I will have chocolate, please," I said, for I had had time enough to think and I did not see how Sir Hilary could try to poison me in such company.

"I did not realize you were fond of chocolate, Miss Rushton," Sir Hilary said.

"Oh, I like it of all things," I replied as carelessly as I could manage. "I am so glad you thought to serve it."

"The pot is meant for chocolate, and I thought it deserved to be used," Sir Hilary said blandly.

"To be sure," I said. I took two cucumber sandwiches and one of the macaroons, then made a show of studying the chocolate pot. It was very like your description; I am quite sure it is either Thomas's or another copy like the one Miranda had at Sir Hilary's investiture. "It is very nice, but it does not go with the rest of your tea set," I observed dispassionately.

"That shade of blue is difficult to match," Sir Hilary replied. He paused, then went on with apparent casualness, "How does your brother go on?"

"Oliver is quite well," I said, and took a bite out of one of my sandwiches.

"I am glad to hear it," Sir Hilary said, swinging his quizzing glass absently on the end of its ribbon. "You have had news of him recently, then?"

"Oh, Oliver has never been much of a hand at writing," I said. "But it is very kind of you to ask."

I gave Sir Hilary my most brilliant smile, tore my eyes away from the chocolate pot, and turned to offer Aunt Elizabeth one of the macaroons, thus putting an end to a most uncomfortable conversation. This maneuver placed me facing the large windows that look out over the side lawn and the little pavilion just in front of the hedge where the maze begins. As I held the plate out to Aunt Elizabeth, I saw a flicker of movement among the bushes. In another moment, someone ran across the open space and disappeared behind the pavilion. I had just enough of a glimpse to make me quite sure that it was James Tarleton.

I swallowed my dismay and irritation—really, the man is impossibly bad at sneaking about—and turned back to the Reverend Fitz. Sir Hilary was looking past me at the window, which made my spirits sink. There was nothing I could do but hope he had not seen James, or that he was uncertain of the identity of whoever was skulking in his bushes.

Somehow, I got through the rest of that tea, but my feelings were in such turmoil that I did not think it wise to attempt to slip away to the library. Aunt Elizabeth and I left at last, and I promise you that I will never again complain of her insistence on limiting our calls on Sir Hilary to the formal thirty minutes.

I spent the remainder of the afternoon at my embroidery, considering Sir Hilary's actions and worrying lest Mr. Tarleton had been discovered. (I spent the evening unpicking all the stitches I had labored over in the afternoon; my mind was *not* on my work.) Mr. Tarleton did not call Tuesday, nor Wednesday. On Thursday, Mr. Wrexton mentioned having ridden out with James the previous day, which let me know that at least Mr. Tarleton was not tied up in Sir Hilary's storerooms somewhere. I am quite out of patience with the man (James Tarleton, not Mr. Wrexton. Mr. Wrexton is a sweet lamb). He might have had the courtesy to call and let me know he was all right and what, if anything, he discovered at Bedrick Hall.

Upon reflection, I have come to the conclusion that Sir Hilary was testing me by displaying Thomas's chocolate pot (or a copy of it, which seems more likely) so openly and under such circumstances. I flatter myself that I did quite well at concealing my reactions, but I have no idea whether I did sufficiently well to convince Sir Hilary that I know nothing of the chocolate pot. It is also very clear that Sir Hilary is, or was, suspicious of me. He would not otherwise have used the chocolate pot, for you know his taste has always been meticulous, and blue porcelain cannot be considered to go at all well with sprig-patterned china in green and purple.

I am also worried by his interest in Oliver. It can only mean that he is well aware that Oliver is hidden away somewhere, and for some reason, he (Sir H.) is anxious to discover where Oliver is. Presumably Sir Hilary fancies that this will, in some way, discomfit Thomas, but it is far likelier to discomfit you and me. Could you find a way to drop a hint to Thomas that Sir Hilary is displaying an unwonted interest in Oliver's whereabouts? As Thomas is the only one who knows where Oliver is just now, it seems to me wise to inform him of the possible danger.

I am enclosing the charm-bags I promised you for Dorothea and Robert. I am not at all sure what the exact effect will be of using the Marquis's handkerchief in your second charm-bag, but from what Mr. Wrexton told me about the violet bloodstains, it may actually enhance the power of the bag. Be very careful of it, however; if Miranda got hold of that charm-bag, she could do perfectly dreadful things to you. For it would not be at all difficult for her to remove the handkerchief, and once the bloodstains have been used for one sort of magic, they are more amenable to being used in other ways. I am afraid I am not being at all clear about this; you will just have to take my word for it, and be very cautious. I will post this entire packet in the afternoon when Aunt Elizabeth and I pay our weekly visit to the Reverend Fitz.

Your curious cousin,
Cecy

12 June 1817
11 Berkeley Square, London

Dearest Cecy,

Nerves of steel aren't sufficient. You must have nerves of adamant to sit at table with Sir Hilary, knowing what we know of him. I admire your calm all the more since you endured James Tarleton's attempted stealth at the same time. Brava, cousin!

That said, I intend to try to follow Aunt Charlotte's favorite advice and tell first things first so that I don't leave anything out. The smallest details may prove to be important.

Saturday last, Thomas invited Aunt Charlotte, Georgina, and me to the opera. It was a revival of Handel's *Atalanta*, which is very silly. The orchestra was first-rate (but despite his reputation, I'm afraid the tenor wasn't), and I enjoyed it very much. Aunt Charlotte was enthralled by the chance to survey the boxes in our circle. From the overture to the finale, for the benefit of Georgy's education, she pointed out all the people of whom she could not approve. She tried several times to get my attention so that I, too, could profit from this instruction, but I kept my eyes stubbornly on the stage.

Rather to my surprise, Thomas did not interrupt the music with conversation, or even pointed remarks. Instead, he simply slouched in his seat, apparently indifferent to everything but the need to stay awake. Aunt Charlotte eyed him sharply at first, but when his lack of interest lasted through the appearance of the opera dancers, she relaxed her surveillance.

At the interval, Georgy insisted on visiting the box adjacent to ours to greet some friends and allow them the chance to admire her new Mexican blue sarcenet gown. Aunt Charlotte accompanied her and I was left alone in our box with the somnolent Thomas.

In the dim light at the back of the box, I could not read his expression, but I thought his apathy most uncharacteristic. Hoping to provoke some response, if only annoyance, I said, "You must have wondered at it when I mentioned James Tarleton to you in our last conversation."

Thomas stirred slightly but his voice held little interest as he replied, "No, I didn't wonder. I was too busy being furious with you."

"I believe he is a particular friend of yours," I said. "My cousin Cecy knows him."

"Yes, yes," said Thomas wearily, "James is a splendid fellow. Bruising rider, crack shot, very handy with his fives—ought to be able to handle a dozen of your cousins. Why don't you leave my friends and your relations out of this and tell me the worst at once. What mischief have you been in since I delivered you in Berkeley Square?"

"Why, none at all," I answered.

"What, none?" he replied. "Not spilt anything, nor tripped, nor fallen down stairs, nor knocked anyone down, nor set them on fire?"

"I have not set anyone on fire this age," I informed him. "I did step on Andrew Grenville's foot, but he's stepped on both of mine so often I can't think that counts."

"Nothing more sensational than that? I commend you," Thomas said. A faint line appeared between his brows. "But I confess it makes me uneasy. I would expect Miranda to have acted by now. Long contemplation is not much in her usual style."

"I thought she might be a rather impulsive person," I agreed. "Her attempt to poison you with chocolate suggested to me that her temper was a hasty one. Why did she do that, if I may ask?"

Thomas looked down his nose at me. "You may always ask, Kate."

"I do think you owe me an explanation," I persisted. "After all, I nearly drank it."

"I doubt it would have done you any good," said Thomas, "but it wasn't poison, you know. I can't think where you got the idea it was."

"What do you mean?" I exclaimed. "She told me it was."

"I doubt that very much," sniffed Thomas.

"She told me it"—I faltered for a moment, then continued—"wouldn't hurt a bit. And that it was appropriate for you to go that way. It was supposed to be your chocolate pot she was pouring it from, after all. And you yourself told me it would have been very unpleasant."

"But it wasn't poison. It was a catalyst of Miranda's concoction. *If* I had drunk it, it would have acted upon that part of myself that the uneducated refer to as 'magical power' and released it from my keeping. An unscrupulous magician, and I assure you that Miranda is as unscrupulous as they come, could then use the magic for herself. The process is painful enough when it is done a little at a time. The catalyst releases it all at once—like draining a cistern of every drop of water. Or opening an artery. Very, very unpleasant."

"Opening an artery—," I whispered, appalled. For a few moments, we sat in silence. Then I said, "Some splashed in Miranda's lap when I spilt it. It seemed to burn her."

"It must have been very uncomfortable," he said. "The

catalyst doesn't have quite such a drastic effect on contact, but it still works. Miranda hasn't been quite as powerful since that day as she was wont to be. She'll recover, though. And it certainly hasn't made her any less malicious in the meantime."

I went on thinking for a moment, then said pensively, "I wonder why it burned my dress? There was a hole in the hem of my gown where it splashed me."

"I doubt that it actually burned the fabric," Thomas replied. "But somewhere in the grass of that garden there are the threads from your gown that the catalyst soaked. After all, you can't bring anything back through a portal of that nature unless it was with you when you came. Which is why I wasn't tempted into the garden myself. Why try to retrieve a chocolate pot across the threshold of a door I couldn't take it through?"

"Well, that was very thoughtless of Miranda," I said.

"Very. But she was never good at theory, so perhaps she didn't realize. Not everyone would. But I worked on the equations with the owner, so I was bound to know." Thomas looked very smug.

"I thought it was Miranda's garden," I said.

"No, she borrowed it for the afternoon. It belongs to Sir Hilary, of course."

"Of course," I said faintly. Really, it is very difficult for me to imagine Sir Hilary as a figure of Byzantine intrigue. What a good thing he has a more even temper than Miranda.

You and I might have been turned into frogs anytime these past ten years.

"I wonder what Sir Hilary thought of that little contretemps over the chocolate set," said Thomas lightly. "Doubtless he made short work of collecting the magic that got loose when Miranda was splashed with her own catalyst."

The door of the box opened and Georgy returned with Aunt Charlotte in tow. They were both in high spirits, for Aunt Charlotte had just given Caro Lamb the cut direct and Georgy was pleasantly scandalized at the discovery that Aunt Charlotte was acquainted with the dashing poetess at all. As the orchestra struck up, both Aunt Charlotte and Georgy craned their necks to see if the eccentric nobleman Lord Byron had come to the opera in his tireless pursuit of the fickle Lady Caro.

Thomas and I had no further opportunity for conversation until he had delivered us back at Berkeley Square. Georgy very kindly engaged Aunt Charlotte in a discussion concerning the next morning's church services, so I was left alone for a moment with Thomas.

I'm not sure what form of leave-taking I expected from him, but I was surprised when he turned to me with a sigh of resignation and said, "Try to avoid Miranda, will you? I don't know when I'll have the leisure to follow you about collecting hairpins again."

I must have let some of my disappointment show, for he paused for a moment to smooth back a lock of my hair that had escaped from its proper place to straggle down in front of my ear. "Save a waltz for me at the Grenvilles' ball next week," he said, and took his leave.

Last night at Almack's, I looked for him in vain. Nothing of moment occurred all evening, save that I stepped on the hem of my new rose muslin gown and ripped out enough stitches to make the flounce sag, and Sally Jersey spoke to me while I was watching Georgy dance a quadrille with Michael Aubrey.

"Thomas was very particular in his attentions to Dorothea Griscomb while you were ill," said Lady Jersey. At least, it took her a great deal longer to say what she actually said, but that was what she meant.

"She is very lovely," I said.

"And her Stepmama has undeniable flair," Lady Jersey agreed. "Miranda had a similar effect on young men when she made her debut. Really quite a sensation. I thought you should know, for often these things seem to run in families."

I felt I must have misunderstood her. "But Miranda is Dorothea's *Step*mama," I said.

"Oh, not her family," Lady Jersey replied. "His."

"Mr. Griscomb?" I asked, in a vain attempt to follow the thread of her conversation.

"Who?" Lady Jersey asked. She gave a little impatient shake of her head. "Oh, I wish you would not confuse me so. I meant Thomas, of course."

"Thomas Schofield?" I asked, determined to go cautiously.

"Yes, yes! Thomas." She shook her head again. "Really, Miss Talgarth, you are betrothed to the man. I might expect you to have a little better recollection."

I chose my words with painful care. "I beg your pardon, Lady Jersey. Were you going to tell me something regarding his family?"

"I think you should be aware of it, yes. You knew he was the younger brother, did you not? Oh, yes, very much the younger. And his elder brother was even more sought after in his day than Thomas. Why, the caps that were set at Edward Schofield—he was far handsomer than his younger brother is, of course, and had twice the address. For, indeed, Thomas never can resist saying exactly what enters his head. Sometimes it is diverting, of course. In fact, it is always diverting to Thomas. But often very awkward for the rest of us. Edward was oblivious to all of them. Until Miranda Tanistry made her debut. Then he was still oblivious, but not to Miranda. Nor she to him, I assure you. For to be sure, she could see how soon she would be a marchioness once she married Edward. His father, the fourth Marquis, was still alive at that time, but Edward was still a most desirable *parti*. Indeed, highly desirable."

I regarded Lady Jersey with wonder. "Thomas's elder brother was in love with Miranda Griscomb?" I asked.

"Head over ears, my dear. Oh, yes, the Ton could speak of nothing else for days."

"But she married Mr. Griscomb anyway," I marveled. "Why was that?"

"Oh, that was much later," said Lady Jersey impatiently. "After Edward died. Why, she would hardly have settled for being mere Miranda Griscomb when she could have been a marchioness, would she?"

I felt a curious lurch in my midsection. "He died? How?"

"It was very tragic," said Lady Jersey, shaking her head. "Carried off by a wasting fever. The doctors were mystified. His father was terribly grieved, of course. They said afterward that the shock hastened him into his grave. The doctors, I mean."

"And Thomas?"

"Oh, Thomas was fighting in Spain. One would have expected him to sell out and come home at once, but he didn't. There's never any accounting for Thomas's behavior. It is as though he delights in puzzling us."

"But Miranda would have married Edward Schofield if he had lived," I said. This report of our conversation makes me sound rather stupid, I'm afraid, but there is something about talking to Lady Jersey that makes me wish to repeat things to be sure I have got them right.

"Very likely," said Lady Jersey, "though, of course, his brother was against it. Violently opposed to it, in fact."

"Thomas?" I repeated. "I thought you said Thomas was in Spain?"

"Well, he was, later. But he would hardly have left England while his brother was ill. Even Thomas is not that unaccountable."

I would have liked to continue on this topic until I worked out the precise order in which things had occurred, but Lady Jersey was growing impatient with my obtuseness. With a final warning, which I took to mean that Thomas might display the same ardor to Dorothea that his brother had for Miranda, she left me to tell Lady Grenville how to conduct her ball on Saturday.

I shall write again directly after I see Thomas, whether at the Grenvilles' ball or sooner still.

Your,
Kate

13 June 1817
Rushton Manor, Essex

Dearest Kate,

This week has been rather quiet, which makes a nice change from the stirring events of the past month. I had hoped to be able to tell you more about the Tanistry book (for I am sure it would tell us something to the purpose, if I could only get hold of it), but I am afraid I have been unable to hit on an acceptable reason to visit Bedrick Hall. I suppose I could call to see whether anyone has discovered my nonexistent fan, but I think this would be more likely to arouse Sir Hilary's suspicions than to soothe them. So, until I come up with a better plan, I am at a stand. I did, however, try a more roundabout approach to the question, with what success you shall judge for yourself.

Yesterday afternoon, I came downstairs to find Mr. Wrexton in the sitting room, engaged in conversation with Aunt Elizabeth. He had obviously been there some time, and I was surprised he had not sent someone to tell me he had come, but perhaps he had noticed Aunt Elizabeth's misgivings about the frequency of his calls. In any case, she was quite in charity with him when I arrived, though she stiffened a little when she saw me. He invited both of us to drive out with him; Aunt Elizabeth was forced to decline, as she was expecting the Reverend Fitzwilliam and his wife to tea. I, of course, accepted, and when we were well away from the house, I complimented him on his stratagem. I assumed, you see, that he had expected Aunt Elizabeth to decline.

"Not at all," he replied. "I would have been more pleased than you may realize to have your aunt accompany us."

"Why is that, sir?" I said, feeling a little miffed.

He turned toward me, his eyes twinkling. "Because it might have kept James Tarleton from glaring at me quite so fiercely next time I visit Tarleton Hall," he replied.

"Mr. Tarleton has no business being annoyed with you

because you are teaching me magic," I said indignantly. "It is nothing to do with him, after all!"

"Oh, you think that is the reason?" Mr. Wrexton said. "Well, perhaps you are right. In any case, as your aunt is not here, have you any questions regarding what I have taught you so far? I am afraid I have not prepared anything new."

It was exactly the opening I had been wondering how to arrange. "I do have a question," I said, "but it is not about anything you have taught me. It is a phrase I heard a little while ago, that made me curious. What are 'epicyclical elaborations of sorcery'?" This, you will remember, was the title of that book by Everard Tanistry that I noticed in Sir Hilary's library.

Mr. Wrexton jerked his head around, and all the humor went out of his face. "Where did you hear of that . . . practice?" He fairly spat the last word, as if he could not think of anything awful enough to call it.

"I don't remember," I lied. "Why? Is it so terrible?"

"It is one of the most unethical, immoral uses of wizardry imaginable," Mr. Wrexton said. "Black magic, if you will. And there is nothing further you need know."

I recognized the tone of voice well enough that I did not bother to argue. It seems, Kate, that even in wizardry there are things it is Not Proper to speak of before Young Ladies. Had I told Mr. Wrexton the full story of all that has happened with you and Thomas and Miranda and Sir Hilary in the past two months, I could perhaps have persuaded him that I did indeed require this extremely improper information. However, I did not feel that this business was mine to tell him of. I have no idea how deeply he is in James's confidence, and he may not know your odious Marquis at all.

So I turned the subject to charm-bags, on which I am fast becoming a positive expert, and we discussed possible implications of adding willow bark to the herbal mixture and substituting Saint-John's-wort for the rosemary. In this unexceptionable fashion, we passed the rest of our drive.

Mr. Wrexton's reaction makes me more anxious than ever to get hold of that book, though I cannot at present see how it is to be done. I hope it may shed some light on Miranda Tanistry Griscomb's methods, if not her motives.

14 June

I have just returned from my morning ride. Things are becoming more tangled than ever, and I cannot see an easy way of clearing up the mess. I am confident, however, that something will turn up; in the meantime, I suppose we must all simply forge ahead as best we can.

I had my saddle put on Thunder this morning, as he is in need of exercise while Oliver is away. (And you know Oliver would never let me ride him, and I have been longing to do so this age.) Thunder is *just* as splendid a mount as I had thought; we fairly *flew* over the ground. I let him have his head for a little and we had a good gallop. After that he was willing to slow to a more sedate pace, so I turned him toward the little wood by the far pasture, which has always been one of my favorite riding places.

No sooner was I well into the wood than I saw a horseman coming toward me through the trees. I reined Thunder in, wondering whether to turn away before I was seen. Then I saw that the rider was James Tarleton.

"I am glad to see you at last," was his greeting to me as he rode up. "I have been waiting half an hour already today, and yesterday I missed you entirely."

"Yesterday I rode by the lake," I said, blinking stupidly at him.

He was frowning at Thunder with evident disapproval, and did not appear to notice my surprise. "That is hardly a lady's mount," he said harshly.

"He is Oliver's," I replied, stung, "and I am perfectly capable of handling him. Would you like me to show you his paces?"

"I saw you coming across the pasture," Mr. Tarleton said in a more normal tone. "You frightened me half out of my wits."

"I like to gallop. Why haven't you come to call since last Thursday week?"

His face darkened. "At first, because I didn't want to give Sir Hilary ideas. After, because—well, because it would have been dangerous."

"Explain," I commanded, for I have been growing very tired of mysterious comments, and I was not about to put up with any more of them.

"Sir Hilary has been watching me since Monday," he said.

"Then he did see you!" I exclaimed.

"What do you know of it?" James said sharply.

I cursed my unruly tongue and told him, as briefly as I could, about the call Aunt Elizabeth and I made at Bedrick Hall. I did not mention the chocolate pot, but I did tell him that Sir Hilary had questioned me rather closely, and that I had seen James crossing the lawn as I turned away.

"And I must tell you again, you are very bad at sneaking about," I added severely. "You should *not* have worn that black coat, and crossing the lawn to the pavilion was a completely chuckle-headed thing to do. If you *must* slink about in bushes again, ask me and I will advise you."

"I will certainly keep your kind offer in mind," he said gravely, but I could tell he was trying not to laugh.

"I am quite serious," I said. "You have made a mull of it at least three times that I know of, and it is only your good fortune that no one but me has noticed until now."

"You are more right than you know," he responded, and all of the amusement went out of his face. "Cecy, you told me once that your cousin, Miss Talgarth, is your dearest friend. Can you get a message to her?"

"I write her regularly," I said in astonishment.

He gave a sigh of relief. "Good. I hoped that was the case."

"Why should you wish to send my cousin——" I stopped as the pieces fit themselves together in my mind like one of Aunt Charlotte's picture puzzles. "You want to send a message to Thom—to the Marquis of Schofield, and since Sir Hilary is watching you, you are afraid he will learn of it if you send it yourself," I said slowly. "But no one will think it at all odd if I write to Kate, and since they are betrothed, she can surely find an opportunity to tell the Marquis."

"Exactly," James said. "I knew I could depend on you to see my reasoning." I felt obscurely pleased by this rather offhanded compliment. "Will you do it?" James went on.

"Of course," I said at once. "What is the message?"

"Ask your cousin to tell Thomas that Sir Hilary has returned and that he is watching me closely, so it is probably unsafe to send any messages directly. Also, that I believe Sir Hilary spent the early part of Wednesday evening working sorcery, probably of a moderately difficult nature. I am certain Hilary has the pot here. I will not make any attempt to recover it until I have heard from Thomas, but I do not think he has much time left. Can you repeat that?"

I did so, adding "chocolate" before the reference to the "pot." James gave me a somewhat disgusted look, but let me finish. "What do you mean, he doesn't have much time left?" I said.

"I suppose you had better say that there isn't much time

left," Mr. Tarleton said. "I would not wish to disturb your cousin."

"I shall tell her exactly what you said, so you had better explain it," I told him.

"Tell her to ask Thomas," he said.

"I've a good mind not to tell her anything at all!" I said angrily.

"In that case, you'll be doing us all a disservice," he said. He looked me in the eyes with a very grave expression, which made me feel most peculiar. "But I don't think you'll fail us."

"I'd better be getting back before Aunt Elizabeth begins to worry," I said in a rather confused manner.

"Yes," he agreed with some reluctance. He started to turn his mount, then looked back at me. "Will you ride this way in the mornings sometimes? I dislike asking you, but if I need to get another message to Thomas, or if he sends a reply . . . It would be safer not to meet openly."

"Of course I will," I said at once.

"Thank you," he said, and rode quickly away.

I rode home in an exceedingly thoughtful mood, and now I wonder what you will make of all of this. I should not, I suppose, have promised your cooperation without first obtaining your consent, but he seemed so worried, and so urgent, that I did so without thinking. I would therefore be much obliged if you would deliver Mr. Tarleton's message to the odious Marquis (for whom I am beginning to feel a little sorry, and about whom I am beginning to be more than a little worried). If you do not wish to act as a mail coach in the future, I assure you I will understand perfectly.

I hope you can pry a little more explanation out of Thomas, by way of return for the favor of conveying Mr. Tarleton's message. I am seriously worried by the reference to Sir Hilary's sorcery, particularly in combination with the comment about not having much time left. It sounds as if Sir Hilary may be getting ready for something. Also, Mr. Tarleton's behavior was not of the sort that inspires confidence and reassurance; quite the reverse, in fact. I begin to feel that Sir Hilary is worse even than Miranda, and the thought that at least they do not seem to be working together any longer is small comfort.

Your letter was waiting for me at home, and I think the conversations you reported are at least as disquieting as James's veiled hints. However, at least we now have some idea what Miranda's intentions are. I had not known it was possible to steal a wizard's magic; I will have to find a way of broaching the topic to Mr. Wrexton. (And I am more determined than ever to get hold of that book on epicyclical elaborations; judging from Mr. Wrexton's reaction, whatever it is about is quite horrid enough to be just the sort of thing Miranda would like.)

I am still unclear as to Sir Hilary's role in all this. Perhaps he is afraid of Thomas for some reason, and does not want Thomas to be as powerful a wizard as he ought to be. This would explain why Sir Hilary aided Miranda in her attempt to steal Thomas's power, and also why Sir Hilary stole Thomas's focus. Unfortunately, it is all conjecture, and I do not like to rely too heavily on it. Also, this theory does not explain why James seems so very worried about Sir Hilary's spell casting. I *wish* we could persuade either Thomas or James to be more forthcoming!

I found Lady Jersey's story about Miranda and Edward Schofield intriguing; I will have to see whether I can discover anyone here who remembers Edward (and who is willing to tell me the story!). Fortunately, Waycross is one of the Schofield estates, and it is certainly close enough to Rushton that *someone* will have been interested in the family's doings! And your betrothal to the Marquis is the perfect excuse to justify my questions.

Aunt Elizabeth wishes me to ask you to remind Aunt Charlotte that she promised to send down a copy of Hannah More's latest work. I trust you will find a moment when Aunt Charlotte is *very busy* with something else to bring up this matter, as it is my personal opinion that there are quite enough books of an improving nature in this household already.

Write soon, and I hope your news is better than mine has been.

Your very worried,
Cecy

Dear Cecy,

My anxiety over Thomas's condition increased after I received your last letter. It seemed intolerable that I should have to wait until the Grenvilles' ball to see him again, so I sent a footman around with a note inviting him to tea that afternoon. The footman returned with Thomas's acceptance and I settled in to endure the hours until I should be able to convey James's message to him.

Teatime arrived, but Thomas did not. Aunt Charlotte poured out for Georgy and me. The butler arrived to announce a visitor. Confident it was Thomas, I put down my cup and saucer so I could turn to greet him without spilling anything.

"Mr. Strangle, Madame," said the butler, and withdrew his bulk to reveal Mr. Strangle in the hall behind him, looking like a garden rake with poor posture.

I concealed my disappointment as best I could, while Aunt Charlotte made Mr. Strangle welcome. By the time Mr. Strangle had concluded an ad hoc oration on the impiety of the lower classes, all the macaroons were gone and I had resigned myself to Thomas's absence. Since he did not even trouble to send a note excusing himself, I could not but believe that the engagement had slipped his mind. An alternative explanation presented itself to me, but I refused to entertain it, even for a moment.

As Aunt Charlotte was sending down to the kitchen for more macaroons, Mr. Strangle leaned his shoulder against mine to whisper in a very conspiratorial fashion. "The truth is," he hissed, "I came here on a quest. I am in search of Frederick Hollydean."

"He isn't here," I said.

"But do you not know his whereabouts?" asked Mr. Strangle.

"No, I don't," I replied, "and I fail to see why you should think for one moment that I would."

"How cold you are," Mr. Strangle replied, "to a lad who was your childhood playmate. And yet I would have judged you a very passionate young lady. Women with wide mouths often are, I've discovered."

I felt a chill run down my spine. I am not sure which alarmed me more, his words, his expression, or his voice, but I felt shocked at his behavior, which is rather strange, when you think of it. There are so many things a properly brought up young lady is expected to be shocked at, it is very odd that this is the first thing that genuinely did shock me. In retrospect, I wish very much that I'd had the presence of mind to box his ears, but all I did was gape at him. Something in my manner alerted Aunt Charlotte, however, for she hovered close throughout the remainder of Mr. Strangle's visit, ready to pounce upon the least vulgarity. He did not stay much longer—nor did I wish him to.

We were engaged for a musical evening at Countess Lieven's, where Georgy was prevailed upon to sing her Italian songs. She got off all the lines in the right order, which was a great relief. I was able to concentrate on the accompaniment fairly well, but once Georgy's songs were over I found myself unable to stop thinking of Thomas, and James's message.

By the time we returned to Berkeley Square it was after midnight. My maid had waited up for me, but I did not let her help me to change out of my gown. Instead, I made her accompany me as I went back down the stairs and ordered the carriage to be brought round again. I was almost surprised when I was obeyed. The servants were certainly startled, but they did not refuse. I was able to sweep out unhindered, merely by saying I had just received news of Oliver.

I was at the doorstep of Schofield House before I realized the enormity of what I had done. The butler, understandably, refused us entry. I explained who I was and demanded to know if the Marquis was in.

"I shall go and see," the butler told us. As he moved off down the hall, I ordered the maid to stay where she was and followed him down the hall and into a dimly lit room, where the butler announced calmly that a young person had called.

"Oh, really, Kimball," said Thomas, "are you out of

your senses?" Then he caught sight of me and said, "Oh, of course. Much becomes clear to me. Well, as long as you're here, Kimball, make yourself useful and dispose of that."

Thomas was seated at a card table set in the center of the room. Across from him sat another gentleman, slumped forward in his chair with his head pillowed on his folded arms. His face was turned away from me, but I could hear his gentle snoring. Thomas indicated the sleeping gentleman with a careless gesture and Kimball stepped forward obediently to lever the man up out of the chair. As he left the room, Thomas added, "More claret, if you please, Kimball."

I watched Kimball depart with his burden and realized only as the sleeper's heels dragged across the threshold that Thomas's guest was Frederick Hollydean.

"You'll forgive me if I don't rise, I trust," said Thomas. "Be a good girl and close the door, will you? You can have the horrible Hollydean's chair if you like. Make yourself comfortable."

I stared at Thomas but to my relief he did not seem much altered since the last time I had seen him. He looked just as weary, not much paler. Perhaps the clearest sign of change was in his eyes, which were too bright and slightly hollow. I held his gaze and said, "I have a message for you from James Tarleton."

He paused in the act of emptying the claret decanter into his glass. "What is the message?"

"Sir Hilary has returned," I began. "He is watching

James Tarleton closely, so it is probably unsafe to send any messages directly. Also he believes that Sir Hilary spent the early part of last Wednesday evening working sorcery, probably of a moderately difficult nature. He is certain Sir Hilary has the chocolate pot at Bedrick Hall. And I can tell you he does," I added, "for Cecy has seen it there."

Thomas began to speak, but I forestalled him. "He will not make any attempt to recover it until he has heard from you, but he does not think you have much time left. And he thought that a week ago, nearly. So that is why I am here. In case you meant to ask," I finished.

"I see," said Thomas. He put down the empty claret decanter and picked up his glass. As he moved, I saw his wrist was stained red. I exclaimed and took an involuntary step forward. He regarded me with surprise for a moment, then glanced at his cuff with mild interest. "It's only claret, my dear. The horrible Hollydean has a head like teak. Under normal circumstances I might have been able to match him drink for drink, but I don't have time to trifle with such things at the moment. So I put much of my share of the claret down my sleeve. It's an old trick, but a good one. And it served my purpose. Sit down."

I took Frederick Hollydean's chair. Between us on the table were two glasses, the empty decanter, a pack of cards, and a whist scorecard. The only light in the room came from the candles on the side table near the door and the fire in the grate. For a long moment, the fire was the only sound.

"Thomas," I said finally, "do tell me what is wrong with you."

Thomas took a sip of claret and put the glass down. It made a ring on the tabletop. He moved the glass and made another, then drew a fingertip across to connect the two. Idly, he went on making patterns with the wine stains all the time he spoke, as if he were reluctant to meet my eyes.

"I told you about the chocolate pot," he said. "Sir Hilary was most unhappy when I left his tutelage. I didn't realize it, but his effort to prevent me from employing my own magic lingered on in the chocolate pot, even when I was expert at wizardry. On my return to England, it served him as a link to me. And when James surrendered the chocolate pot to him, it was only a matter of time until Sir Hilary discovered how useful such a link could be."

"James gave him the chocolate pot?" I asked. From your description of how suspicious James Tarleton is of everyone, including you, I found this hard to credit.

"He thought he was giving it to me," Thomas answered. "Dear old James." He took a sip of claret and regarded me with his brilliant, hooded gaze. "What a diplomat—I recall the winter after Salamanca. We were with Wellington in Frenada. James was one of his aides-de-camp, and found a way for us to hunt the Duke's pack of hounds. It was the one source of amusement all that dreadful winter—Frenada was quite the dirtiest village I ever saw on that whole campaign. Anyway, we hunted the foxes to extinction and had to start in on the neighborhood wolves. When the Duke learned of it, *we* were nearly extinct, I can tell you. But trust James to find a way to turn old Hooky up sweet. He had the Duke off to Cádiz and the lovely ladies there in a trice, and the whole staff along with him. Well, almost the whole staff. I was ordered to remain behind in Frenada, but that was small punishment in light of the crime."

He broke off and eyed me fiercely. "You're not drinking your claret."

"It's Frederick Hollydean's claret," I said.

"Well, don't you like it? Or do you only drink tea and ratafia?"

"I've never tasted anything stronger than ratafia," I confessed.

"What? You mean to tell me that your cod's head of a cousin never even gave you a taste of your uncle's brandy?"

I shook my head.

"Well, then, what are you waiting for? I'd give you some from my glass, but it's nearly gone. Drinking from Hollydean's won't hurt you."

It seemed the only way to get him to stop carping at me. After the first sip flared and faded, I took another.

"Well?"

"It's not as nasty as ratafia," I admitted. "But I hardly think it can be very good claret."

Thomas gaped in amazement. "The devil you say, girl—

how could you tell that from your first two sips? You're roasting me."

"I don't think you would serve the best claret to Frederick Hollydean," I pointed out. "Particularly if you planned to pour the greater share of it down your sleeve."

"Oh," said Thomas. "I begin to see how you find yourself in scrapes like taking chocolate with Miranda. Your trouble, my girl, is that silly trick you have of nodding and looking intelligent while you produce the most amazing pieces of information. How the devil am I to guess what you know and what you don't know?"

"You might try explaining things to me," I suggested. "For one thing, what did you hope to accomplish by pretending to be in love with Dorothea?"

"I hoped to keep Miranda to a program of events I was already familiar with. I knew what to expect from her while she thought Dorothea had some influence over me. Miranda requires me to be close at hand, you see. At any point up to actual matrimony, I would have been safe enough. I didn't expect her to be quite so ruthless about terminating our engagement. According to Frederick Hollydean, she has taken a really amazing dislike to you, Kate." Thomas sighed and drained his glass. "Where can Kimball be with the other decanter?"

He rose and crossed the room to ring for Kimball. Watching Thomas move, I found it difficult to believe he was the same man who had waltzed with me at Almack's. He walked like an old, old man. The claret might account for some of the hesitation in his step, but I was sure his unnatural fatigue played a part as well.

"Who is doing this to you?" I asked. "Sir Hilary or Miranda?"

"For all her bad intentions, Miranda hasn't harmed me yet," Thomas replied. From the bellpull he moved to his writing desk where he rummaged industriously. After a brief search, he returned to the table with a ring, which he handed to me as he took his place. I examined it closely. It was a narrow band of dull metal, marked inside and out with curious little glyphs.

"Does it fit?" Thomas asked.

I put the ring on my left index finger. Thomas took my hand and examined the effect. "Good," he said. "Keep it. And mind you wear it. If Miranda tries to turn you into a goat, I should like to be able to find you in short order. The horrible Hollydean says she finds you perfectly mystifying. On the one hand, it's obvious you are merely a social nuisance. But on the other, how is it that you were able to find the door to Sir Hilary's garden without help? Miranda's taken the corkbrained notion into her head that you are working with him."

"Absurd," I said hastily. "How *did* I find the door?"

Thomas smiled, for once without a trace of derision. "It might be interesting to conduct a few tests when this is all over. I expect you must have some degree of natural aptitude in order to see the door with an utterly untrained eye. After all, I worked on the equations."

"Yes, so you told me," I said.

Kimball entered the library without the formality of knocking. "Your pardon, my lord," he said, "but there is a lady here to see you."

"Come now, Kimball," said Thomas, "this is most unlike you."

"So this is where I find you," said Aunt Charlotte in a voice of iced vitriol, "playing cards and drinking claret with this—nobleman." She stepped around Kimball and seized me by the tip of my left ear. "You sadden me, Katherine."

I winced and rose in obedience to her grip on my ear. Thomas got to his feet and began an explanation as bonelessly smooth as it was utterly false.

"As for you," Aunt Charlotte said, fixing him with a look so filled with scorn that even Thomas's glib words slowed, "there is only one thing that could spare you from disgrace."

"Oh, Aunt Charlotte," I said, "rip up at me all you please, only not here. He had nothing to do with it, I promise you."

"Yes, very likely," she agreed with a savage tug at my ear to demonstrate her skepticism. "I feel quite certain he has nothing to do with 'news of Oliver.'"

"Oh, yes," I faltered, "news of Oliver."

For a moment I dared to hope that my calm voice might produce some plausible lie without interference from my brain, but the moment passed and I felt myself surrender hope. Silently, I awaited Aunt Charlotte's wrath.

"Yes, Madame," said Thomas in a tone of bland interest, "what precisely was it that you wished to know about young Oliver?"

Aunt Charlotte gave my ear a savage twist but in perfect fairness to her I think it was done in astonishment, not anger. "His whereabouts," cried Aunt Charlotte. "I wish to know where the boy has gone! He was in my keeping, sir!"

"Perhaps you would care to see a letter written to me by one of the friends with whom he is staying?" replied Thomas. "A very well respected gentleman, highly thought of by Wellington himself."

Aunt Charlotte said nothing, but Thomas returned to his writing desk and conducted another brief rummage, which produced a single sheet of paper. Aunt Charlotte accepted it from him without releasing her grip on my ear in the slightest. For a moment or two the fire made the only sound in the room, then Aunt Charlotte sniffed disdainfully and handed the letter back to Thomas.

"And just who is this Michael person?" she inquired. "He has neglected to furnish the direction of his letter. This says no more than those vague scrawls of Oliver's to his father—that he arrived safely and seems to be well looked after."

"Well, Aunt—," I began.

Thomas cut in before I could begin the vague protest I meant to utter. "You wished to know his whereabouts, Miss

Rushton. He is staying in the country with this gentleman. If this news does not allay your anxiety, I apologize, but it is all the news of Oliver I possess."

"And for this news," said Aunt Charlotte with a twist of my ear that I'm sure was done deliberately, "you have risked utter social ruin. I hope you are perfectly satisfied with yourself, Katherine."

"Miss Rushton," said Thomas very softly, "I see no need whatever to indulge in idle speculation of this kind. Perhaps I am more than usually vain, but I do not think the Ton will count Kate's marriage to me as social ruin. If you wish, I am prepared to procure a special license and marry her at once. The Archbishop was a great friend of my Father's, and I fancy he would be able to hasten the matter along at whatever pace you wish."

"Nonsense," sniffed Aunt Charlotte. "It is no intention of mine to allow a breath of this encounter to come to the knowledge of anyone outside this room. As far as I am concerned, the coachman misunderstood my orders and left without me. We shall drive back together, of course."

"I think that's perfectly clear, don't you, Kimball?" said Thomas.

"Indeed, my lord," said Kimball.

"Good," said Thomas. "By the way, Kimball, where's my claret?"

"We shall say good evening, then," said Aunt Charlotte, and we took our leave of Thomas. He resumed his place at the card table and began to fold the letter from Michael into a cocked hat as Aunt Charlotte tugged me out into the hall.

Aunt Charlotte was perfectly silent all the way home. The maid yawned and I spent the drive rubbing my ear and wondering about Miranda's plan for Thomas, and Sir Hilary's method of harming Thomas even from a distance. The trouble with talking to Thomas is that even when he is in a perfectly forthcoming mood, I seldom have the opportunity to cross-question him. For example, I now wonder very much about his order to Kimball concerning Frederick Hollydean's disposal. Dare Thomas release the horrible Hollydean if he is in Miranda's employ? Dare he lock him up? After all, however horrid he is, people will be bound to inquire if he simply disappears. And what about Mr. Strangle? If Frederick is working with Miranda, might I not assume that Mr. Strangle is, too?

And if Aunt Charlotte had insisted, could Thomas really have persuaded the Archbishop to grant him a special license?

Your,
Kate

P.S. And if Aunt Charlotte is determined to hush up my night's outing, how will she be able to punish me suitably? She can scarcely keep me confined to my room for a crime I am not supposed to have committed. And by this time, I know my collect backward and forward.

18 June 1817
Rushton Manor, Essex

Dearest Kate,

I have finally got hold of that *Epicyclical Elaborations of Sorcery* book of Sir Hilary's, and I must confess that it is even worse than I had suspected. I do not blame Mr. Wrexton in the least for not wishing to discuss it with me. I was strongly tempted not to tell you anything about it, but that is exactly the sort of trick James or Thomas would play, and I refuse to stoop to such a level. Also, I think it wise for you to have some idea of what Miranda is up to.

After my failure with Mr. Wrexton last week, I was more determined than ever to find out about epicyclical elaborations. Since it was clearly inadvisable for me to return to Sir Hilary's library, I cast about for a way to have the book brought to me (or at least, brought somewhere easier for me to get it). I hit upon a method almost at once. (I cannot think why it did not occur to me sooner. It is probably all this conversation with the all-too-straightforward Mr. Tarleton.)

I went to see Papa. He had, as usual, a dreadfully long list of books he wishes to examine for his latest paper (Aunt Charlotte will probably be receiving another request in the near future). I was able to remind him that Sir Hilary had offered him the use of the Bedrick Hall library, and that, as Sir Hilary was now in residence once more, Papa could perfectly well send someone over to borrow the books. (I do not know why Papa will not do this when Sir Hilary is absent; it is all handled by the servants, after all, and I doubt that Sir Hilary ever knows anything about it.)

I am sure you can guess the rest. I offered to give Papa's list to one of the grooms, and before I did so I added the Tanistry book to the bottom. Then I sent Jenkins off to Bedrick Hall quite early in the morning (because I thought it likely that Sir Hilary would be out shooting then, and because Mrs. Porter has a fondness for Jenkins). I haunted the hallway until Jenkins returned, collected the books from him, and took them in to Papa. It all worked quite perfectly, Kate; the Tanistry book was the second volume, and I was able to abstract it without any difficulty whatever.

I spent the remainder of the morning developing a most convincing sick headache, so that I was able to spend the afternoon and much of the evening reading Tanistry's *Epicyclical Elaborations of Sorcery*. And I must tell you, Kate, that it is quite the most appalling book I have ever read. It is all about how to steal another person's magical ability and use it oneself, and the very best ways appear to involve binding the person to one in some way (such as marrying him or being his tutor) and then, well, *sucking* all the magic out of him. This quite frequently kills the unfortunate person whose magic is being stolen, and the author actually appears to approve of it!

There is a whole chapter on how to pick out the best person to steal magic from (magical ability apparently runs in families, and the author recommends choosing someone who is adult but relatively young, at the height of his power, and preferably untrained) and another on how to get the person one has chosen into the most convenient position for having his magic stolen. If Miranda is related to this Everard, she comes from a truly dreadful family, and I am not at all certain Thomas was right when he told you she did not intend to poison him with that chocolate. At least, that may not have been the main thing the chocolate was supposed to do, but I would not be in the least surprised to discover that he would have died all the same. And he referred to it as "uncomfortable"!

I have managed to get about halfway through the book, and I am strongly tempted to burn it instead of returning it to Sir Hilary. I continue on in hopes of discovering whether there is anything that can interfere with this insidious process. For it seems obvious from reading the book (and from your rather elliptical conversations with Thomas) that both Miranda and Sir Hilary are trying to get hold of Thomas's magic. (I must say, I would never have thought it of Sir Hilary, but why else would he own such a dreadful book?) Their success would, I am sure, be quite unfortunate for Thomas.

I am inclined to think that Miranda is the more pressing threat, for the distance between Rushton and London is far too great for Sir Hilary to have any success with the epicyclical spells. (And I must add that it is entirely possible that Miranda is related to the author, for he mentions a daughter named Miranda. Miranda Tanistry Griscomb is far too young to be the same Miranda [she would have to be about seventy!], but perhaps she was named for an aunt.)

I shall continue to study the dreadful Tanistry book, and if I find any way of interfering with the spells I will add it to this letter. In the meantime, I must give you the rest of the Rushton news.

Mrs. Everslee paid us a morning call yesterday (before I retired with my "sick headache"). Apparently Sir Hilary does indeed intend to have a party to celebrate his elevation to the Royal College. (It is not clear to me whether this has been his intention all along, or whether Mrs. Everslee managed to bring him to a sense of his obligations.) Mrs. Everslee is extremely pleased by this; her expectation was marred only by the possibility that Aunt Charlotte might bring Georgina back from Town prematurely (that is, in time to attend). Upon being assured by Aunt Elizabeth and myself that this was unlikely, she expressed her regret that you and Georgy would miss such a glittering affair, and returned home in perfect happiness to flutter over Patience's preparations.

While I am on the subject, Kate, do you suppose you could find me a length of taffeta or organdy that I could have made up into something stunning for Sir Hilary's party? I could, I suppose, wear my pomona green crape again, but I wore that to Lady Tarleton's ball already. It is not that I have a desire to shine down Patience Everslee (and, indeed, she is an amiable girl and deserves a more pleasant mother), but I really do not think Mrs. Everslee should have it all her own way. In the absence of you and Georgy, it will be up to me to represent the family properly. I suppose it is *possible* that Sir Hilary will not send us a card, but it seems unlikely. It would be much too obvious a slight, for no reason that anyone here would know, and Sir Hilary is not foolish enough to make himself (and us) a nine days' wonder in the County.

 20 June

Your letter arrived yesterday, and I was shocked and appalled by how thoroughly I had been misled. For from what you said (or rather, what Thomas said), it seemed clear that he believes it is not *Miranda* but *Sir Hilary* who is responsible for his weariness, and that Sir Hilary has somehow been using the chocolate pot to achieve his most reprehensible ends. As soon as I reached this conclusion, I brought out your letters and reread them most carefully, paying special attention to everything your odious Marquis has told you about his wretched chocolate pot. And, of course, as soon as I did so, I realized that it must be the "whiff of Sir Hilary's magic" in the chocolate pot that is allowing Sir Hilary to do whatever he is doing.

I was quite sure of this in my own mind (and, indeed, I felt rather foolish for not seeing it before), but upon consideration I decided that it would be best to get some confirmation of my fears. I thought of applying to James, but quickly rejected that idea. I doubt very much that I could get James to reveal anything regarding Thomas; he is so irritatingly discreet. I decided, therefore, to ask Mr. Wrexton, instead. Fortunately, he has got into the habit of calling in the afternoon to take me for my magic lessons.

It took me a little time to work around to the subject in a way that would not arouse his suspicions, but I managed it at last. I recalled one of those old tales Papa is so fond of, the one about the twin sorcerers who used the same emerald as their focus, and I told him the story; then I asked, as if it were mere idle curiosity, why on earth they would wish to do such a thing. "For it seems to me that it would be most inconvenient, always having to go and get the thing from someone else when one wanted to do a spell," I said.

Mr. Wrexton smiled. "It would indeed be inconvenient, but there are compensations. If two people mix their magic in a single focus, each can draw on the other's power in the same proportion it was used in making the focus. I don't advise it. One must trust the other person absolutely, and if the trust is misplaced . . . And even if both parties mean well, the trust may be accidentally abused."

"Abused?" I said. "What do you mean?"

A shadow crossed his face. "It can kill a man, to have too much of his magic drawn into a joint focus by someone else."

"I thought that focuses were harmless!" I said. I was beginning to be really frightened, but I was determined to get to the bottom of it.

"You are quite correct, in the normal course of things," Mr. Wrexton said, smiling at me reassuringly. I believe he thought that I was worried about creating a focus of my own, and whether it might be used against me. I hope I am not so poor-spirited, but I did not wish to correct his misapprehension and cause him to stop his explanation. "When a wizard uses a single focus, his magic is used and returns to him, and no harm is done. When a joint is used, however, the power leaves both of those who made it, but it returns to only one, the spell caster. By drawing on his power without replenishing it, a joint focus weakens the magician who is not using the focus. If too much is done too quickly, the nonusing magician dies."

"How horrid!" I exclaimed involuntarily. "Why would anyone ever make such a thing in the first place?"

"Some do it because they do not know the hazards," Mr. Wrexton answered. "More commonly, a joint focus is created by two magicians who wish to pool their magic for a specific project. When the spell is successfully cast, the joint focus is smashed so that it can never be used again, and each wizard returns to the personal focus he had been using before."

"I see," I said slowly. "It sounds very complicated."

"You won't have to worry about it for some time yet," Mr. Wrexton said. "Now, how are you doing with those animation spells?"

I am afraid I did not do at all well with the animation spells. Magic requires concentration, and my mind was elsewhere. Fortunately, Mr. Wrexton is very patient, but even so I sensed his disappointment with me. I was very glad to leave him to visit Papa when our drive was over, and go up to my room to consider.

I considered for much of the rest of yesterday afternoon and evening. Unfortunately, I do not think my conclusions are particularly useful. I do not see that it is any better to have Sir Hilary draining Thomas's magic slowly through the chocolate pot than to have Miranda draining it quickly with her catalysts and epicyclical spells. And in either case, I do not see what we can do about it. The charm-bag I made might slow things down a little, but it is far too simple a spell to be very effective against such advanced magic. Especially when Sir Hilary has the chocolate pot to use as a link.

 Later

I went riding this morning after I had partially answered your letter. I thought it would clear my head and give me time to think, but James Tarleton was waiting for me in the woods. He had not been there the day before, and Tuesday and Wednesday were the days I had pretended to have the headache, so I had neglected my ride by way of convincing Aunt Elizabeth I was truly unwell.

"Good morning, Miss Rushton," he said as I drew rein beside him. He looked very tired. "Have you heard anything from your cousin?"

"She has given Thomas your message," I said, and stopped, wondering how to convey to him the scene you described without either worrying him excessively or damaging your reputation beyond repair.

"And?" James prompted.

"He didn't give her a reply," I said cautiously.

"Why not?" James demanded. He looked at me very closely and said gently, "I think you had better tell me the whole, Miss Rushton. There is more, and it is not good news, is it?"

"I am afraid not," I said, and hesitated. "I must tell you that my cousin Kate's determination to deliver your message made her act in a way that was not—not altogether wise."

"My memory is most adaptable, Miss Rushton," he said reassuringly.

I smiled at him uncertainly, and plunged into the tale. James's face became stiff and expressionless as I spoke. "I see," he said when I finished. "Miss Rushton, when you write your cousin next, please ask her to tell Thomas that if I do not hear from him soon, I shall make an attempt to recover the pot on my own, wizards or no wizards. There is such a thing as too much caution."

"I'll tell her," I said. I hesitated. "Do you really think it will be necessary?"

"I hope not," James replied. "Thomas is a good wizard, and things do not seem to have progressed very far as yet. If there's a loophole, he'll find it." He smiled reminiscently.

I swallowed the comment that Sir Hilary's possession of the chocolate pot did not appear to me to leave any loopholes, and said instead, "You must know him very well."

James laughed. "Too well, perhaps. We've been friends for a long time."

"How long?" I said. "Did you know his brother, Edward?" I had been wondering for days about that confused story Lady Jersey told you, and I was hoping that I had finally found someone who could tell me about it.

"So you've dug up that tale, have you?" James said. He did not look at all pleased.

"Lady Jersey told Kate," I said. "But I am afraid she was not very clear about what happened."

James gave a bark of laughter. "'Silence' Jersey doesn't have it in her to be clear. What exactly did she tell your cousin?"

"That Edward Schofield was in love with Miranda," I said cautiously, "and that he died of a wasting fever that sounds to me remarkably like what is ailing Thomas now."

James's expression darkened. "Not exactly. Edward

wasn't a magician; Miranda couldn't do to him what Sir Hilary is doing to Thomas."

"What *did* she do, then?" I demanded crossly, for I was very tired of mysteries.

"I suppose I'd better tell you the whole story," said James, and he did.

Apparently, Miranda Tanistry made even more of a splash in Society when she made her debut than Dorothea has, and for exactly the same reason. She snared Edward Schofield almost at once, and she would probably have married him before the Season was even over if Thomas hadn't come dashing up to Town to stop it. Thomas had been studying magic privately with Sir Hilary and had run across something that disturbed him. (I suspect it was that dreadful book on epicyclical elaborations, but, of course, James did not know exactly.)

When Thomas got to London, he was able to tell that Edward was under the influence of a spell of some sort, but convincing his brother of this was quite another matter. (Apparently Edward was just as stubborn as Thomas seems to be.) So Thomas laid a charm on Edward's snuffbox to protect him from Miranda's spell. (And yes, it was the same snuffbox that James was using to keep himself safe from Dorothea.) That put an end to Miranda's game at once, for, of course, Edward quickly discovered that he was not in the least in love with her.

Miranda was so annoyed that she went to Sir Hilary and

offered to teach him those horrid epicyclical spells if he would keep Thomas from interfering anymore. He agreed (which leads me to believe that Sir Hilary is even more unscrupulous than I had previously supposed). I expect he thought that since Thomas was one of his students, he would be easy to deal with, but it was no such thing. Because, of course, Thomas was already suspicious. Still, Miranda and Sir Hilary caused such a deal of trouble for Thomas that he was practically obliged to fly the country. (James did not put it quite like this, of course.) It was after that that Thomas's brother took sick and died.

"Thomas was certain Miranda was behind it," James told me, "but he couldn't do anything without proof. And he couldn't get any proof without returning to England, which would have been fatal at that point."

"I'm surprised he didn't come dashing back anyway," I commented.

"He wanted to," James admitted, "but I talked him out of it. He was cross as a bear for weeks afterward, and became positively reckless whenever he had to fight. That was how he came to be mentioned in the dispatches."

"When was that?" I asked.

"Near the beginning of Wellington's campaign on the Peninsula," James replied. "That was where we met."

"Kate says you were A.D.C. to Wellington himself," I said, feeling that a change of subject was in order.

He looked embarrassed and pleased at the same time. "Well, yes, I was."

"Then someday you must tell me all about it," I said. "I warn you, though, that Kate and I will compare your stories with Thomas's, so you had better not try to roast us with impossible tales."

He smiled and made some disclaimer, and we rode in silence for a little way. I could see that he was very worried, in spite of his outward lightness, so I stayed a little longer than usual in hopes of raising his spirits. I cannot flatter myself that I was more than marginally successful; I think that only good news of Thomas will do anything to cheer James.

I arrived home just in time to go to the parsonage with Aunt Elizabeth. I would never have expected it, but that visit with the Reverend Fitzwilliam turned out to be quite fortunate. For Martin De Lacey had stopped in to borrow a cricket bat, and he had received a note from Robert Penwood! Robert has apparently found Mr. Griscomb, and the two of them hit it off extremely. Robert has permission to pay his address to Dorothea, and he and Mr. Griscomb are to be in London by the end of the month. (I am not at all sure this is a good thing, knowing Miranda. So if you see Robert, be sure to give him the charm-bag I sent to you for him.)

I shall look for a letter from you next week, and I sincerely hope your news of Thomas will be good. I am sure

James will do something foolish if I cannot tell him your Marquis is in better health, or at the least that Thomas has something specific for him to do.

Give Georgy my love. I do not send it to Aunt Charlotte, as I think she has behaved abominably in following you about and bullying you in front of Thomas. It is the outside of enough, especially from someone who spends so much time prosing on about manners and proper behavior. Of course, she would consider it very wrong of you to have gone to a gentleman's lodgings, even with your maid. (And really, Kate, could you not have waited until morning? If you are determined to do things openly, you ought not to do them in the middle of the night. Particularly if you are going to call the servants and order up a carriage. That sort of thing is quite unexceptionable during daylight hours; at midnight it is bound to cause comment. Really, you are nearly as bad as James.) But Oliver was never in her charge at all; he came up to London *weeks* after you and Georgy left, and he only stayed in Berkeley Square to keep an eye on Georgy. Aunt Charlotte is simply trying to puff up her own consequence, as usual, and you ought to have told her so. And you really must get a spare key made for your room, Kate, in case she tries to lock you in again. What if Miranda were to do something dreadful, and you were stuck in your room?

I was surprised to learn that Frederick Hollydean has become involved with Miranda, but upon reflection I see that it is exactly the sort of thing he would do. I have a vivid recollection of the worm he tried to put down my back when I was eleven, and while this is not quite the same, there is something wormy about Miranda that would probably appeal to Frederick. And I cannot but approve of Thomas's description: "Horrible Hollydean" suits Frederick perfectly. Nor can I help hoping that Frederick will find being disposed of to be properly uncomfortable.

I think it quite likely that Mr. Strangle is also in Miranda's confidence, if not her employ. The Reverend Fitzwilliam, you will recall, had no knowledge of him, though Mr. Strangle claimed they had been at school together. If Frederick is out of the way, however, I doubt that you will have much cause to associate with his tutor. Under the circumstances, this is just as well. Your description of his behavior makes me certain Mr. Strangle is an utter toad.

I think that if I have one of the grooms take this to town immediately, it will still catch today's London mail coach.

Yours in haste,
Cecy

23 June 1817
11 Berkeley Square, London

Dear Cecy,

I have just received your letter concerning epicyclical elaborations of sorcery. Perhaps it is a mercy that I did not know how very serious the threat to Thomas has become, for I doubt I would have been able to keep still at the Grenvilles' ball, and Thomas detests a fuss.

Taking the day in strict order, breakfast was marred by a contretemps between Georgina and Aunt Charlotte. As I hoped, Aunt Charlotte's determination to keep my misbehavior a complete secret has prevented her from punishing me in any of her usual ways. The effect this has had on her temper is startling. Georgina asked, understandably enough, for the news of Oliver that had taken us from the house at such an unreasonable hour the night before. When Aunt Charlotte did not reply at once, I explained that Thomas had received a letter from Oliver's host. Georgina pressed me for details. For a moment I was tempted to tell her that Aunt Charlotte had refused to let me read it myself, but I merely said, "Oliver is very well."

"Very well!" exclaimed Georgina. "Is that all? Who knows what he might be up to? Cockfighting, bearbaiting— even gaming!"

"A lady has no knowledge of such pursuits," sniffed Aunt Charlotte.

Georgina's response to this was a wonderful combination of indignation and illogic. Aunt Charlotte lost her temper to such an extent that she sent back the toast to the kitchens. The civil war that resulted when the cook discovered Aunt Charlotte's crime took all her resources to quell. Georgina was engaged to drive out with the Grenville twins, and was thus able to escape while Aunt Charlotte was occupied with the cook.

So I went to my room to conduct a thorough search for my pearl eardrops. It seemed to me most unfair that I should lose not just one but both earrings, and at the same time, too. But after I looked through my things twice and checked every spot I could think of where they might have fallen, it occurred to me that Georgy might have borrowed them and forgotten to mention it to me. (I'm sure this reminds you of your coral bracelet. I admit I was thinking of that misunderstanding when I looked in Georgy's jewel case.) It seemed to be simpler to borrow the eardrops back than to provoke a brangle. So, with a ruthless exercise of what Oliver calls "eldest's rights," I searched Georgy's jewelry.

The eardrops were not there. Neither was her brooch set with aquamarines. But at the very bottom of the case lay a slim little memorandum book bound in limp green leather. It was very wrong of me, but I am only human, and I opened it. My punishment came when I read the first page. Frederick Hollydean had reason to ask me if I shared Georgy's talent for the tables. The little green book contains a list of her wagers. Unfortunately, most of the entries record losses, my eardrops and the blue brooch included.

I don't have to describe my feelings. You must share them. While the sums involved are not large, our family history makes it a very grave symptom. If the Talgarth passion for gaming has recurred, Georgy may easily ruin herself while Aunt Charlotte is busy lecturing her on her posture. What should I do? What *can* I do? Will scolding Georgy myself have any effect? It never has before. How I wish, for the thousandth time, that you were here or that we had never left Rushton.

This revelation sent me to my room to think until it was time to prepare for the ball.

On our arrival at the Grenvilles', Alice took me aside at once to say, "Thank goodness you are here, Kate. The Marquis of Schofield has been here for nearly an hour and he hasn't a civil word to say to anyone. Perhaps you can amuse him."

She showed me where he sat, watching the guests arrive from a chair in the corner. The change in him was more marked now. Even with his dark coloring, he seemed pale, and his dark eyes seemed to burn. When I greeted him, I thought for a moment he did not recognize me, so fierce was his hooded gaze. But his voice was perfectly matter-of-fact as he greeted me. "Well, Kate, so your Aunt Charlotte decided to let you live. I'm gratified."

"She seems to have changed her attitude the instant you mentioned a special license," I said. "Life in London has made her most unpredictable. Her volte-face was astonishing."

"Yes, astonishing," said Thomas, with an unpleasant smile. "Really, Kate, she's not a stupid woman. The instant you marry, her influence over you ceases. I don't think your Aunt Charlotte is a woman to surrender influence willingly."

I let this remark go unanswered and asked if he wished to convey a message to James Tarleton through a letter from me to you. At the very idea he drew himself up a little straighter in his chair and said, "Yes, by all means. Tell James not to trouble himself. I am perfectly well able to manage things alone."

"What a gudgeon you are, Thomas," I replied. "Are you sure you are well enough to waltz? You are looking very ill."

"I shall sit out our waltz, with your permission," Thomas replied grandly. He made a sweeping gesture with one hand. "I shall sit them all out. I only came to tell you to be sure to beware of Miranda. She has some scheme afoot, and Harry Strangle is still on the loose to put it into practice. I had hoped that my abduction of the horrible Hollydean would lure Strangle into my clutches as well, but there isn't a trace of him anywhere."

I felt a reminiscent chill as the memory of that dreadful day when Mr. Strangle came to tea presented itself. "I will be careful," I said.

Thomas looked at me with an expression of skeptical surprise. "Don't let your aunt pitchfork you into Strangle's company for a brisk sermon on vice, either," he said. "The fellow has done altogether too much research on that topic. And *don't* take that ring off. Now, I must tell you how much

I admire your tactful remarks about my health. I wish I could insult you in turn, but you are looking very healthy indeed. And I do admire this new fashion of wearing your hair half-tumbled down in back."

As I engaged in a desperate effort to restore my coiffure without benefit of a mirror, Miranda arrived with Dorothea in tow. From our vantage point in the corner, we could watch them sweep into the ballroom, Dorothea looking perfectly enchanting and Miranda fairly glittering with self-satisfaction. Dorothea disappeared behind a wall of young men, and Miranda surveyed the room with an air of calm disdain that suggested she found the marble floors and crystal chandeliers poor stuff indeed compared to her customary surroundings. I could tell the instant she caught sight of Thomas, for her eyebrows rose halfway up her forehead and then drew down into a frown. After a moment her bland expression returned and she began a circuit of the room, her progress bringing her steadily toward us in a procession of greetings and snubs.

"What a dreadful woman," said Thomas, watching her approach.

"But how well she dresses," I replied.

"Thomas," purred Miranda, "how divine to see you here. How very seedy you are looking these days. Have you been ill?"

"Not at all," Thomas replied. "I see you've trained

Dorothea to look at her partner when she dances and not at her feet. What a wonder you are, Miranda. Why don't you take Frederick Hollydean in hand?"

"Dear Thomas, always such delightful company," said Miranda. "Do you know, from your appearance I would judge I am about to lose a little wager I made with a dear friend of mine. But I can't regret it. Remember the promise I made you once, that I would dance at your funeral? Perhaps that glad day is not so far off. And even if I am unable to take full advantage of your company before your departure, no doubt your charming fiancée will provide me with diversion of her own." Her eyes when she said this rested upon me with cold merriment.

I glanced from Miranda to Thomas to see his response to this savage pleasantry. To my surprise, he was not looking at Miranda, but past her, with an expression compounded of equal parts exasperation and fondness. I followed his gaze to see, sweeping up to stand beside Miranda, the most striking woman I have ever beheld.

She was old. I am not certain how old, but over sixty at least. She was tall, as tall as Thomas (and a great deal taller than Miranda). Her hair, which must once have been as dark as Thomas's, was touched with silver and dressed in a heavy knot at the nape of her neck. She wore a black gown of such elegance that she seemed almost foreign, and the only outward mark of her age was the ivory walking stick she carried.

"Sylvia Schofield," hissed Miranda, at the same moment that Thomas rose smiling and said, "Good evening, Mother."

"Good evening, Thomas," said Lady Sylvia. "Do sit down dear boy." She let her dark gaze sweep Miranda from top to toe. "How very daring of you to wear that shade of yellow, Miranda. What a pity whoever tinted your slippers was unable to get a closer match. Still, it is the price one pays to live in England. In Paris they know about these things. And who is this young lady, Thomas?"

Thomas presented me.

Lady Sylvia's brown eyes narrowed as she studied my curtsey. "Talgarth. Not one of George Talgarth's girls?" I nodded and she went on. "Isn't it amazing, Thomas? George Talgarth was a great friend of Sir Percy's. What an excellent liar the dear boy was, too. A man after Sir Percy's own style. A face like an angel and a voice like silk. Now I fancy he married a Rushton, did he not? Ah, I have it. Celia Rushton. You must be the eldest. I've heard it is the younger girl who has George's looks. Not that you haven't a great deal of your mother's charm, my dear. That very insouciant fashion of wearing your hair, for example."

Thomas paid no attention to his mother's suggestion he seat himself again. Throughout Lady Sylvia's speech, he stood swaying silently beside me, growing steadily paler. I slipped my hand under his elbow to steady him.

"I understood you were living in Paris," said Miranda.

"How obliging of you to travel so far to inspect your future daughter."

"But how fortunate I did," replied Lady Sylvia. "Now, Thomas, you may be annoyed with me, but I have sent my things directly on to Schofield House, so you must come away with me at once and see me settled in. Very boring for you, dear boy, I'm sure, but I shall let the Grenvilles know the fault is entirely mine. Forgive me, Kate, for taking him away from you so early in the evening. Come to tea when I am settled at Schofield House, and I shall tell you all the dreadful scrapes Thomas got in as a child."

"How charming," said Miranda, "but doubtless it will require several days to cover so much material."

"I shall only tell Kate of the ones I heard about, of course," replied Lady Sylvia. "In general, Thomas was a most resourceful boy, very well able to manage on his own. It has been interesting to meet you again after so many years, Miranda. You haven't changed at all, I see."

Miranda seemed troubled by this remark, though it was delivered in very cordial tones, for she excused herself and went away, doubtless to tally up Dorothea's latest admirers. Lady Sylvia watched her go with unconcealed dislike and then turned to Thomas.

"Thank heavens," she said softly. "I thought she would never leave. Now, dear boy, tell me. If you hold my arm as if to steady me, can you walk out of here, or ought Kate to keep hold of your elbow?"

"I can manage," said Thomas grimly.

"Excellent," said Lady Sylvia. "Then good night, Kate. Don't forget. Come to tea."

They departed with deliberate care, but from my vantage point it did not look as though Thomas were retreating. It seemed to me as though the pair of them swept out together in slow and deliberate dignity.

Need I say, I shall accept the invitation to tea at the earliest opportunity?

Your,
Kate

26 June 1817
Rushton Manor, Essex

Dearest Kate,

Your letter arrived late this morning, and I must say that I am glad that for once the post was a trifle slow. For this morning James was waiting in the woods when I went for my ride, and I am sure that had I had your letter I could not have kept from telling him the whole. (Well, not about Georgy's shocking behavior, of course. That is nothing to do with James or Thomas. I do not see that you can do much about it, either, except to keep a sharp eye on your remaining jewelry. I am afraid Aunt Charlotte would be far more likely to scold you for looking through Georgy's jewelry box than to blame Georgy for taking your earrings.)

James looked very tired when I met him, and he greeted me with an abrupt demand to know whether I had any word from you yet.

"No," I said. "But I'm sure Kate will write as soon as she gets my letter. I should hear something today or tomorrow."

James shifted restlessly in the saddle. "You're sure?"

"Of course I'm sure!" I said indignantly. "Kate knows how important it is."

"Does she?" He sounded as if he were talking to himself, more than to me. "But it may be too late already. Sir Hilary has been at work in his laboratory for four nights running."

"How do you know what Sir Hilary has been doing?" I asked.

"I've been watching Bedrick Hall until past three in the morning every night for the past two weeks," he said. "And before you begin making comments about my sneaking abilities, may I inform you that I'm quite sure I wasn't seen."

"You were quite sure the last time, too," I pointed out. He had sunk back into gloom again and did not seem to hear me.

"If Sir Hilary has finally found out how to use that damned chocolate pot—," he said in a dull voice.

"Then we must do something," I said briskly. It felt like

a rather obvious thing to say, but I could not stand hearing James talking in that miserable, half-dead tone. "But *not* until we are sure that things are as bad as you seem to fear."

"*We* are not going to do anything at all," James said. "This is my responsibility, Miss Rushton, not yours."

"Oh, stuff!" I said. "Kate is as much my friend as Thomas is yours."

"You don't understand," he said. "This is my fault."

"How is it your fault?" I demanded. "Really, you and that Marquis of Kate's are quite impossible. How do you expect us to do anything sensible if you won't tell us what is going on?"

"My dear Miss Rushton," Mr. Tarleton said with a smile, "I do not think I would ever expect you to do anything sensible."

"What an odious thing to say!" I commented. "And you still have not explained why you think the Marquis's condition is your fault."

"I let Sir Hilary have the chocolate pot," he said. "If I'd known—but I'm not a wizard, and Thomas didn't tell me."

"Then it's Thomas's fault for not telling you," I said firmly.

James shook his head. "Thomas trusted me, and I let him down," he said in that infuriatingly stubborn tone men use when they are discussing things like cards and politics and the military, which they don't think females understand.

"Oh, well, if it's a matter of honor," I said. "You should

have said that to begin with. Not that it has anything to do with deciding what we ought to do next, but I am sure you would have felt better for saying it."

He gave me a surprised look, tinged with amusement. "Quite so. But may I repeat, Miss Rushton, that this is my responsibility, not yours."

"You may repeat it as many times as you like," I assured him. "Only I wish you will leave off calling me 'Miss Rushton'; it makes me want to look around for Aunt Elizabeth."

He laughed, which was what I had intended, and spent the remainder of the ride attempting to convince me that he ought to do whatever needed to be done alone. I refused to agree to anything, and ended by telling him to go back to Tarleton Hall and get some sleep before he decided anything at all.

"For even Papa admits that it is impossible to come to a sensible conclusion about anything when one is very tired," I pointed out.

Eventually I got him to agree. You can, therefore, imagine what a quandary I was in when I returned home to find your letter waiting, with news every bit as bad as James Tarleton seemed to fear. Fortunately, Aunt Elizabeth was going over next week's menus with the cook, so I was able to slip up to my room to consider.

I thought for quite a long time. I saw that if Sir Hilary had been using the chocolate pot in his spells for four nights running, as James feared, then Thomas might well be in a dreadful state. I also saw that as soon as James discovered this, he would very likely do something foolish. He might decide to break into Bedrick Hall after the chocolate pot, for instance, and if he tried he would certainly be discovered. He has no talent whatever for subterfuge. Unfortunately, I knew I would have to tell him the whole when I saw him next morning. (I was quite certain he would be waiting, and quite apart from the fact that I promised to give him any messages from Thomas, he has a remarkable talent for worming things out of one.) So I determined to do something myself, immediately.

I then went downstairs to find Aunt Elizabeth. I managed to persuade her to pay a morning call on Sir Hilary, to inquire about the proposed party. This was a rather difficult task, because she dislikes wizards so, and calls at Bedrick Hall only when she must, if Sir Hilary is there. I dropped a hint that Mrs. Everslee ought not to have things all her own way, and Aunt Elizabeth was forced to agree.

I wore Georgy's made-over dress and my blue shawl again with the dreadful Tanistry book in one pocket. It had occurred to me, you see, that if Sir Hilary was using the epicyclical spells, he might well need to refer to the dreadful Tanistry book, and if he did he would certainly discover that it was missing. Returning the book had, therefore, become a matter of some urgency, and I knew that Papa would not be sending his stack back to Bedrick Hall for at least a month. So I took the book with me. I was quite sure that I could come up with some excuse to wander about the house while we were visiting, and I could easily return the book to Sir Hilary's library while I was looking for the chocolate pot.

Mrs. Everslee was already at Bedrick Hall when we arrived, and to my utter amazement Sir Hilary was once again using Thomas's chocolate pot with the rest of his tea things. "Ah, Miss Rushton and her admirable aunt," Sir Hilary said as he rose to greet us. "And have you, too, come to advise me about my party?"

"We will be happy to do so if you wish it, Sir Hilary," Aunt Elizabeth said stiffly. "I cannot think why you should suppose it the reason for our call, however."

"Can you not?" he said, and his eyes flickered briefly to Mrs. Everslee, who colored. "Then perhaps we can find something else to discuss. Your family is well, I trust?"

I listened with half an ear while I studied the chocolate pot, trying to decide whether it was the real thing or simply an imitation like the one Miranda used. It seemed to me very foolish for Sir Hilary to use the chocolate pot so openly; then I remembered that Mrs. Everslee had been present when Aunt Elizabeth and I payed our duty call. No doubt Sir Hilary thought she would find it odd if he did not use the same dishes. And, I told myself, he would not worry about any of us seeing it if he thought we knew nothing of its history and use. (Beyond, of course, the obvious use of pouring chocolate.) I decided that it probably *was* Thomas's chocolate pot, and resolved to take the chance.

Sir Hilary's smooth voice broke in on my reflections. "You seem fascinated by my chocolate pot, Miss Rushton," he said. "I do not recall your being so intrigued on your previous visit."

"It has occurred to me that my cousin would look simply wonderful in that shade of blue, and I am trying to fix it in my mind so that I may match it later," I said, for that was the first thing that came into my head. I do not know why Sir Hilary has this effect on me lately; I used to be much better at facing him.

"Your cousin?" he said, and there was an undercurrent to the words that I did not like. "If I remember correctly, her coloring is much like yours. This particular shade of blue would never do for her."

"You are thinking of Kate," I said, feeling my mouth go dry. "I was speaking of Georgina."

"Quite right," said Sir Hilary. "I was indeed thinking of the elder Miss Talgarth."

"Dear Kate!" said Mrs. Everslee in sentimental tones. "Do you know she is betrothed, Sir Hilary? And to the Marquis of Schofield!"

"Yes, I saw the announcement in the *Gazette* some weeks ago," Sir Hilary replied. His eyes flickered back to me. "Your cousin is to be greatly complimented on her good fortune."

"I will tell her you have said so, when I see her again," I said.

Aunt Elizabeth had poured herself a cup of tea, and was

just beginning on a second cup for me. "No thank you, please, Aunt Elizabeth," I said. "I will have chocolate. It was so good the last time we were here," I added to Sir Hilary as I leaned over and picked up the chocolate pot.

As soon as I touched it, I was quite sure that it was Thomas's, for I could *feel* the magic in it sending tingles up my arm. I kept my composure as well as I could and poured half a cup of chocolate very slowly. Then I raised my head and stiffened, as if I had heard something. "Oh, what was that?" I said, looking toward the windows. As I spoke, I started to rise, still clutching the handle of the chocolate pot.

Everyone, including Sir Hilary, looked automatically toward the windows for the briefest fraction of a second. And in that second, Kate, I put my knee under the edge of the tea table and tipped it over. It was rather difficult to manage in a casual fashion, but I believe I succeeded admirably.

"Oh, dear!" I cried, and gave a little jump backward. This, of course, let me knock into the chair, and as I pretended to struggle for balance I threw the chocolate pot (with as much force as I could conveniently manage) down on top of the whole tangle of tea things. For an instant I was afraid it would not break, but it hit the edge of the tea table with a most satisfactory crash and splintered into a thousand pieces, sending chocolate flying everywhere.

I fell on top of the chair, and for a moment everyone was busy sorting things out. Mrs. Everslee fussed, Aunt Elizabeth scolded, and Sir Hilary rang for the servants to clear up the mess. I, of course, was busy scrubbing at the chocolate stains on my gown, spreading them around as much as I could so as to ruin the gown completely, if possible. I was determined that this would be the very last time I would wear this particular make-over of Georgy's.

Aunt Elizabeth noticed, and changed course in midscold. "Stop that, Cecy, you're only making things worse," she said. "I shall have to get you home at once. How *did* you come to be so clumsy?"

"I thought I heard something outside," I answered. "And, *indeed,* Sir Hilary, I am very sorry."

I looked at him as I spoke, and went cold all over. Sir Hilary was looking at me with all the affability of a cobra, and when I saw his eyes I was suddenly quite sure that he *knew* that what I had done was deliberate. I clutched at my reticule, feeling very frightened and small, and it was just then that Aunt Elizabeth tried to wrap my shawl about me to hide the chocolate stains.

"There, Cecy, I think this will— What have you got in your pocket?" she said. "Cecy, you know I have told you not to carry books in your shawl; it spoils the hang, and—" She drew the book out of my pocket as she spoke, before I even realized what was happening. And so I could not stop her from seeing *Epicyclical Elaborations of Sorcery* on the spine.

Aunt Elizabeth immediately had an absolutely frightening attack of the vapors. When she began to recover herself a little, I braced myself for another, far worse scolding. To my utter amazement, she did not tear into me, as I expected, but began abusing *Sir Hilary* in the most amazing manner.

"How dare you, sir?" she demanded, shaking the book in Sir Hilary's face. "How dare you attempt to corrupt my niece? Well, I shall not allow it!"

"Aunt Elizabeth, pray—," I started, but she cut me off with a wave.

"You be quiet, Miss! I'll speak with you later." She looked back to Sir Hilary, and her eyes were positively flashing fire. "I could not keep you from destroying my William with your filthy magic, but this time I will not be alone in my efforts. You may be sure Cecy's Papa shall know the whole before the day is out."

"I believe you are seriously overset, Miss Rushton," Sir Hilary said calmly. He appeared no more put out than was reasonable for a gentleman having an inexplicable scene enacted in his sitting room, but when he looked at me his eyes were even colder than before. By this time, however, I had resigned myself to his realizing that I was involved in Thomas's affairs, and that I might well have some magical ability of my own, so I was able to meet his glare with tolerable composure.

"Overset!" Aunt Elizabeth raged. "I'll show you overset!" And she threw the book at Sir Hilary's head.

Sir Hilary ducked, and the book knocked a bit of plaster out of the wall behind him. Aunt Elizabeth glared at him, then turned to me with magnificent unconcern. "Come,

Cecy," she said in a controlled voice. "It is high time we were going."

I could not have agreed more. The next half hour was, however, the worst I have ever spent in my entire life. Aunt Elizabeth berated me in low tones for the entire drive home. She appears to labor under the impression that Sir Hilary has been teaching me magic, and that he had provided me willingly with the dreadful Tanistry book. I did not feel able to set her straight, as it would have involved lengthy explanations of Thomas's business, as well as that of James and Mr. Wrexton. Upon reflection, however, I cannot help but wonder why she was so certain the book was Sir Hilary's, and what exactly she meant by the accusations she hurled at his head. Who, for instance, was William? And whatever did Sir Hilary do to him?

I shall not, I fear, have much chance to investigate these interesting tidbits. When we arrived home, Aunt Elizabeth stormed up to my room and went through all my things. Naturally, she discovered my charm-bag and my supplies for making others. She confiscated everything, and opened the charm-bag despite my protest that it was only a protective spell. It is just as well, therefore, that I am now confined to my room until further notice. I do not think I would feel at all safe going about in public without the protection of the charm-bag, particularly now that Sir Hilary is aware that I know more than I had let on.

I expect Aunt Elizabeth will write to Aunt Charlotte very soon. I suggest, therefore, that you find a *very good* hiding place for all the various charm-bags I have sent you, though I suppose you might contrive to pass them off as presents from Thomas. I don't suppose Aunt Charlotte would find it at all out of the ordinary for a wizard to give such things to his betrothed.

You may also tell Thomas that I apologize very much if he does not like it, but I have smashed his chocolate pot to smithereens. It is unfortunate that it was necessary to do so, but the pot was not doing Thomas any good where it was, and I saw little likelihood of its being recovered. This way, Thomas will have to make himself a new focus, but at least Sir Hilary will not be able to use the chocolate pot against him any longer. (Thomas and James seem to have been determined to get the thing back, instead of being practical, which is just the sort of thing men do when they are being stubborn. You need not tell him I said so, however.)

27 June

I had intended to write more of my conjectures today, as I am still confined to my room and have little else to do. I find, however, that I am nearly too tired to lift my pen; I believe that I may be sickening of the influenza. So I shall ask

Mary, the little upstairs maid, to smuggle this off to the post. I do wish I had had the chance to reassure James, but even if Aunt Elizabeth would have allowed me to do so, I do not think I have the energy to have ridden out.

Your loving cousin,
Cecy

30 June 1817
11 Berkeley Square, London

Dear Cecy,

Bless you and keep you, cousin! *Bless you* for smashing that wretched chocolate pot. And keep you from the influenza. Fortunately, Aunt Elizabeth is a splendid nurse. Please take great care of yourself. It is sometimes hard on one's temper to be treated as an invalid.

On Thursday, I accepted Lady Sylvia's invitation to tea to Schofield House. She was kind enough to send a carriage round to collect me, so I was able to visit unattended by Aunt Charlotte. By the time the invitation arrived, I had taken pains to inquire about Lady Sylvia Schofield and was able to discover that although she is perfectly respectable, she has a considerable reputation for eccentricity.

In the first place, she has never put off mourning since her elder son's death. In the second place, after her husband's death she left England and has since traveled about the world.

In the past year she took up residence in Paris and no one expected her to return, even for Thomas's wedding. In the third place, she has a reputation for outspokenness that puts even Thomas to shame. Apparently she once told the Archbishop of Canterbury that marriage among the clergy was the only factor that prevented English village life from degenerating into utter savagery. (No wonder Thomas did not say the Archbishop was a particular friend of his *mother's*.) In the fourth place, and I have saved the best for last, Lady Sylvia Schofield enjoys considerable notoriety for her skills as a wizard. (In addition to her independent interests, she is said to have given Sir David Brewster the idea for his kaleidoscope.)

Thus it was that I arrived at Schofield House with my reticule stuffed fat with the charm-bag you stitched for Thomas.

As I feared, Thomas was not well enough to come down to tea, but Lady Sylvia received me in the library, over a tea table laden with good things.

"Now then, Kate," said Lady Sylvia, pouring tea, "you must tell me how long this nonsensical behavior of Thomas's has been going on."

I took a steadying sip of India tea and began with the day of Sir Hilary's investiture. When I was finished, I produced your charm-bag for Thomas. "It requires a lock of Thomas's hair to complete," I said, as I handed it to her, "but I thought it might prove useful—or at least do him no harm. He seems so *weary*—" I broke off helplessly.

Lady Sylvia refilled my teacup and gave the charm-bag her full attention for several minutes. "Good work," she said at last. "Nothing extravagant, just good wholesome basic craft. A five-finger exercise. Your cousin's doing, you say? Hmm. There's talent there. I should like to hear her orisons and invocations. Still, that can wait. By all means, I shall crop a lock of Thomas's hair for it. I'm sure it cannot harm him. And they do say cutting hair is most beneficial to some fevers, do they not? Oh, come. Don't look so stricken." She poured herself more tea, but neither of us drank any.

"If only we knew what Sir Hilary is *doing*," I said finally. "Thomas gets worse and worse and we're powerless."

"Now, stop that, dear child," said Lady Sylvia, moving the plate of ratafia biscuits away from me. I realized belatedly that I had ground several of the biscuits into powder while my thoughts wandered. As I brushed futilely at the crumbs, Lady Sylvia rose and went to rummage in Thomas's writing desk. After a moment she returned with his ink pot, which she put down on the tea tray.

"This should show us a little of Sir Hilary's actions," she said, "though the knowledge may do us no good at all. Unfortunately, the spell only works with the single sense of vision. Still, it may prove interesting."

She clasped the ink pot in her hands for a moment, her dark eyes steady on mine, then passed her left hand over the top, unstoppered it, and seized my right hand in hers. She spoke, but I could not catch her precise words. They sounded to me like classical Greek as Uncle speaks it. "Now we both look," she said, and tilted the ink pot a little in her free hand. It took several moments for her to find an angle where we could both peer into the ink pot, but when she did, I could see the bright, distorted reflection of the library windows on the surface of the ink. "Oh, good," said Lady Sylvia. "It's very clear. Perhaps it helps that you're a virgin."

Despite this rather shocking remark, I kept my eyes on the reflection in the ink, for as I watched, I saw the brightness change. As if from a great distance, I could see Sir Hilary presiding over a crowded tea table. I saw you jump up from your chair, chocolate pot in hand, and in a series of movements as devastating as my most inspired clumsiness reduce the entire tea table, chocolate pot and all, to wreckage. You fell down as Aunt Elizabeth sprang up—and the ink rippled as Lady Sylvia's hand trembled.

From upstairs came the sound of glass breaking.

I glanced up. Lady Sylvia had lifted her head to listen. Swiftly, she put the ink pot down and rose, ivory walking stick in hand. I followed her as she rushed from the room and upstairs to the open door of Thomas's room.

He was in bed, awake, propped up against many pillows. On the floor in the center of the room, a shattered drinking glass lay in a pool of viscous milky liquid. At our entrance, Thomas looked up and smiled. He was still very pale, but his smile was his old derisive one, and his voice, though weak, held unmistakable satisfaction as he said, "If you have come to give me more barley water, Mother, I warn you I am feeling far too well to drink it."

On my next visit, this afternoon, I arrived to find Lady Sylvia presiding over the tea tray as before and Thomas feeling so much more the thing that he had actually gone out.

"Yes," said Lady Sylvia as she offered me a cucumber sandwich, "he has gone to see about Frederick Hollydean. Evidently the dreadful boy was forever prosing on about the Grand Tour, so dear Thomas has made a booking for him on a ship bound for Piraeus via Alexandria. Very broadening for the lad, but I doubt the horrible Hollydean will appreciate it. Still, I must admit I'm proud of Thomas. When he disposes of people, they stay disposed."

When I finished my first cup of tea, I brought out your most recent letter. I hope you will not object, though I know it was never meant for anyone's eyes but mine, but I asked Lady Sylvia to read it. I felt that she was not only personally involved, but also interested on the basis of her expertise as a wizard. She read it through rapidly and returned it to me, saying that she did not blame me in the least for my concern at your closing paragraph. She said it was very clever of you to have worked out the double focus, that she considered Thomas a great gudgeon for not breaking the chocolate pot himself long since, and that she would speak with Thomas the instant he returned. "But in the meantime," she said, pouring us each another cup of tea, "tell me exactly what your cousin was referring to when she says you went to a gentleman's lodgings in the middle of the night."

I told her the whole, stressing the fact that time *was* of the essence, and that a call during the day would have included Aunt Charlotte, who would have insisted on chaperoning me herself.

"Your Aunt Charlotte," Lady Sylvia said. "Surely that must be Charlotte Rushton?"

I nodded.

"Would that be Elizabeth Rushton's sister?"

I nodded again.

Lady Sylvia's brows rose. "Well, well. Your cousin Cecelia comes by her magical aptitude very understandably then. These things do run in families, you know. Oh, yes. They do indeed."

And no more would she say.

Please write to tell me the very *instant* you receive this letter. Your illness worries me very much.

Love,
Kate

P.S. You will not attend Sir Hilary's party now, of course, but I send with this letter a dress length of amber taffeta. It was ordered for me but the modiste never cut it out. I hope there is enough fabric to provide a dress for you, despite your greater height. Perhaps when all this is over, you will be able to wear it in happier circumstances.

Dearest Kate,

I am so sorry that my last letter worried you; I did not intend that it should. It was very foolish of me to have added that last paragraph, but I was not thinking too clearly at the time.

Thanks to Mr. Wrexton, I am quite well now, and very glad to know that my efforts with the chocolate pot were not ineffective. I am beginning to think it a pity that you have promised to jilt Thomas at the end of the Season; he appears to need someone around with more wit than he has. It is a good thing his Mother has returned. Between the two of you, you may be able to bring him to his senses.

Also, I must thank you for the amber taffeta you sent with your letter. I am taking it to Mrs. Hobart this afternoon to choose some ribbons and have it made up for Sir Hilary's party on Saturday. For I must tell you, Kate, that we will be going to it after all. The invitation card arrived this morning. This is not so unlikely as you may think, for Aunt Elizabeth has apologized to Sir Hilary for her behavior. It is exceedingly provoking of her, for she seems to think she has misjudged him, and while it is quite true that it was not Sir

Hilary who was teaching me magic, it is also true that Sir Hilary has been doing things which are *far* worse.

I had better explain how all this has come about. After I wrote you last Friday, Papa came up to my room to see me. Aunt Elizabeth had told him the whole story (as she knows it) of the incident at Sir Hilary's, with particular emphasis on the wicked magic that Sir Hilary was supposedly teaching me. Papa had come to hear my side.

I was feeling very tired, and was lying on the daybed in the satin dressing gown that Aunt Charlotte gave me last year (blue, of course, but the embroidery is so pretty that I do not care). Papa stopped short, frowning, when he saw me, and said anxiously, "Cecilia, are you unwell?"

"I am not feeling quite the thing, Papa," I admitted.

"I came to find out what was behind the tale your aunt brought me," he said, "but I can return some other time if you would rather not discuss it now."

"It is quite all right, Papa; I am only a little tired," I said. I was more than just a little tired, but I had decided that I would much rather explain things to Papa then, no matter how much effort it took. I knew that if I let him leave, I would spend the rest of the day worrying about whether he was fretting, which would not have been at all restful.

"Very well, if you are sure, Cecy." Papa pulled one of the chairs over beside the daybed and sat down. He looked at me very gravely. "Your aunt says that you have been letting

Sir Hilary Bedrick teach you magic, against her express wishes," he said. "Is this true, Cecy?"

"No, Papa," I said. "At least—I *have* been learning magic, but not from Sir Hilary. And Aunt Elizabeth never actually *said* I was forbidden to do so. Though I must admit that I knew she would not like it," I added conscientiously.

"Elizabeth says you were carrying a book—," Papa started, and he looked so sorrowful that I had to interrupt before he finished.

"*Epicyclical Elaborations of Sorcery* by Everard Tanistry," I said. "And it is a perfectly dreadful book, and I quite understand why she was upset, at least— How did Aunt Elizabeth know how horrid it was?"

"What were you doing with it, Cecy?" Papa asked. His expression had gone very stiff when I said the name of the book, but he relaxed just a little as soon as I said that it was perfectly dreadful. "Who gave it to you?"

"No one gave it to me, Papa," I said. I raised my chin and looked at him. "I fooled Sir Hilary's servants into sending it over along with some of the books you asked for last week. I had seen it in Sir Hilary's library, and I wanted to look at it because—Papa, will you promise not to tell Aunt Elizabeth?"

"Cecy—"

"Please, Papa! She'll write to Aunt Charlotte, and Kate will be in dreadful trouble, and she does *not* deserve it."

"I see. Very well, Cecelia, I will not tell your aunt—either of your aunts—why you wanted to look at that particular book."

"Thank you, Papa. It was like this—," and I explained to him about Miranda. Not the whole story, of course; just that you and I had discovered that Dorothea's Stepmama had been Miranda Tanistry before her marriage, that she did not seem to be a particularly pleasant person, that we thought she was a sorceress of some kind, and that you have told me that she has a strong dislike for Thomas. All of which is quite true, even if it is nothing like the whole.

"And when I saw the name Tanistry on a book in Sir Hilary's library, I thought perhaps it might have been written by a relative of hers," I finished. "And I thought that I might find out something that would be useful for Kate to know about her family if I looked at Sir Hilary's book closely."

"I see," Papa said again. "And did you?"

"Well, only that if she *is* related to the man who wrote that book, then her whole family is a great deal more wicked than I had thought," I said. "Do you know what that book is about, Papa?"

"Yes," he said, and smiled at me. "That is precisely why I was worried when Elizabeth told me you had been studying it."

"You mean Aunt Elizabeth thought I was trying to learn those dreadful spells for— Well, that is the outside of enough!" I said indignantly. "Just because she dislikes magic, she thinks everyone who uses it must be wicked! Even if it's me!"

Papa laughed, then sobered and shook his head. "Try not to judge your aunt too harshly, Cecy," he said. "She has more reason than you know to dislike Sir Hilary. I think it was that, as much as the magic, that made her react so strongly."

"Why does Aunt Elizabeth hate magicians so?" I asked. "I have wanted to learn about magic forever, and she will not even let me talk about it!"

Papa sighed. "Cecy—" He paused, and shook his head again. "Your aunt does not hate magicians," he said deliberately. "She is an excellent magician in her own right, or she was once."

"*Aunt Elizabeth* is a magician?" I said incredulously "But . . ."

Papa nodded, and began to explain. When she was younger, Aunt Elizabeth was apparently not only a magician, but an extremely good one. She became engaged to a man named William Camden, who was also a wizard. Papa says he was very devoted to his craft, which is where the trouble started. For the more magic he learned, the more he wanted to learn. This is not necessarily a bad thing, Papa was careful to explain, but in this case the results were quite tragic. William Camden became obsessed with magic and neglected all his other duties (including Aunt Elizabeth).

Finally, he went to Sir Hilary Bedrick for tutoring (Sir Hilary apparently has quite a name for training up young wizards). But William was still dissatisfied with his progress, and tried to hurry things up by studying some of Sir Hilary's magic tomes on his own. He was killed experimenting with one of the more sinister spells. (Papa would not be too specific about exactly what William was trying to accomplish. From this I conclude that it was something truly dreadful, for Papa does not usually pay much attention to whether his tales are suitable for females.)

Papa says that this is the real reason why Aunt Elizabeth does not like magic, magicians, or Sir Hilary Bedrick. She gave up her own practice when William died, despite Papa's urging her to continue. I think perhaps she felt she ought to have done something to keep William from blowing himself up (or whatever it was), and gave up her magic out of guilt.

"Well, I am very sorry for Aunt Elizabeth," I said. "And I understand a little better why she was so upset with Sir Hilary. I suppose I can even see why she doesn't want me to learn magic. But Papa, I *like* magic, and Mr. Wrexton says I am very good at it."

"Mr. Wrexton? Is that who you've been getting your lessons from?" Papa said.

"Yes, and he doesn't know anything about that dreadful Tanistry book," I said. "He's only had time to teach me about charm-bags and animation spells."

"You don't need to reassure me about Michael Wrexton's principles," Papa said. He looked at me closely, and sighed. "You really want this, don't you, Cecy? Very well, then; I'll speak to your aunt. But no more investigations in Sir Hilary's library. Is that understood?"

"Yes, Papa," I said. "And thank you!"

I ought to have been quite elated by all this, but when Papa left I was too tired to write you with my good news and the astonishing story of Aunt Elizabeth. I do not know what I will say to Patience Everslee when next I see her, for she has always maintained that Aunt Elizabeth suffered a grave disappointment in her youth, and I have always told her that it was most unlikely. And now Patience has turned out to be quite right. It is most annoying.

Aunt Elizabeth came in in the afternoon and gave me back my supplies for making charm-bags. She made it quite clear that she disapproved of the entire matter, and said that as Papa had explained the true circumstances she had written Sir Hilary Bedrick a most apologetic letter. (It is quite provoking, for I could not tell her that Sir Hilary was just as bad as she had thought without bringing in Thomas and Miranda and everything. So now she thinks she has misjudged Sir Hilary, and that is why we are to go to the party after all.) She gave me a sharp look and added there was no reason for me to mope about when I had got my way again. I told her I was not moping, I was really very tired. I do not think she believed me then, but when I spent the rest of that day and most of the next sleeping, she was forced to change her mind.

Saturday morning I was still just as tired as I had been the previous day. Having so recently recovered from a bad cold yourself, Kate, you will understand why I was determined not to spend another day staring at the same four walls. It was not as if I were truly ill, for I promise you I was not—I did not even have the headache. I was only tired. And as there have been mornings in the past when I was very tired (the day after Aunt Elizabeth found us in the Twelve-Acre Field at one in the morning, struggling with the goat, for instance), and as I had previously been able to continue my ordinary activities in spite of my tiredness, I decided to do the same that day.

My resolution did not carry me very far. To be precise, I managed to dress and make my way down to the sofa in the library. I was quite put out, though I must admit that it was a great relief not to be in my bedchamber any longer. Papa came to find me a little later, looking worried, so I pretended to be absorbed in a novel and did my utmost to appear just as usual. He seemed somewhat reassured when he left, and I collapsed gratefully back onto the sofa. It is a great strain to have to reassure people that one is perfectly well when all one really wishes is to be left alone to sleep.

I was not, however, left alone for long. A few minutes after Papa left, Danvers tapped at the library door to inform me that James Tarleton had called. "He asked for you expressly, Miss," Danvers said, and there was a note of disapproval in his voice. I am told that butlers do not generally approve of occurrences that are out of the ordinary, and Danvers has always been the most correct of butlers.

"Show him in here," I said, struggling to a sitting position. "And have someone bring in a tea tray. Oh, and I believe Aunt Elizabeth has gone down to inspect the herb garden; send someone to inform her of Mr. Tarleton's arrival." I was very pleased with myself for thinking of this last, for the longer it was before Aunt Elizabeth learned that James had called, the more time I would have to speak with him alone. The herb garden was the farthest place I could think of that also sounded entirely reasonable.

Danvers unbent a little at this evidence that things were not going to be completely irregular, and a moment later he brought Mr. Tarleton into the library. James looked a trifle pale and very worried indeed. I felt a stab of guilt. I really ought to have made more of a push to let him know about the chocolate pot, so that he would not have kept fretting over Thomas. As the door closed behind him, he came swiftly across the room toward me. "Cecelia! What is the matter with you?"

"There is nothing whatever the matter with me, Mr. Tarleton," I said. "I am a little tired, that is all."

He pulled a chair up beside the sofa and sat down. His eyes never left my face, which made me feel very odd. "Gammon," he said bluntly. "You're pale as a ghost. I was afraid there was something wrong when you missed your ride three days running."

"I tell you, I am quite all right!" I said. "And if you must inquire about my health, do so later. Aunt Elizabeth will be here at any moment, and I must tell you about Thomas before she arrives."

"Devil take Thomas!" James said vehemently. "I should never have dragged you into his affairs."

"You did no such thing," I said. "If anyone did, it was Kate." This did not appear to mollify him, so I hurried on. "I have had a letter from her. Thomas has sent you a nonsensical message that he can manage things perfectly well alone, and you are not to trouble yourself. Kate says he was looking very tired and unwell, and she thinks he is a gudgeon to tell you such a thing, but he did say it. But it is quite all right because—"

Aunt Elizabeth and the tea tray arrived simultaneously at just that moment. I sighed in frustration as James rose to greet her, for I had wished very much to discuss matters openly with him. However, there was nothing I could do about it, so I set myself to make polite conversation, and to work in bits of important information as best I could.

Fortunately, Aunt Elizabeth began by asking what we had been discussing when she arrived. "We were talking about Kate," I said quickly. "Do you know that Mr. Tarleton is a friend of her fiancé, the Marquis of Schofield?"

"I was not aware of that, Mr. Tarleton," Aunt Elizabeth

said. "The Marquis spends so little time at his estates here that it had not occurred to me that he had any local acquaintance."

"We served together in Spain," Mr. Tarleton said. "We were both staff officers. The Duke of Wellington found our abilities complementary, so we shared a number of assignments and became very well acquainted."

"Have you ever met the Marquis's Mama, Lady Sylvia?" I said. "Kate writes that she has come to London quite unexpectedly."

James gave me a sidelong look that told me he understood. Aunt Elizabeth sniffed. "Kate is the only one who would find it unexpected," she said. "Of course Lady Sylvia wishes to inspect her future daughter-in-law."

We chatted for a few moments about the various balls and events that you have attended during the Season, and the people you have met. James appears to know a great many of them, and was able to answer most of Aunt Elizabeth's questions concerning their appearance, manners, and respectability. (She is not, apparently, completely satisfied with Aunt Charlotte's account, and needless to say I have not shown her your letters.)

Finally I saw an opportunity, and I said in a cross tone, "And I do wish you had let me go to London with Kate, Aunt Elizabeth."

"You know quite well why you were not allowed to have

a Season this year, Cecy," Aunt Elizabeth said. "And after the way you have behaved this week, I cannot be sorry for that decision."

"Surely you are being rather severe, Ma'am," Mr. Tarleton said. I could see a little frown line between his eyebrows, but his tone was perfectly civil.

"It was an accident," I said mendaciously. "I did not *mean* to break Sir Hilary's chocolate pot."

James stiffened. Aunt Elizabeth did not notice; she was too busy being relieved that I was not going to bring up the subject of my magic lessons. "It was extremely careless of you, Cecy," she said repressively.

"I am afraid I do not understand," James said cautiously. "Miss Rushton broke Sir Hilary's chocolate pot?"

"Into a million pieces," I said. "It was so unfortunate! Aunt Elizabeth and I had called on Sir Hilary on Tuesday, you see, and I was pouring myself a cup of chocolate when I thought I heard something. I am afraid I jumped and dropped the chocolate pot. Sir Hilary was most annoyed, and I cannot say I blame him. It was *such* a lovely blue, even if it did not match the rest of Sir Hilary's tea things."

James stared at me, aghast. I smiled reassuringly, wishing again that Aunt Elizabeth had waited even a few minutes longer to arrive. For I could see that he was angry with me for what I had done, and with Aunt Elizabeth present there was no way that I could explain to James why breaking

Thomas's chocolate pot was *necessary*. A wave of tiredness swept over me and I swayed, spilling a little of my tea into my saucer.

Aunt Elizabeth, of course, noticed at once. "Cecy, dear, do take care," she said reprovingly.

"I am sorry, Aunt Elizabeth," I said. "I am afraid I have the headache."

"Then you must go upstairs and lie down," Aunt Elizabeth said. "I am sure Mr. Tarleton will excuse you."

I rose a little shakily. James was still frowning at me, but I tried to smile. "I am very sorry to run off like this, Mr. Tarleton," I said. "Do forgive me."

He said nothing, and my heart sank. I took a firm hold on the arm of the sofa and dropped a curtsey. "If you see Mr. Wrexton," I said, "would you be so kind as to tell him I am not feeling quite the thing? I was engaged to go driving with him this afternoon, and I would not like him to make the trip for nothing."

Aunt Elizabeth stiffened at the impropriety of this request, but I was watching James. All the expression washed out of his face when I mentioned Mr. Wrexton's name. "I will be happy to do you the favor," he said in a toneless voice. "Your servant, Miss Rushton."

I nodded and left the room as quickly as I was able. Upstairs, I went to my bedroom and indulged in a hearty bout of tears, which I can only put down to my extreme tiredness, for you know I am not usually a watering pot, Kate. But it seems most unfair for me to have gone to such trouble to extract Thomas from his difficulties with the chocolate pot and then have James scowl disapprovingly at me because of it. I comfort myself with the thought that he is not a wizard and does not see the necessity of what I have done, but it is still very melancholy.

I was quite exhausted after the encounter with James, and I slept for the remainder of the day. Mary told me, when she brought up my dinner tray, that Mr. Wrexton had called in the afternoon, so James must not have seen him. Fortunately, Papa came through the hall just as Danvers was conveying my regrets to Mr. Wrexton, and the two of them went off to Papa's study for a comfortable cose about the ancient Sumerians, or the Babylonian Empire, or whatever Papa is currently eager to talk about with anyone who comes by. So I need not feel guilty that Mr. Wrexton drove out to Rushton Manor for nothing.

Aunt Elizabeth allowed me to sleep all day Sunday, but she came to my room very early Monday morning and fussed over me until I was driven nearly to distraction. She did not stop after I got downstairs, but kept on giving me tea and tucking up my lap robe. Finally I said something very cross, but Aunt Elizabeth did not scold me as she usually does. She did go quite stiff for a moment, but then she reached into her sewing basket and pulled out a charm-bag with my initial on it!

"I made this for you, Cecelia," she said, and I could tell

she was quite uncomfortable. "And I must apologize for ruining the one you made yourself." She held out the bag and a pair of scissors.

I took them from her in silence and clipped off a lock of my hair for the charm-bag. As I closed it up, I studied the bag closely, and suddenly I gasped. "The charm-bag in Oliver's room!" I said. "You made it!"

"It was the only way of protecting him from that Griscomb girl's spell," Aunt Elizabeth said stiffly.

"Oh, Aunt Elizabeth, I am sorry! I opened it the day we went on the picnic with Dorothea, because I did not know what sort of charm-bag it was and I was afraid it would do something horrid," I said. "But I made another for him right away."

"It was an understandable mistake," Aunt Elizabeth said. "How are you feeling now, Cecy?"

"I am not so tired as I was," I said, "but I still do not feel much like riding. I think—"

There was a rap at the sitting room door. "Mr. Wrexton," Danvers announced.

Aunt Elizabeth paled slightly and sat up very straight. "Do join us, Mr. Wrexton," she said. "Will you have tea?"

"Thank you, Miss Rushton, I will," Mr. Wrexton replied. He took his teacup and sat down between Aunt Elizabeth and me. "I've come to see Cecelia; I believe you know why."

"Magic lessons," Aunt Elizabeth sniffed. "Arthur told me."

"Your brother is wise enough not to wish to stifle talent," Mr. Wrexton said gently. "I know you cannot like it, but I hope you will understand."

Aunt Elizabeth did not reply, and Mr. Wrexton gave a little sigh. Then he turned to me. "I understand you have not been feeling well, Cecelia. What's that you have?"

"I have been rather tired," I said. I fingered the charm-bag and glanced at Aunt Elizabeth. When she did not say anything, I held it up for Mr. Wrexton to see. "Aunt Elizabeth made it for me," I told him.

"I see." Mr. Wrexton's voice was noncommittal, but he threw Aunt Elizabeth a speculative look. "May I examine it?"

I looked at Aunt Elizabeth again, but she made no sign, so I handed it to him. He studied it in silence a moment, then nodded. "Excellent work. Unfortunately, I do not believe it is quite enough for what is troubling the young lady."

Aunt Elizabeth's eyes narrowed. "You have some other suggestion?"

"I do, indeed," Mr. Wrexton said. He drew a small jeweler's box from his pocket and handed it to me. "Put that on, Cecy, if you would."

I opened the box and gasped. It was the little gold locket and chain that Mama left me. "Mama's necklace! But how did you get it?"

"Your father gave it to me when we discussed the matter on Saturday," Mr. Wrexton said. "He felt it would be better for me to place the protective spells on something that you were accustomed to wearing. Please, put it on."

I did so, and the moment I had the chain fastened around my neck I felt positively energetic. It was as if I had been wrapped up in cotton wool for several days, and it had all just dropped away. I gave a gasp of surprise and sat up very straight.

"Excellent," Mr. Wrexton said with some satisfaction.

"Just what is going on here, Mr. Wrexton?" Aunt Elizabeth said in freezing tones.

Mr. Wrexton hesitated. "Nothing you need worry about any further, I assure you," he said carefully.

I was thinking furiously, for it seemed that the cotton wool had dropped away from my brains as well as my muscles. Suddenly it was quite obvious that Sir Hilary had set some kind of spell to make me feel so very tired. I wondered for a moment whether it was the same kind of thing that he had been doing to Thomas, but I was forced to abandon this theory. For one thing, I had not had even a ghost of a fever; for another, Sir Hilary and I have not got a joint focus he could use to torment me. (And you may be quite sure I shall make certain he never gets one!) It is quite possible that he was simply trying to keep me out of the way for a while for there seemed to be no ill effects whatever now that Mr. Wrexton had given me the locket. I am not certain of this, however, as I am not knowledgeable enough to be aware of all the various things Sir Hilary might have been attempting to do.

While I was thinking, Mr. Wrexton gave Aunt Elizabeth some tale that did not at all satisfy her. She was extremely cool toward him for the remainder of his visit, though she warmed a little toward the end when it became obvious that I was my old self.

And so, Kate, I am wearing Mama's—and Mr. Wrexton's—locket everywhere, and I feel perfectly well. I even went riding this morning after your letter arrived, but James was not in the woods. So I have not had the opportunity to tell him why I broke the chocolate pot, nor that it worked just as I had hoped and Thomas is on the mend. If he is not there tomorrow, I will have to find some other way to let him know that Thomas is feeling better, for even if he is angry with me, I think he would want to be told.

I have made no effort to visit Bedrick Hall; there seems no need whatever, now that the chocolate pot has been taken care of. I hope that this has occurred to James, and that he has ceased lurking in Sir Hilary's bushes. And you may be very sure I shall be on my best behavior at Sir Hilary's party Saturday evening. I shall not leave Aunt Elizabeth's side for a minute. So you see, I am being extremely sensible, just as you would like. I only wish Thomas and James would do the same; then perhaps this entire business would be quickly concluded.

Your,
Cecy

6 July 1817
11 Berkeley Square, London

Dear Cecy,

Robert Penwood is here in London at last. He ran Mr. Griscomb to earth in Leeds and accompanied him to London where they were both putting up at Mr. Griscomb's club. Given Miranda's short temper, I suppose it is understandable that Mr. Griscomb stays at White's while Miranda and Dorothea lease a very desirable Mayfair residence.

I learned all this last Tuesday when Robert came to call. He stayed barely a quarter of an hour and questioned me about Dorothea almost the entire time. I was able to persuade him to accept an invitation to take tea on Thursday, but he was far more interested in learning everything he could about the attentions shown to Dorothea by the Duke of Hexham. All I could tell him was what everyone in London knows: The Duke is wellborn, well-known, well-to-do, and well over sixty. Much cast down, Robert left scowling.

On Wednesday I was asked to tea at Schofield House, where I expected to see Thomas. I did not. Instead, Lady Sylvia received me in the most formal drawing room I have ever seen. I had scarcely taken my place when Lady Sylvia fixed me with a searching look and asked in a very serious tone whether I preferred milk or lemon.

"Milk," I said, tugging off my gloves and crumpling them in my lap.

As she poured, Lady Sylvia continued to scrutinize me. A little discomfited by the intensity of her regard, I took a bite of my biscuit and asked, "When did you first discover Thomas's talent for magic? I expect he must have been very young at the time."

Lady Sylvia said nothing but went on gazing at me as though she wished to peer through me like a window. Unnerved, I inhaled a biscuit crumb and went off in a coughing fit. When I blinked my vision clear, she was still regarding me with the same expression of stern interest.

"Is something the matter, Lady Sylvia?" I asked.

"You seem a nice girl," Lady Sylvia replied, "and I know Thomas well enough to guess the sort of tricks he is likely to get up to. You needn't be afraid to tell me the entire truth, you know."

I spilt half my tea in my lap. It was still quite hot and the gloves did not soak up enough to make much difference. I dabbed ineffectually with my napkin as I tried to think of something to say that would relieve my feelings without giving Lady Sylvia the idea that I was badly brought up. "My goodness," I said finally. It wasn't very satisfactory. "Drat!" I said. That was better. "I don't know what you mean," I said to Lady Sylvia.

"I mean that Thomas might have made you think there was some reason for you to pretend to be betrothed, for his protection perhaps." Lady Sylvia's dark gaze had not altered. "You might feel very awkward about ending the betrothal before you were quite sure he was safe."

Cecy, you *know* I can tell falsehoods. No matter who looks at me, for how long, I can tell bouncers so enormous even Aunt Charlotte does not think to question them. I *know* I can. Only, sitting in that perfect room of ivory and gold, dripping tea on the Axminster carpet, I just couldn't tell a lie to Lady Sylvia. So I took refuge in silence. For several minutes (it seemed like several years), I gazed into the cloudy remainder of my tea and tried to think why I felt so miserable at the chance to rid myself of the burden of betrothal to Thomas. In a way I thought it would be better than jilting him, for I felt quite certain his Mother would disapprove strongly of his sham offer of marriage.

"He was perfectly honest with me," I said at last. "He said I was the only young lady he could ask who would not misunderstand him. There is something about Dorothea, you see, that no man can resist. And he wasn't certain he could resist either, until he saw her. He didn't like to take the risk."

Lady Sylvia was silent so long I looked up from my teacup. She was no longer gazing at me. She was staring at the teapot with an air of faint disgust. "So you were the only young lady in the Ton who would not misunderstand him," she said. There was a twist in the corner of her mouth that boded ill for someone.

"He said I could jilt him whenever I please," I continued. "I have given it a great deal of thought. I think perhaps the ball at Carlton House would be best. But perhaps you would prefer something more discreet."

"That is entirely your affair," replied Lady Sylvia. Her voice was still remote but much of the chill had gone out of it. "In the meantime, we must do the thing properly. There is a set of rubies that Thomas ought to present to you—"

I made an inarticulate noise of protest.

"—and I'm afraid I've been dreadfully selfish with the Schofield pearls. There is also a sapphire necklace, which won't do for your coloring, of course, but will come to you all the same, and a brooch with a really splendid intaglio."

"Lady Sylvia, I could not—truly—"

"There will be more tedious things to see to in the way of settlements and so on, but I won't bore you with all that now," said Lady Sylvia. "No, don't argue, child. We'll have the solicitors see to everything. After all, you don't want to betray Thomas's useless, stupid little charade now, do you? People will talk if you don't do the thing properly. And those rubies will be really stunning with your complexion."

"No, Lady Sylvia," I said. "No."

Lady Sylvia gave me another long, measuring look. The ill-natured twist of her lips smoothed itself away as she smiled at me. "No?" she asked. "Well, perhaps not just yet. Will you take more tea, Kate?"

To my relief, she let the subject drop and did not refer to

it again. We spent the rest of the afternoon drinking tea and discussing Thomas's youthful misadventures. Apparently Oliver was not the only child to have the firm conviction he could fly from the peak of the stable roof. Thomas did something very similar, only instead of breaking his arm, he broke his leg. I ought to write these things down so that if you and I ever have children, we will know at about what age these notions arise.

On Thursday, Dorothea came to tea in Berkeley Square. Robert was already here when she arrived and he stared at her, quite speechless with happiness, all the time Aunt Charlotte was pouring out for Dorothea.

"Will you have a cream bun?" I asked Robert, in an effort to distract him from Dorothea.

Robert merely shook his head and went on stirring his tea absently. Dorothea drank an entire cup of tea before she overcame her bashfulness sufficiently to look up at him, and when she did, he lost his grip on his spoon altogether. It flew in a sharp little arc over the tea table and landed on the carpet at Georgy's feet.

"Oh, I beg your pardon," said Robert, flushing scarlet. "Let me get it."

He rose and circled the table the long way around. As he walked behind Dorothea he made a sudden attack on the plate of cream buns and under cover of this distraction dropped a folded scrap of paper into Dorothea's lap. Aunt

Charlotte would certainly have discovered this piece of amateur subterfuge if I hadn't had the presence of mind to upset the sugar bowl into the slops dish. To my disappointment, Dorothea was not goose enough to open the paper and read it there and then. She slid it into her glove while Aunt Charlotte was addressing me and ringing for more sugar, and was able to put her gloves on with perfect composure when it was time to take her leave.

On the whole, I would say romance becomes Robert Penwood. He does not talk nearly so much as was his habit, and he ate scarcely anything, not even his cream bun.

It is a pity that I cannot give them another opportunity to meet, but since Thomas warned me of Miranda's intentions toward me, I have been avoiding her to the best of my ability. Unfortunately, this means I must also avoid Dorothea, except in those rare cases, as at tea, when she can escape Miranda's company. Georgina teases me about it, telling me that this betrays my jealousy of the attention Thomas paid Dorothea while I was ill. But Georgy is usually teasing me about something. It is almost pleasant to have her roast me about something that I know isn't true for a change. Much better than her usual instinct—she has only just stopped making references to gilding my toenails. This has been doubly annoying as the whole idea was Georgy's to begin with. If she keeps on with her arch remarks on the topic, Aunt Charlotte is sure to find out after all, and it will be me that she makes sorry. An awful thought just struck me. Aunt Charlotte will certainly blame me for Georgy's gaming—but do you suppose she would be right in doing so? Am I to blame?

Love,
Kate

9 July 1817
Rushton Manor, Essex

Dearest Kate,

Of course you are not to blame for Georgy's gaming. If anyone is to blame (besides Georgy), it is Aunt Charlotte, for (as she has pointed out to everyone so often) she is Responsible For You Both. However, I doubt that she will see it this way. She probably *will* claim it is your fault, for she always does. I cannot imagine why she is so unjust. Nobody can do anything with Georgy when she takes a notion into her head, and she never listens to your advice any more than Oliver listens to me. It is a great pity you cannot tell Aunt Charlotte so to her face, and so bring her to a sense of her obligations, but it would never work. If you tried, she would probably lock you in your room for the next twenty years, and Miranda would make away with Thomas in the meantime.

I am glad to hear that Robert has reached London, and

gladder to know that Miranda has not yet arranged to have him set upon by footpads or poisoned with chocolate or thrown by his horse (though the way Robert rides, I do not think I could set such an accident down to Miranda's account with any great degree of certainty, however much I might like to). I do hope Robert will do something useful, now that he is there. Staring happily at Dorothea over the tea table may be very enjoyable for them both, but I cannot see that it accomplishes anything. I suppose I must pin my hopes on the note he passed her, though it is probably only bad verse to her eyebrows. (And I cannot commend too highly your presence of mind in distracting Aunt Charlotte. Had she noticed what Robert was doing, she would certainly have considered it her duty to inform Miranda, and you know what that must have led to.)

I must confess that I cannot completely make sense of Lady Sylvia's remarks to you regarding your betrothal to Thomas. However, she seems to have accepted the current state of affairs, which must make things far more comfortable for you. You must have found it excessively awkward, dealing with Lady Sylvia these past two weeks and knowing that she believed you to be really engaged to her son. I do think it rather unkind of her to refer to it as "Thomas's useless, stupid little charade," but no doubt she was slightly overset on first hearing the truth. And she is quite right; rubies would be perfectly stunning on you.

I have spent much of this week at Mrs. Hobart's, having

fittings on the gown she made for me from the amber taffeta you sent. Mrs. Hobart is nothing if not painstaking, and I cannot justly say, therefore, that the major part of my week has been lively.

Monday morning I went out for my ride as usual. I did not expect to see James Tarleton, though out of habit I rode toward the wood where we had agreed to meet. He had not been waiting for me since that dreadful tea the week before, when he seemed so upset at my having broken Thomas's chocolate pot. I considered this most unfair, as it meant that I had still not been able to tell him why I had done it or that subsequent events had justified my actions (i.e., Thomas had begun to recover). So it was with mixed feelings that I saw James Tarleton's bay coming toward me through the trees.

He was looking very stern and solemn, but not, I thought, actually furious. Considering that he had had all of a week in which to let his temper subside, this was not notably encouraging. However, it was at least an opportunity to provide him with my explanation and news, which I felt honor-bound to do in spite of his attitude.

"Good morning, Miss Rushton," he said coldly as he came up with me.

"And to you, Mr. Tarleton," I said in similar tones. I could not but feel that this was an inauspicious beginning, so I added more warmly, "I suppose you have come at last to hear the rest of my news of Thomas?"

"No, Miss Rushton, I have come to ask you to stop your

well-intentioned interfering in Thomas's affairs. There is no further need for it."

I gaped at him, amazement warring with indignation. Indignation won out very quickly. "If I had not broken that chocolate pot, Thomas would probably be dead by now," I said in as cold and stiff a tone as ever Aunt Elizabeth managed. "It was *necessary*, Mr. Tarleton, and if you do not see that, you are as feather-headed as—as my brother, Oliver. Furthermore, I will have you know that I have no particular interest in the affairs of the Marquis of Schofield. My cousin Kate's affairs are, however, another matter, and I hope I shall always be willing to lend her my assistance when she is in need of it."

Mr. Tarleton's eyes narrowed. "Then it is to oblige your cousin that you are attending Sir Hilary Bedrick's dance on Saturday?"

"Is *that* what you're cutting up stiff about?" I said. "I was sure you were still annoyed about Thomas's chocolate pot."

"*Damn* Thomas's chocolate pot!" James said. "Can you think of nothing else?"

"Mr. Tarleton!" I said, more surprised by his vehemence than shocked by his language. "Have you and Thomas had a falling-out?"

"You might say that," he replied. "But you are not going to divert my attention this time, Miss Rushton. Are you going to Sir Hilary's party?"

"Yes. Aunt Elizabeth has accepted on behalf of all of us," I said.

"And I suppose you had no hand in that?" he said skeptically. "No plans to slip into Sir Hilary's library during the party? No intention of poking around the house to see what you can discover?"

"None whatever," I assured him. "Now that the chocolate pot is disposed of, there seems not the slightest need for such stratagems."

"I am glad to hear you say so," he said in a dry tone.

"Well, it is obvious," I said. "Without the chocolate pot, Sir Hilary cannot do much to Thomas without returning to London. He cannot do that before the party, so Thomas will have plenty of time to recover from any lingering ill effects. And as long as neither of us does anything to annoy Sir Hilary, he can have no reason to put spells on us to keep us out of his way."

"So you do suspect that Sir Hilary was behind that convenient illness of yours," he said, and his tone was not so hard as before.

"Well, of course," I said reasonably. "And I will take the greatest care not to irritate him again, you may be sure."

He laughed suddenly, but there seemed very little humor in it. "The only thing I'm sure of is that taking great care is not something you're particularly good at," he said. "I suppose I'll have to come to Bedrick Hall and keep an eye on you."

I frowned. "Is that wise? I shall be quite all right because I will stay with Aunt Elizabeth all evening, but if Sir Hilary suspects you of spying on him, you won't be safe."

He looked at me with a twisted little smile. "Don't worry about me, Miss Rushton. The only danger I'm likely to be in comes from quite another quarter."

"Miranda? But she's in London—" Then I remembered the garden you stumbled into at Sir Hilary's investiture, and Thomas's remarks about a portal. "Oh, dear, I hadn't thought of that at all," I said.

"Not Miranda," he said. For a moment he seemed about to explain further; then he shook his head. "I seem to have spent our last few conversations ripping up at you, Miss Rushton," he said after a moment. "I beg your pardon for it."

"It is quite all right," I said. "For I know how worried you must have been about Thomas, and being worried always seems to make people cross." His expression seemed to be darkening again, so I hurried on, "Kate's news of Thomas has been very good; if you would not mind riding a little way back with me, I can tell you of it."

"Of course," he said with a sigh, and nudged his horse to walk. "Tell me about Thomas."

I gave him a complete description of what you had told me in your last letter but one. I was forced to confess that you had not actually seen Thomas this past week, but I was careful to point out that Lady Sylvia did not seem the sort of person to allow him to be out disposing of Frederick Hollydean if he were not entirely recovered from Sir Hilary's machinations. Mr. Tarleton made no objection to this; in fact, he seemed somewhat preoccupied. I enjoyed our ride nonetheless. I was even rather sorry when we reached the hill near the house, and James took his leave.

I did not have time to fall into a groundless fit of the mopes, for Aunt Elizabeth pounced on me directly I came in, and we went out to collect my dress from Mrs. Hobart. Then Mr. Wrexton came in the afternoon to resume my magic lessons (and I must say, Kate, it is far easier to apply oneself to such things indoors instead of perched in a carriage with a groom riding ahead).

Mr. Wrexton says that the spell that made me feel so tired has faded, and has not been renewed. He seems inclined to think that it was simply in the nature of a warning, but he recommended that I continue to wear the locket, just in case. I had already formed that intention, but I thanked him gravely for the advice.

Sir Hilary has sent Aunt Elizabeth a note acknowledging the apology she sent him and particularly requesting our presence at his party. This may be only because he wishes to stop the rumors that resulted from the tales Mrs. Everslee has been telling of Aunt Elizabeth's behavior that day I broke the chocolate pot. On the other hand, he made a point of saying that if Oliver came home unexpectedly, we were not to stand on ceremony but to bring him along.

It occurs to me that the last few times we have seen him, Sir Hilary has made a great point of inquiring about Oliver. That strikes me as sinister, for you know he has never before shown a particular interest in any of us. It bothers me even more that I cannot imagine why Sir Hilary should be concerned with Oliver. If he were inquiring about you, I could understand it (since you are engaged to Thomas). But what can he want with *Oliver*? I find that I am very glad your odious Marquis has Oliver safely hidden away somewhere.

Your puzzled cousin,
Cecy

11 July 1817
11 Berkeley Square, London

Dear Cecy,

Forgive me for this letter. I shall give you all the news, I promise, but I must be merciless and tell it all in order or my head will start to spin and I'm sure to leave things out. I'm sure to leave things out anyway, but this is the only way I can make sense of it for you at all. You would not have me be like Lady Jersey and tell the story hopscotch fashion, would you?

On Friday, Lady Sylvia and Thomas came to supper before we were to depart for Carlton House. Just as we were going in to dine, a message arrived from Dorothea. She said that Miranda was indisposed. Unless she could find a proper chaperone she would be unable to attend the ball, and would Aunt Charlotte be able to oblige? After much coaxing from Georgy, Aunt Charlotte agreed we would call at Miranda's on the way to Carlton House and collect Dorothea. (Doubtless the importance of the party counted for something with Aunt Charlotte.) I was surprised at Dorothea's willingness to be leered at by the Duke of Hexham, but suspected she might have learned that Robert Penwood would be there. Lady Sylvia and Thomas exchanged dark looks over the news that Miranda was not planning to attend the Prince's ball after all. As soon as the meal was over, Thomas took his leave, with the unstated intention of investigating Miranda's sudden change of plan. It developed that with Dorothea along there would be no space in the carriage for me, so I was able to accept Lady Sylvia's offer of a place in her coach, instead. The others departed and we waited in the blue saloon for word that Lady Sylvia's coach was ready.

From the instant the others left, my heart began to lift. It was true that Thomas and I were not really engaged. It was understandable that he had abandoned the ball to hunt Miranda. But it was also true that on the strength of my sham betrothal, I had been allowed a silk dress—far grander than anything I've ever had—the color of a ripe peach: rich gold with shifting highlights of deep rose. And it was also understandable that I felt my spirits rise when I was alone with

Lady Sylvia, whose opinion of me, even when she is frowning at my coiffure, is so much easier to bear than Aunt Charlotte's.

"I can't understand how you produce that effect," she said, squinting at my hair critically, "but I wish you would not, my dear. Do you have a comb?"

I did, of course (*and* a clean handkerchief), but to get at it I had to turn out my reticule on the side table. Among the hairpins and other small debris I carry, she spied the pair of charm-bags you made for me. I returned my own to my reticule when I bundled up my things again, but she took the one containing Thomas's handkerchief and turned it over and over in her hands with a pensive expression.

"So you carry this with you," Lady Sylvia said.

I explained what you told me about the bloodstains.

"They turned violet?" repeated Lady Sylvia. She regarded the charm-bag in thoughtful silence for a moment, then nodded. "You are wise to guard it well. The handkerchief links you with Thomas, did you realize? Oh, yes. And such a link may not always be to your benefit. Remember the headache he gave you at Countess Lieven's? You had a charm-bag and it ought to have protected you from such slight magic as that. Of course, charm-bags can't protect you from everything. They work best when their existence goes undetected, or when a spell has been cast and left to do its work unattended. If Miranda were to try to enchant you this evening, for example, it would be very little use against her, save perhaps to delay the spell's effects a trifle. Of course, it would be the worst of bad taste for Miranda to employ magic at Carlton House. The magical precautions cast over that place are very precise; it would be rank folly to interfere with them. And after all, whatever his personal habits, the Prince is still our heir to the throne. Still, you must remember that since you and Thomas are both in this charmbag, you are linked. It is a small thing, but sometimes small things can cause more misery than you might expect. These magical bonds can sometimes prove painful."

I remembered the day Thomas came to cry off, when I thought Dorothea had enchanted him. Thomas needed no magical assistance to make people miserable. "What should I do, Lady Sylvia? I don't wish to prolong such a link, but I daren't do anything to harm the charm-bag if it is protecting us—and even if I opened it, I don't know where I'd be able to keep the handkerchief safely."

"If the blood were out of the silk," said Lady Sylvia, "the pair of you would be disentangled. I think I shall try, with your permission. May I keep this?"

I agreed and she tucked the charm-bag into her own reticule.

"And now," she said, "your comb, my child."

In the three minutes before the carriage arrived, she unpinned my hair, made me bend over until it nearly brushed the carpet, and combed until the tears came to my eyes. Then she twisted it all up into a loose coil, told me to straighten, and produced an intricate knot at the crown of my head. She thrust six hairpins in, apparently at random, and turned me to the mirror to judge the effect, which was, to my eyes, entirely lovely but very precarious.

"It's perfect," I said glumly, "but it will never stay up."

In the mirror I could see Lady Sylvia standing behind me. Her reflection held my eyes as she said very distinctly, "It will stay up. It will stay up *all evening.*"

Our arrival at Carlton House was festive, for many of the guests were old friends of Lady Sylvia's, anxious to welcome her home to England. I could see Georgina among a swarm of young men, and from the presence of the Duke of Hexham in the group, I judged Dorothea must be there, too. Of Thomas there was no sign.

Lady Sylvia made me known to her friends and conducted me on a brief tour of the marvels of Carlton House. There are marvels there, too, and you will be amazed, as I was, when you see them. In one long corridor they display some of the artifacts the Prince brought back from his tour of the American colonies last year, some very fine beadwork and a Mohican shaman's drum, which casts out illness (Mohican illness only, unfortunately). There was also a gleaming obsidian disc that belonged to Doctor John Dee, and an exquisite chessboard with enameled pieces. I bent close to admire the detail of the white queen's cloak (I could see the black-tipped ermine) and jumped.

"Oh, it moved!" I exclaimed—for as I watched, the

queen had taken a step to her left, to a black square, where her cloak showed to best advantage. As I stared, the white knight beside her stepped aside politely to clear the next square. "That's not a proper knight's move," I protested. "They're just wandering around at random."

Lady Sylvia smiled. "This is the King's pride and joy," she explained, "but the enchantment merely animates the pieces. It doesn't instruct them in the finer points of play."

"How dreadful," I replied, "to be caught up in a game and have no idea of the rules."

"It's not a plight unique to this chess set," Lady Sylvia observed dryly.

"Well, someone should teach them," I said.

Lady Sylvia nodded. "It's been tried. All they do is display their clothes, jostle for position, and, very occasionally, crawl back into their velvet case to sleep."

"Oh," I said. "Just like real people."

"Indeed," replied Lady Sylvia, and continued the tour.

A little past midnight, I received a message via Michael Aubrey that Dorothea wished to speak with me particularly, and that she waited for me with Georgina in the conservatory. Thinking she had some message to give me for Robert Penwood, who was not among the guests after all, I accompanied Michael to the little assembly of bamboo chairs set in the heart of the glass-roofed and walled conservatory. Dorothea and Georgy were sitting with their backs to the door. At our arrival, Michael claimed Georgy's hand and took her off to search for refreshments. I took one of the delicate bamboo chairs beside Dorothea.

I arranged my skirts carefully, folded my hands over the reticule in my lap, and composed myself for another lengthy discussion of Robert's virtues. And realized that Dorothea's eyes were not blue, but dark and very hard. The woman sitting next to me was not Dorothea, but Miranda.

I had to squint a little to see her as she really was, and as I did so something in my expression must have betrayed my recognition, for she smiled at me icily and said, "I *have* been looking forward to this moment, you meddlesome little chit. It is about time I discomfited you as you have discomfited me, don't you think?"

"Is that the reason for this little masquerade?" I asked. Really, it was so satisfactory to speak bluntly to Miranda for a change that I almost forgot to be frightened. "To discomfit me?"

Miranda put her hand up to conceal the smile on her lips. "In part," she said. "You will prove useful to me. But I work best with an audience. Time to arrange for the rest of my entertainment. Thomas is being so slow about finding me, I think I'm entitled to give him a hint."

She put out her hand to me. I found myself lifting my left hand and holding it out to her. It was a strange sensation—my hand had fallen asleep and there was the same feeling I'd had in Sir Hilary's garden in it, first pins and needles and then numbness. Miranda made a slight sound of annoyance and pulled off my long glove. Beneath the glove, on my index finger, I wore Thomas's ring. Miranda plucked it off and inspected it with a sneer.

"Quite the ugliest betrothal ring I ever saw." She tossed it on her palm, caught it, and clenched it in her fist. Her knuckles went white—there was a flash of brilliant light— she opened her fist and the ring was gone.

"That ought to fetch him," Miranda said.

For a moment I wished it would; then the thought of Thomas confronting Miranda's reckless malice made me wish him a thousand miles away. From that thought, it was a small step to wish myself a thousand miles away, too. But wishing accomplished nothing.

It would have been nice to call for help, or even turn my head toward the door to see if Michael and Georgina were returning, but I could not. The pins and needles spread from my hand up my arm and slowly all through me—more slowly than that first day in Sir Hilary's garden, but just as thoroughly in the end. I was held fast in the deep hard chill of Miranda's gaze.

"You ought to have settled for life as a tree," Miranda informed me. "I have always heard it is a most restful way to spend time. I won't offer you such a pleasant fate now. You've had your chance at painless alternatives. When it seemed Dorothea had enchanted Thomas it should have been simple enough to break your neck, but you managed not to—and later it became plain that although you were solidly in the way, your death would do nothing to forward Dorothea's cause with Thomas. So it is your own fault that you are finally providing me with a method of inflicting the pain that Thomas so richly deserves."

As in Sir Hilary's garden, I found I was able to speak, though my tongue was woolly and my words slow. "What did he ever do to you?" I asked muzzily.

Miranda rose and began to pace back and forth in front of my chair. It hurt me to follow her with my eyes, but I could not look away. I think, from the expression on her face, that she realized this and enjoyed it. "He interfered," Miranda replied. "He has always interfered. He objected to his brother's devotion to me, and interfered with it. He objected to my research with Sir Hilary and interfered with that. He had the audacity to threaten to expose us. We put a stop to that, and when he had run away, we put a stop to his brother, too. It seemed an appropriate means of replenishing our resources. And from the moment he arrived back in England, Thomas began to interfere again. He might have been of some practical use to me before Sir Hilary leached away most of his magic—but now my only interest in him is the entertainment value he provides. It will be amusing to witness his reaction to your death."

"What do you intend?" I inquired. "Will you turn me into a chocolate pot and break me?"

"Don't tempt me," said Miranda. "No, I see no reason why you shouldn't provide me with your youth. You'll have no further use for it, after all. It is a delicate procedure, but worth the fuss."

From somewhere on her person she produced a stick of blue chalk. Stepping delicately in a circle around me, she drew a ring of glyphs on the floor. As she worked, I was able to look away and see the reflection in the glass of the conservatory wall opposite me. The night beyond the glass threw back the candlelight in the conservatory to produce a reflection of me, sitting as stiff and stupid as a tailor's dummy on a little bamboo chair, and Miranda working intently. In the reflection I could see her as she really was, a little woman with fair hair.

"I will be as old as you are," she said, chalking symbols rapidly. "You will be seventy-five. As I recall, I enjoyed being your age very much. You won't enjoy being seventy-five, and I'm quite sure Thomas won't enjoy seeing you that way, either."

She put the chalk away and surveyed the effect of the ring, dusting her palms with a fastidious little gesture. "A little off center, but nothing to signify," she said. "I shall enjoy being young again. Disguising myself as Dorothea has given me a taste for youth. Pity it didn't work out between her and Thomas. I would have taken her place soon after the wedding, of course. If he noticed, he could have done nothing. Now, of course, the chit's worthless to me. Not even a virgin by this time, I suspect."

"What!" I knew it was absurd to be in my predicament and still find myself shocked by a remark from Miranda, but shocked I was.

Miranda laughed merrily at the expression on my face. From what I could judge of it from my reflection in the glass wall opposite, she was entitled to her amusement.

"Yes, Dorothea's gone off with some bumpkin she met in Essex," Miranda said. "They had Griscomb's consent to marry; they could never have arranged for a special license without it. I shall have his liver for it, of course, just as soon as I've taught Thomas what it means to interfere with me. Men—they think marriage solves all a woman's problems."

I thought of Robert Penwood's little scrap of paper dropped in Dorothea's lap at tea. "It solved Dorothea's," I said. "And it is the outside of enough to hear you complain of men. What do you know about men, anyway, you nasty little fright? What do you know about anything except how to hurt people?"

Miranda drew herself up and glared at me. "I know enough about that to deal with you, at least," she informed me.

"What will that accomplish?" I demanded. "Thomas stood up pretty well to the worst that Sir Hilary could contrive. He's sure to deal with him eventually. No matter what becomes of me, he has enough scores to settle with you to keep you busy for seventy-five more years."

Miranda was still glaring at me. In the reflection in the glass wall opposite I could see her back, my front, and behind me, Lady Sylvia moving slowly to stand in back of my chair, her ivory walking stick held across her path as a shield. Miranda did not appear to have noticed Lady Sylvia as yet, and I determined to delay that moment as long as I could. More interested in making noise than sense, I went on talking.

"You've been buzzing around like a fly," I said, "and all this time Thomas has had more important matters to deal with. But sooner or later you are certain to be swatted. And I must say I think the swatting is already sadly overdue."

"If this accomplishes nothing else," said Miranda, lifting her arms, "at least the spell will silence you."

As she spoke in a high, exultant voice, I heard Lady Sylvia speak in my ear, as close as the moment she told my hair to stay up, saying, "All the years in this ring to you, and all your own years, too."

In the reflection of the glass conservatory wall, I saw Lady Sylvia's black figure behind my chair, ivory walking stick lifted over my head. There was a double flash of light—one from the real scene before me, a brighter one from the reflection—and Miranda screamed.

The numbness withdrew from my arms and legs and I found I could move again. I felt Lady Sylvia's hand on my shoulder, a gentle pressure keeping me in my chair. I turned my head and saw nothing, though in the reflection I could see her quite plainly. But looking in the reflection revealed all too clearly what was becoming of Miranda. It was easier to watch her real body than the reflected one, even as the years she had lived and wished away came flooding back to leave her an empty husk, brittle with age, in the center of the conservatory floor.

"I came in as you were discussing flies," murmured Lady Sylvia. "Had she cared to concentrate on her work, she would certainly have detected me as I crossed the circle. Thank you for your excellent work in distracting her." As she spoke, Lady Sylvia grew visible to me in person as well as in the reflection. She leaned upon her ivory walking stick and said, "Miranda and I were at school together long ago. *Long* ago. When she received her own age back, the very slight addition of my age and yours, even briefly, upset the balance of her youth spell. Distressing to witness, but I doubt the demise of such an unscrupulous wizard will cause much recrimination."

At the moment she finished her sentence, the glass wall opposite me shattered to fragments. Shards of glass were still ringing on the marble floor as Thomas leapt over the wreckage and into the conservatory. He crossed the room in two great strides and pulled me up out of my chair. With an embarrassed glance at Lady Sylvia, I realized she was fading tactfully away again, leaving the two of us in the conservatory with Miranda's corpse.

"Kate!" exclaimed Thomas harshly. "—You're not hurt? The ring—" He held me too close for me to get a clear look at him, but I could tell he had undergone some adventure, for his hair was disordered, his dark eyes were wide, and his evening clothes were ruined. His neckcloth was undone, the sleeve of his coat ripped from wrist to elbow, and there was blood on his knuckles. Before I could reply, Thomas stiffened, staring over my shoulder.

"Miranda is dead," I informed him. "She was waiting for you, but grew impatient."

Thomas went on looking past me. I turned to follow his stricken gaze—and found myself facing the Prince of Wales and a phalanx of his companions.

"Good gad, sir," said the Prince to Thomas, "what do you mean by all this?"

I looked from the Prince's scarlet face to Thomas's pale one and freed myself from Thomas's embrace to sink into my deepest curtsey.

The details of my story, told in my very best truthful voice, evolved and expanded during the next half hour. I explained Miranda's treasonous use of magic within the confines of Carlton House, Thomas's heroic intervention, the unfortunate but trifling loss of the glass wall in the conservatory (broken when Miranda tried to halt Thomas), and Miranda's ultimate defeat. The highly unpleasant condition of Miranda's remains proved a convincing piece of evidence. The Prince accepted the entire tale eventually and ordered the mess cleared up. Despite the heroic character I gave him, Thomas received many horrified glances, as much for his appearance as his alleged behavior. When the Prince pronounced himself satisfied, Thomas withdrew, taking me with him.

As we made our way out, Lady Sylvia stopped us, just long enough to return the second charm-bag to me. "You'll have to decide between the two of you what should be done with this," she said, "but without it, I'd never have been able to throw Miranda's spell back upon her without ill effects for you, Kate." I accepted the charm-bag, slipping it into my reticule as we left Carlton House.

Thomas said nothing as we left. In fact, beyond civilities to the Prince, he had said nothing since his arrival in the conservatory. A little concerned by his uncharacteristic reserve, I said, "I hope I didn't offend you when I explained matters to the Prince."

Thomas lifted an eyebrow. "Oh, is that what you call it? Explaining matters?"

"I did offend you."

"Don't be silly. You saved me from the consequences of my own folly. And you, er, explained matters beautifully. If you'd been less plausible or the Prince less persuadable, *then* you might have seen me take offense."

We descended the stairs outside Carlton House. Thomas paused on the steps to gaze into the darkness. "I forgot," he said. "I didn't bring a carriage."

"How *did* you end up outside the conservatory windows?" I asked.

"Walked. Or, rather, ran," Thomas answered. "I was at Miranda's house, where I had just forced the news of Dorothea's elopement out of Mr. Strangle. It seemed to me that if Dorothea had gone off to marry Robert Penwood, then the 'Dorothea' attending the ball had to be Miranda. I could sense where the ring had been when it was destroyed— but I had to take the most direct path to that point or I would have lost my bearing on it. My route to Carlton House led me through half the kitchen gardens in Mayfair, and brought me into the Carlton House grounds behind the conservatory. I thought my heart would burst before I got to you."

"She destroyed the ring to fetch you," I said. "She wanted to let you watch while she took my youth and aged me to seventy-five."

A little pause fell in which we fidgeted on the steps of Carlton House. I broke the silence to ask, "Did you say you forced the news out of Mr. Strangle? Does that mean you hit him?"

"It certainly does," said Thomas.

"Oh, I'm so glad. Do you think you could hit any footpads who might set upon us if we walked home from here?" I asked.

"Tonight I would hit Cribb himself," Thomas replied.

We set off into the darkness with a great and delicious sense of wrongdoing. After we had gone a good way, Thomas asked, "What was that my mother gave you as we left?"

I explained, including the fact that his mother knew our betrothal was a sham and her warning that a magical link between us might prove painful and distressing.

"Gammon," said Thomas. "What do you think spared me from Dorothea's enchantment? You keep that charm-bag safe. And as for our betrothal, you may cry off if you insist, but I wish you won't. I like the idea of marrying you."

I came to a halt in the street. "Oh, do you?" I asked.

"Yes, I do. I think we shall deal extremely." Something in my manner penetrated his notice even in the dark. "Why? Do you have some objection?" he inquired uneasily.

"Only a very trifling one. You have never proposed to me," I answered.

"Oh, well—if that is all," said Thomas with relief. "I recollect making you the offer quite distinctly—"

I cut him off. "That was a matter of your convenience, conditional on my willingness to jilt you. I should like some indication that your desire to marry me extends beyond this evening's whim."

"Oh, you are being a perfect pig about this, Kate. What do you want me to say to you?"

"'I love you,'" I informed him. He misconstrued me.

Fortunately, by the time we were quite finished kissing in a public thoroughfare, he had said it himself, with considerable feeling. I admit I, too, repeated the words several times. And we agreed that we should, indeed, deal extremely.

What with one thing and another, it took us quite a long while to walk back to Berkeley Square. When we were at the spot where the street opened out into the square, I stopped Thomas and held him for a moment with my hands on his shoulders.

"What is it, Kate?" he asked. I didn't have to see him to know he was smiling; I could hear it in the dark.

"Miranda is dead," I said, "but Sir Hilary is not."

I felt the laughter leave him.

"Miranda is dead," he said. "I'll find a way to deal with Sir Hilary."

"Thomas," I said, exasperated, "you don't by any chance *believe* all that rubbish I told the Prince about what a marvelous wizard you are, do you?"

Thomas laughed, and despite my irritation my heart lifted a little at the sound. "Very well," said Thomas, "you and I will find a way to deal with Sir Hilary."

He took my right hand in his left and put his other hand on my waist. With a monotone but rhythmic buzz, which I took to be his attempt to hum a waltz, he led me into a dance in the middle of the dark street.

"You and I and Lady Sylvia," I said, obeying his lead.

Thomas stopped humming to say, "And James."

"And Cecy," I added.

"But not Aunt Charlotte," said Thomas, as he changed direction.

"Definitely *not*," I said, following him through a sophisticated turn.

So, in the dark, to music only Thomas could hear, we waltzed the rest of the way up Berkeley Square. And when I was alone before the mirror in my bedroom, I realized that Lady Sylvia was right. Despite the exertions of the night (and despite Thomas's affectionate nature), my hair stayed up *all evening*.

Love,
Kate

14 July 1817
Rushton Manor, Essex

Dearest Kate,

Your letter arrived this morning, and I was so delighted by your news I could scarcely contain myself. (Your news about marrying Thomas, I mean; your description of Miranda's fate was, I admit, welcome, but I hope I am not so lost to propriety as to rejoice over it with such glee.) It was rather difficult to explain my emotion to Aunt Elizabeth, as she was, of course, unaware of the circumstances behind your betrothal. I must own that I have wondered for some time whether you were quite so indifferent to the odious Marquis as you claimed. I have told James everything, and he was relieved to know that Miranda will create no further difficulties; Sir Hilary alone has caused quite enough trouble, to his way of thinking. James also said that if you were anything at all like me he did not know whether to send Thomas his felicitations or condolences. I believe he intends to send both (though I assured him you were far more sensible than I and would suit Thomas admirably), so I thought I ought to warn you in case Thomas makes one of his sharp remarks.

Things have been very lively here as well. Saturday was completely taken up with all manner of last-minute preparations for Sir Hilary's party—procuring a fan that would look well with the amber taffeta, helping Aunt Elizabeth with her hair, etc. I took a great deal of trouble over my appearance, for if I was going to have to face Sir Hilary, I wished to do so looking as well as I possibly could. There is nothing that is quite so reassuring in an awkward situation as knowing that one is well turned-out, and while I hope I am not so fainthearted as to *require* such stratagems, I am not so foolish as to overlook their value. The dress suited me to perfection—Mrs. Hobart trimmed it with a brown velvet ribbon that is very nearly the same shade as my hair, and I wore brown satin slippers and Mama's locket.

In spite of all this work, I am afraid I was nearly as nervous as Aunt Elizabeth when we arrived at Bedrick Hall. Sir Hilary did not appear to notice, but greeted us both as though nothing at all out of the ordinary had occurred.

Aunt Elizabeth tried to make a stiff little apology for abusing him at tea, but Sir Hilary cut her off with a bow and told us to enjoy the party.

James Tarleton arrived a few minutes later. I was in the middle of a country dance with Martin De Lacey when I saw him, and I nearly forgot the figure in my annoyance. For he *knew* that Sir Hilary would be watching him, and he did not have to come. He glanced over the company in a bored fashion, and I could not help but notice that he was dressed with as much elegance as ever—black satin knee breeches, a white silk waistcoat with pale blue stripes, and a very dark blue evening coat of a superior cut.

I returned to Aunt Elizabeth as soon as the dance was over. Mr. Tarleton did not come near us, but strolled along the opposite side of the room, chatting with acquaintances, and looking perfectly at ease. I determined to do the same, to help make it plain to Sir Hilary that there was no connection between us. So I had a perfectly miserable time for the early part of the evening, forcing myself to make bright, cheerful conversation with everyone else while still keeping an unobtrusive eye on James.

That was my undoing, for in the middle of a waltz with Jack Everslee someone behind me stepped on the flounce of my gown and I felt the stitches rip. I turned to find Sir Hilary apologizing profusely for his clumsiness. I was afraid he was going to offer to escort me to one of the private rooms to pin up my hem (which offer I should certainly have declined!) but, instead, he found Patience Everslee and asked her to accompany me. I was not entirely reassured by this, for it seemed peculiar that Sir Hilary would practically *force* on me the opportunity of prowling about Bedrick Hall. I therefore insisted that Patience stay and help me (which she did without objection), and returned to the ballroom with as much haste as I could manage.

My first thought on reentering the ballroom was to look about for James. He was not there. I looked again to make certain, and my heart sank. I had no way of knowing whether Sir Hilary was responsible for James's absence, or whether James was sneaking about the grounds somewhere, but I could not feel sanguine about either possibility. I looked about again, hoping to find Sir Hilary (on the theory that if he was in the ballroom he could not be casting spells on James), and saw him just vanishing through the door of one of the card rooms.

I hesitated only briefly before making my way around the room. I was quite sure that Sir Hilary would not attempt to do anything to me while I was in company, and I was also sure that I should keep a close watch on him. When I reached the door of the card room, I glanced quickly around the dance floor to make certain James had not returned. Then I opened the door and stepped through.

As I crossed the threshold, light flared all around, momentarily blinding me. I blinked and shook my head. Then my eyes cleared and I saw that I was not in the card room at all. Instead, I was standing in a pleasant little cloistered garden. The light came from seven tall torches thrust into the ground just inside the wall. The flames wavered in a cool evening breeze, and by their light I saw a chair on the opposite side of the garden occupied by a man in evening dress. I realized at once that it was James.

I whirled to run, but my arms were caught in a grip of steel and I heard Sir Hilary's voice in my ear, "You really should not be so inquisitive, my dear."

I kicked him and screamed as loudly as I could for help. Sir Hilary did not seem the least discomposed, and his grip on my arms did not loosen. "You may stop that dreadful noise, my dear," he said when I paused to draw breath. "An entire artillery brigade could fire a salute inside this place and not be heard outside the walls."

As he spoke, he dragged me halfway across the garden toward James. He stopped in the center and jerked my locket off without bothering with the catch, which stung rather painfully. He tossed the locket in a corner, turned to me, and muttered a word. Then he let go of my arms. I tried to run, and discovered that I could not move at all, except to blink. I was completely numb. I could not even speak (which was exceedingly frustrating, as there were any number of very uncomplimentary things I would like to have said to Sir Hilary just then).

Sir Hilary smiled mockingly, as if he was aware of my efforts, and glanced from me to James. Then he reached out and turned me a little, so that I was facing straight at the chair where James sat.

"There," Sir Hilary said with satisfaction. "I believe that will do. I regret that I must leave you temporarily; I cannot have my guests wondering over the disappearance of their host. Don't fear I shall forget you, however. I will be back as soon as the last of them leaves. In the meantime, do enjoy yourselves as best you can."

He stepped out of my sight, and I heard his footsteps leave the pavilion. I was left in a blaze of candlelight, staring at James and quite unable to move. He appeared to be in exactly the same case as myself, for he sat like a wooden statue. I could see the anguish in his eyes, and I felt very little better myself. It was horrible to have to stand there, waiting, unable to do anything whatever to save either of us, and unable even to *speak* to James. For I was quite sure that he blamed himself for my predicament, when it was my own folly that drew me out into the garden, and I wished very much to explain it to him and apologize for being such a goose. I ought, at the very least, to have informed Aunt Elizabeth.

The thought of Aunt Elizabeth made me feel a little better, but only briefly. Sir Hilary was not foolish enough to kidnap me at his own party without having concocted some tale that would satisfy Aunt Elizabeth, at least temporarily. I did not think that she would be fooled for very long, whatever story he told her, but I was sure he had taken that into consideration, too.

I will not dwell on the next several hours. I had no way of telling how much time had passed, or when Sir Hilary would return. It was maddening to be so helpless, and the worst of it was having to watch James sitting like a corpse with living, tortured eyes. It was almost a relief when I heard the door behind me open and Sir Hilary's voice say, "How kind of you both to wait for me."

Neither James nor I, of course, could say anything in response. I heard noises behind me, and shortly Sir Hilary appeared, carrying three white candles in silver holders and a large bag. He dropped the bag beside James and set one of the candles carefully on the ground between James and me, then moved on. In a few minutes, he returned, this time carrying black candles in gold holders. He placed one just to the left of the white candle, lit both of them, and moved out of sight again. He returned a third time, empty-handed, and stood between me and James for a moment, studying whatever he had done. Then he set his quizzing glass firmly in one eye and muttered something long and involved.

The candles flared all around me, and suddenly I could move again. I leapt for the door, hoping to catch Sir Hilary by surprise, and bounced off an invisible wall. Just beyond, I could see a ring of black and white candles, six of each set in mismatched pairs surrounding me.

"I wouldn't bother trying to escape, Miss Rushton," Sir Hilary said. "The boundaries are quite solid, once they've been properly established. I'm afraid you'll find your movements rather restricted, but it won't be a problem for very long."

"Why not?" I said before I could stop myself, and I am afraid my voice was a trifle shaky.

Sir Hilary smiled. "I'd rather not disturb you by explaining."

I snorted, trying not to show how frightened I was. "You are being ridiculous, Sir Hilary," I said. "Aunt Elizabeth and Papa will surely be looking for me before long."

"On the contrary, my dear." His smile grew wider and thinner, and I wanted to throw something at him. "Your aunt is under the impression that you went home with Patience Everslee, at the invitation of her mother. Mrs. Everslee is a most ... suggestible woman. By the time Elizabeth discovers that you are not with the Everslees, she will also have information indicating that you and Mr. Tarleton have, er, eloped."

"Aunt Elizabeth won't believe it," I said.

"Oh, but she will, Miss Rushton," Sir Hilary said in smug tones. "When she hears the full tale of your clandestine meetings with Mr. Tarleton during your morning rides—a most unwise thing for a young lady of quality to do—she will have no trouble whatever in believing you have run off with him."

"And when she finds out I haven't?" I demanded.

"Ah, but she won't discover that at all, my dear. Why do you think I bothered to decoy both of you? I'm afraid Mr. Tarleton is only of incidental value to me, you see, though I certainly won't waste him. The two of you will be found tomorrow, on the road to Ipswich, I think. It's clearly not in the direction of the Great North Road, and I believe Mr. Tarleton owns a quiet little place up in that area. It won't take long for people to conclude that he had no intention of marrying you, Miss Rushton. No, Mr. Tarleton cleverly abducted you, right in the middle of my ball. Everyone will consider it fortunate that he broke his neck in the curricle accident— Did I mention that there will be an accident? How careless of me to forget. Yes, Mr. Tarleton will have broken his neck, and I am very much afraid that your wits will have been permanently turned by your harrowing experience. I shall, of course, be as horror-struck as everyone else, and most sympathetic to your poor relatives. I believe it will serve admirably. Don't you agree, Mr. Tarleton?"

Sir Hilary made a complicated gesture with his right hand as he spoke, and James began cursing in a steady, vicious monotone. "Really, Mr. Tarleton, and in the presence of a lady, too. You forget yourself." Sir Hilary gestured again, and James was completely frozen once more.

"It will never work, Sir Hilary," I said. "You'll be caught."

"On the contrary, my dear. No one will connect it with me at all."

"Kate will," I said before I could stop myself. "And so will the Marquis of Schofield."

Sir Hilary's expression became, if possible, even more smug than before. "That is the cream of the jest, my dear. Neither your cousin nor the Marquis can do anything against me without proof, and I assure you, there will be none. They will each feel hellishly guilty for having involved the two of you, and with a very little prodding they can each be brought to blame the other for the sad fate of their dearest friends. So I shall have the pleasure of dividing Thomas from the woman he loves, as well as watching him writhe with guilt every time Mr. Tarleton's name is mentioned."

All I could think of was to say, in a most unconvincing tone, "But the Marquis doesn't love Kate!"

Sir Hilary snorted. "Don't play the innocent with me. I know Thomas far too well to think he'd behave as he's been doing for any other reason."

"And you're going to kill James and ruin me, just to make the Marquis suffer?" I said numbly. "You're worse than Miranda!"

"Not at all." Sir Hilary looked annoyed. "Miranda let revenge distract her from what should have been her main goal. I, on the other hand, would be quite willing to forget about Thomas if necessary—indeed, for a while I thought I would have to. It is simply my good fortune that you will serve both my purposes at once. Which reminds me; there is one last bit of Thomas's interference that I should like to clear up. Excuse me, my dear."

Sir Hilary walked over to the bag that lay beside James, taking care to stay outside the ring of black and white candles that surrounded me. He took a silver-rimmed mirror from the bag and muttered over it for a minute. Then he pulled out a small, ivory-handled knife and came toward me. I shrank away, pressing against the invisible barrier behind me, and Sir Hilary frowned.

"Don't be a fool, girl," he said. "Give me your hand."

"I wouldn't give you a greeting at church," I said.

Sir Hilary snorted and muttered something that sounded like the classical Greek Papa speaks upon occasion. I found myself frozen in place once again. Sir Hilary circled the candles until he reached my side. I saw him take my hand and nick my finger with the dagger, though I could not feel a thing. He squeezed my hand in a way that I am sure would have been painful if I could have felt it, and let the blood drip onto the mirror. He dropped my hand and stepped away, muttering a single word. This time I was quite sure it was classical Greek, though I did not quite catch what it was he said. An instant later, I could move, and my hand was throbbing most unpleasantly.

Sir Hilary ignored me completely, staring into the mirror. Suddenly he gave a harsh laugh. "Waycross! Of course! And I've been looking for the brat everywhere else in

England! My lord the Marquis of Schofield is nearly as clever as I am."

He wiped the mirror clean and replaced both it and the knife in the bag, then turned to me. "I do hope you will excuse me for a little, my dear. I realize it must be very trying, but I have just stumbled across an opportunity that is far too good to miss. I shall return in a little while." He made the same complex gesture as before in James's direction. "Keep the lady company, dear boy. And do try to moderate your language." He bowed mockingly and left.

I ran across my invisible prison until I hit the wall just opposite James. "James! Are you all right?" I demanded.

"How should I know?" he said, still glaring after Sir Hilary. "I can't feel a thing from the neck down." He transferred his gaze to me and said in a gentler tone, "Don't cry, Cecy. Please don't cry. There isn't anything you can do, and it only makes both of us feel worse."

"But there *has* to be something," I sniffed. "There is *always* something one can do."

"If you have any ideas, just tell me," James said. There was an undercurrent of bitterness in his voice as he added, "Not that I can do anything to help in this condition."

I sat down on the grass, considering. "I don't suppose you're close enough to blow out one of those candles?" I said without much hope. "I'm sure they're part of the spell that's holding me in."

"No," James said. "I'm afraid not." He turned his head

away, as if looking at me hurt him. "I should never have got you involved in this," he said softly.

"You keep saying that," I said. "For the hundredth time, you did *not* involve me."

"If I hadn't asked you to send Thomas that message—"

"Nothing would be any different," I said firmly. "I would still have taken that book from Sir Hilary's library, and I would still have smashed that chocolate pot into a million pieces." I took a deep breath. "And I'm not sorry for any of it, James."

He raised his head to look at me, and the corners of his mouth quirked. "None of it?"

"Well, I do wish I had guessed that Sir Hilary was getting me out of the way tonight when he stepped on my hem," I admitted. "But that isn't the same thing at all."

"No, I suppose not."

Neither of us spoke for a few minutes. Then I sighed. "And I wish I'd told you I wouldn't go to Sir Hilary's party," I said, and my eyes started to fill with tears again. "I could have told Aunt Elizabeth I had the headache; I've done it before. And then Sir Hilary wouldn't have got either of us."

"Maybe." James's voice was thoughtful, and I looked up in surprise. "And maybe he would have tried something else. Don't blame yourself, Cecy."

"I'll try not to," I said. "But, oh, James, I am so sorry!"

"So am I, Cecy," he said, and we were silent again. The flickering torchlight threw shadows across his face that made his expression difficult to read. After a time, I could not bear to look at him anymore, and I slumped down against the invisible wall. The night was quite cool, but I controlled my shivering as best I could so as not to further distress James. To add to my discomfort, I was feeling quite hollow, for I had not eaten since before the party. I stared at the candles, hoping that they would perhaps burn down and flicker out before Sir Hilary returned, but they showed no sign of such desirable behavior.

There was an idea nagging at the back of my mind, but I could not quite catch hold of it. "If we only knew what Sir Hilary *wants* of us!" I burst out at last in utter frustration.

"But my dear Miss Rushton!" Sir Hilary's voice said from the doorway behind me. "You've read the book from my library on epicyclical elaborations. Surely you've guessed?"

I stood up hastily and turned to face him. "What do you—" I stopped short, staring. Sir Hilary was carrying a limp form over one shoulder, and as he turned, the torch-light gleamed on the man's wavy brown hair. *"Oliver?"* I gasped.

"Just so," Sir Hilary said. He sounded terribly pleased with himself.

"What have you done to my brother?" I said.

Sir Hilary lowered Oliver to the ground. "Nothing, as yet, my dear. For the future—well, I intend to do very nearly the same thing to each of you. I've had my eye on young Oliver for a long time, but no safe opportunity had presented itself. Miranda almost had him once, but she didn't know what she'd had hold of and she let Thomas steal him away. I've been searching all over England for him for weeks. And all the time he's been practically next door!"

"I don't understand," I said, though I had a horrid suspicion I was about to. "Where did you find Oliver? And what are you going to do to him? To us?"

"Waycross, my dear. Your brother has spent the last several weeks at Waycross. I've spent days trying to get a peek inside Schofield Castle, but I never thought to check on the Marquis's estate not ten miles from my own door. It was really remarkably clever of Thomas."

It did not seem to me that Sir Hilary had been gone long enough to have ridden ten miles, but then I remembered that Miranda had apparently been able to get into Sir Hilary's garden through a door in London. I found myself hoping that such an unorthodox manner of traveling would be something of a strain on Sir Hilary's resources. One of Mr. Wrexton's first lessons had been that every magician's strength is limited, and one must take the greatest care not to exceed those limits. Sir Hilary did not, however, appear to be much discomposed.

Sir Hilary was arranging Oliver in a spread-eagled position on the ground. I could see Oliver's chest rising and falling as he breathed, which reassured me slightly. There was something unpleasantly familiar about his position, however, and suddenly I remembered one of the diagrams in that dreadful Tanistry book of Sir Hilary's.

"But *Oliver* isn't a wizard!" I blurted.

"So you figured it out at last," Sir Hilary said. He straightened and turned to look at me with a supercilious smile. "But I'm afraid I must correct you. The Talent runs very strongly in your family, my dear, whether it's put to use or not. Your half-witted brother admittedly has no training, but that only makes him more useful for my purposes. Why do you think I've been watching him for so long?"

"You can't steal Oliver's magic!" I said. "If he does, in-deed, have any."

"Oh, he does, my dear, he does, indeed. I doubt very much, however, that he has the capacity to make use of it." Sir Hilary smiled. "So I shall merely be taking from him a gift he does not need. It is unfortunate that doing so will kill him, but I am afraid that is how these things work. You needn't fear for yourself; I shall be careful not to take enough of your power to cause your death. I only want you to go mad, you see, and with Oliver here to draw on, I can afford not to drain you of everything."

James made a strangled noise, and Sir Hilary turned his head. "I'd forgotten about you," he said, and gestured. I knew that James was frozen completely motionless again, and I felt very alone.

"Oliver isn't bound to you," I said desperately. "And

neither am I. That awful book said that the spell to transfer power wouldn't work well if there wasn't a bond."

"Oh, but there is, Miss Rushton," Sir Hilary said. He seemed to be enjoying himself. "It took me an extremely long time to discover it, but the connection is there."

"What connection?"

"Your dear Mama was descended from my great-great-uncle," Sir Hilary said. "On the wrong side of the blanket, I'm afraid; that's why it took me so long to track it down. Still, even the faintest of blood connections is enough to allow the Tanistry spells to work, now that I am aware of it. I don't even require Miranda's assistance with the invocations any longer."

"Miranda's assistance?" I said. I saw that as long as he was explaining to me how clever he was, he couldn't do anything to Oliver, so I was determined to keep him talking as long as I could.

"You don't really think old Everard Tanistry was fool enough to put everything he knew in that book he wrote, do you?" Sir Hilary said contemptuously. "Some of the real secrets were handed down in the family. It's a pity Miranda wasn't more like him, in a way. She'd have managed better. Fortunately, I don't need her anymore."

I hardly had time to wonder what had been happening in London before he turned away and walked toward the bag he had left on the ground beside James. He pulled out the ivory-handled knife and a little packet of herbs. He sprinkled some of the herbs over Oliver's face and raised his hands. "Wait!" I said in desperation. "What did you mean about Miranda?"

Sir Hilary glanced back at me over his shoulder. "You've had enough explanations, my dear, and it's nearly dawn. I prefer to get the … unpleasant portions of this business over with quickly, now that all the preliminaries have been taken care of."

"Then it's a shame you didn't take better precautions against interruption," said a voice from behind me.

Sir Hilary and I both turned, and now I know exactly why people are said to faint with relief, Kate. For Mr. Wrexton was standing just inside the door to the garden, and I was so glad to see him that my head swam. Aunt Elizabeth was right behind him, her eyes positively blazing with fury. "Wrexton!" Sir Hilary spat. "Where did you come from?"

"Waycross," Mr. Wrexton said. His voice was very calm, but his eyes were hard and a little wary. "I've been there for weeks, but I took care to keep out of your way. Thomas Schofield asked me to keep an eye on that young gentleman lying at your feet, you see, and I thought it would be simpler if you didn't know I was nearby."

"How did you find me?" Sir Hilary demanded.

"I took the precaution of placing a locating spell on Cecy's locket along with the protections," Mr. Wrexton said.

"As soon as Elizabeth discovered she was missing, she came to me, and the rest was easy."

"It should have taken days, even for you, to figure out how to cross that portal!"

Mr. Wrexton smiled nastily. "You forget, Sir Hilary. Thomas worked on the equations. This was one of the first things he warned me about when he asked me to come out here to watch over the boy."

"So." Sir Hilary put his shoulders back slightly. "What do you plan to do, now that—" In the middle of the sentence, he threw up his hands and began shouting in Greek.

Mr. Wrexton began making hasty gestures of his own, and Aunt Elizabeth slipped out to stand muttering beside him. I backed away as far as I could. I could tell that there was a great deal of very powerful magic being flung about, and I had no idea if Sir Hilary's invisible walls would keep it out. I tried to follow the spells for a moment, but Mr. Wrexton and Sir Hilary were going much too fast for me. Mr. Wrexton was frowning intently, and I began to worry. I knew that Mr. Wrexton was very good (he was with the Duke of Wellington, after all!), but Sir Hilary had stolen the magic from heaven only knows how many people, and Sir Hilary was on his home ground (in a manner of speaking).

I looked back at the battle. Aunt Elizabeth looked quite white, and Mr. Wrexton stepped in front of her. I could see beads of sweat on his forehead, though his muttering was as rapid as ever. Sir Hilary looked cool and supercilious, and his eyes were hard with triumph. It was clear that he, at least, was sure that he would win.

The idea that had been nagging at me earlier returned, and I tried desperately to shut out the sights and sounds of the wizardly battle and *think*. Suddenly it came to me. I turned my back on Sir Hilary and Mr. Wrexton and, facing James, I made the same gesture I had seen Sir Hilary use twice to let James talk.

James's face came alive. Before he could say anything, I hissed urgently, "James! What is the Greek word for 'release'?"

"*Apheteon*," he said, and I saw comprehension in his eyes. "And hurry, Cecy."

I swallowed and closed my eyes. Concentrating with everything I had, I made Sir Hilary's gesture again and said, "*Apheteon*."

My eyes flew open as I spoke. James stood up, picked up the chair, took two steps forward, and brought it down on Sir Hilary's head. It connected with a most satisfactory crash, and Sir Hilary collapsed. At precisely the same instant, all of the candles went out, and a moment later I heard Oliver groan.

I stood where I was, as I felt rather weak about the knees and was not at all sure I could walk without falling over. James stared down at Sir Hilary with a positively vicious expression on his face. Then he turned, and a moment later I was caught up in his arms. It was remarkably comfortable and reassuring, and after all we had been through I did not care a jot whether Aunt Elizabeth gave me a lecture on propriety later. Then James bent over and kissed me. I do not think it would be quite accurate to describe that as "comfortable and reassuring," but I assure you I had no objection whatever. In fact, I cooperated as well as I was able (which was not very much, as James was holding me tightly enough to make it seem that he wished to squeeze all the breath from my body. This made it rather difficult for me to render him much assistance in kissing me.).

An unfortunately short time later (or so it seemed to me), James pulled his head away. "Why are you stopping?" I asked somewhat hazily.

James chuckled, and I felt it in my bones. "Because if I didn't, I wouldn't be able to ask you to marry me," he said. "Will you, my love?"

"Oh, *yes,* James," I said, and kissed him. This time I was able to do rather better at aiding him, which was very satisfying for both of us.

"Marry you!" said Oliver's disapproving voice from behind me. "I should dashed well think she'll have to, if this is the way you've been carrying on. What do you mean by getting up to such tricks while I'm away, Cecy?"

James and I fell apart, though he kept a hand in mine to steady me. "Don't be a prig, Oliver," I said. "Of course I'm going to marry James, but not for such a stupid reason as that!"

Mr. Wrexton and Aunt Elizabeth were muttering over Sir Hilary's unconscious form. Oliver looked at them with disapproval and started to say something. "Don't interrupt them!" I said quickly.

Oliver scowled at me, and Mr. Wrexton looked up. "It's quite all right, Cecelia; we're finished here." He smiled warmly at Aunt Elizabeth. "Thank you for your help, Elizabeth. I will have to take him up to London at once and let the Royal College know the sort of thing he's been up to. I expect they'll be very severe with him."

"What do you think they'll do to him?" I asked.

"I would say that they're sure to strip him of his powers. Beyond that, I'm not certain."

"Don't leave before I've had a chance to talk to you, Wrexton," James said in a grim voice. "You ought to know the whole of what that cur was planning."

Mr. Wrexton nodded and looked at Aunt Elizabeth again. "I won't be gone more than a week," he said. "And you know how to reach me if you should happen to need me."

"Of course, Michael," she said softly. "Hurry back."

"You may be sure of it," Mr. Wrexton said. He took her hand and kissed it, and Aunt Elizabeth blushed.

There is very little more to tell. James drove me back to Rushton Manor; Aunt Elizabeth and Oliver followed in Mr. Wrexton's carriage. Mr. Wrexton stayed behind to seal up Sir Hilary's garden and to remove Sir Hilary to a safer place. I spent the rest of the day in bed (Aunt Elizabeth did not even suggest that I go to church!), and am now quite recovered. Oliver, too, seems none the worse for his experience. He read me a dreadful scold when he discovered that I had had the temerity to ride Thunder, but I was too happy to care, and Aunt Elizabeth shooed him away very quickly.

James spoke to Papa as soon as we reached home, and Papa sent the announcement of our engagement to the *Gazette* this morning. Actually, he sent two announcements, for Aunt Elizabeth is to marry Mr. Wrexton. I am very pleased by this news, for I think they suit almost as well as James and I. You will understand when you meet Mr. Wrexton. I can hardly wait to see what Aunt Charlotte makes of it all!

I have asked James whether he would object to a double wedding with you and Thomas, and he seemed quite receptive to the idea. I do not wish to steal your thunder, however, so if either you or Thomas has any objection to this suggestion, do tell me at once. Papa and Aunt Elizabeth are bringing me to Town next week to have my bride-clothes made, and I can hardly contain my excitement. We shall have *such* a lot to talk about! For letters, no matter how satisfactory, can bear no comparison to seeing you face-to-face, and I am absolutely *wild* to meet your Thomas. From what you and James have told me, I feel as if I know him already.

Do let me know about the wedding, and don't forget to tell me about Aunt Charlotte. She'll probably turn purple.

Your ecstatically happy,
Cecy

17 July 1817
Schofield House, London

Dear Cecy,

Thomas says he might have known James would display his usual masterly grasp of tactics (I believe this is his way of saying that he is jealous of James for getting to hit Sir Hilary), and that he wishes you both very happy. You know I am delighted—I shall tell you so next week. It doesn't seem possible that you haven't even seen 11 Berkeley Square yet, let alone met Thomas.

Mr. Wrexton has been in London for two days. After he conveyed Sir Hilary to the Royal College, he came to inform us that Sir Hilary is to be stripped of his magic (and his membership in the College) and exiled to the continent. Once he delivered this very welcome news, he remained to consult with Lady Sylvia about the effect the double focus had on Thomas's health in general and magic in particular. After twenty minutes spent scrutinizing Thomas from top to toe, they dismissed him, so he came to Berkeley Square to listen to me practice the spinet. Really, when inclined, he can sulk amazingly. Oliver simply isn't in it.

Lady Sylvia and Thomas spent all afternoon yesterday asking me questions and conducting peculiar tests with items

Lady Sylvia brought in on a tea tray. They have agreed on the verdict, apparently, but neither could be persuaded to tell me what it is. I should warn you that ever since her conversation with Mr. Wrexton, Lady Sylvia has been most anxious to meet you.

Thomas has no objection to a double wedding (nor do I, of course), provided you are willing to have a very hasty one. Thomas intends us to accompany Lady Sylvia when she returns to Paris, which she means to do as soon as possible. From there he wishes to go on to several cities he thinks I ought to see. (Among other things, he insists he will perish if he cannot take me to Venice and watch me fall into a canal.) These schemes of his for a rapid departure to the continent date from Sunday, when he called for me in Berkeley Square.

When he arrived, Aunt Charlotte was at her very worst. She was reading out religious tracts to me in an effort to bring me to a proper sense of shame concerning my behavior at Carlton House. (Not walking home or waltzing in Berkeley Square, mind you—consorting with Lady Sylvia's friends.)

His arrival put a stop to that. After a very civil greeting to Aunt Charlotte and Georgy, he said, "I thought I would see if you cared to drive in the park with me, Kate. We could see if the ducks have returned to their pond after your rude invasion of their quarters."

"Kate cannot go out today," Aunt Charlotte said. "It will certainly rain later."

Thomas appeared to be considering several alternative remarks, but he said nothing.

Abruptly it seemed to me to be a great shame that I should miss even one of Thomas's remarks because of Aunt Charlotte and her ridiculous notions. So I said, "Nonsense, Aunt Charlotte. I shall go out. And if it rains, the ducks won't care."

Aunt Charlotte stared aghast as I prepared to depart. Then, spacing her words as carefully as if I were the half-wit Thomas has so often accused me of being, she said, "You cannot go. I have not given you leave to go."

"I am going, Aunt Charlotte," I replied calmly. "I don't see why you insist on making my last few days in this house as uncomfortable as possible, but I recommend you find some other diversion to occupy you when I am married and gone. Perhaps you should read a few tracts to Georgy—don't you think she ought to know how improper it is for young ladies to dance on the Sabbath? The Grenvilles will have dancing after supper tonight, won't they, Georgy?"

Georgina looked daggers at me.

"And perhaps you should remind Georgy that Michael Aubrey is only a second son," I continued unscrupulously.

Aunt Charlotte's voice dropped into trembling disbelief. "Katherine Talgarth, do you presume to tell me how to look after Georgina?"

"Well, yes, Aunt Charlotte, I must. Particularly since she's learned to play silver loo and shows every sign of turning into as reckless a gamester as Grandfather, despite your chaperonage."

"Kate!" Georgy sprang up with a shriek. "You beastly sneak! Cut line!"

"And you've let her pick up the most dreadful sporting cant, Aunt Charlotte," I added. "Another thing you should know—that goat of Squire Bryant's? Well, it was all Georgy's idea—she said it would be pointless to confess after you and Aunt Elizabeth had already punished Cecy and me anyway."

Georgy and Aunt Charlotte advanced on me, shouting in counterpoint until the prisms of the chandelier chimed softly overhead. "And moreover," I informed Aunt Charlotte, "Papa always referred to you as 'that interfering harpy.'"

Georgina blanched and Aunt Charlotte stiffened, speechless. I felt Thomas grip my arm. "Come away, Kate. Come tell me all about Squire Bryant's goat, before you give your aunt an apoplexy."

So we went driving in the park. I shall spend the next week at Schofield House with Lady Sylvia, since I have, in Thomas's words, "made Berkeley Square too hot to hold me." He adds that you have a fortnight to get here before, double ring or single, he brings me up before a clergyman and marries me. He is set upon flying the country for the continent. Typically, he has decided (without consulting anyone's wishes but his own) to make our wedding trip into a peculiar sort of Grand Tour. I hope you don't mind too greatly. I don't mind at all. In fact, I'm looking forward to it very much. (Not the canal, though.)

Love,
Kate

Afterword

CAROLINE

I don't know who invented the Letter Game (which I have heard called Persona Letters, or even Ghost Letters) but Ellen Kushner introduced it to me. I believe it originated as an acting exercise, one character writing a letter "in persona" to another.

The game has no rules, except that the players must never reveal their idea of the plot to one another. It helps to imply in the first letter why the two characters must write to each other and not meet in person.

The Letter Games I've played previously were usually a matter of two or three letters each, spaced about a month apart, during summer vacation. When it was time to return to school, we abandoned our characters in mid-intrigue, usually on the verge of a duel, a crime, or a coup d'état. Our letters were long on gossip and short on plot, but they provided good clean fun for the cost of a postage stamp.

PAT

Caroline first mentioned the Letter Game over the tea table, appropriately enough, in April of 1986. I was among the fascinated listeners who pumped her for more information,

317

more directions, more details. I was intrigued by the possibilities and anxious to try it, so I badgered Caroline into agreeing to play, with the provision that I write the first letter. I dashed home at the end of the afternoon, full of enthusiasm.

As the opener of the letter exchange, I was responsible for choosing a setting, as well as for defining my own character. I decided on England just after the Napoleonic Wars, in an alternate universe in which magic really worked, just to spice things up a little. I knew Caroline shared my interest in both subjects, and I figured we would have a lot of fun working out a more detailed background as we went along. Little did I know what was in store!

CAROLINE

For the first few letters, things went quite calmly, with Pat writing as Cecelia and me writing as Kate, both of us having fun making up alternate history. Then, about the time Oliver disappeared at Vauxhall, I started to get a little obsessed with the game. A letter every few weeks wasn't enough anymore. Luckily, Pat felt the same way. We began to exchange letters more frequently. Although we still didn't reveal plot details, we met for lunch once a week and found ourselves discussing the characters as though they were members of our families. We were caught in a perfect balance between the desire to show off for each other and the desire to know how the story would come out. The day I knew this particular Letter Game had a life of its own was the day I came home to discover the latest letter from Cecelia tucked under my door. Written on the back was, "Don't be *too* amazed. I sent it by one of the footmen."

So the summer went, with Pat and me exchanging letters at every opportunity and driving our friends to the screaming point with gossip about the characters. (Never about the plot, I hasten to add.) I began to break china. Pat began to say things like, "We simply must *do something*!" without realizing it. We had *fun*.

The Letter Game ended around Labor Day. Pat and I took one entire Saturday to go through the letters and pull out loose ends that distracted from the story as it finally turned out. We sent the results off and we got lucky. We were able to publish the Game. But we didn't play the Letter Game to publish it. We played because it was fun.

PAT

Caroline is entirely correct in saying we did not discuss plot with each other. In the interest of complete disclosure, however, I must confess that we did, to some extent, discuss timing. Specifically, sometime around the middle of August I asked her, "How many more letters is it going to take you to get rid of Miranda? I need to know so I can get rid of Sir Hilary pretty much at the same time." She thought for a while and said, "Two or three, at most." And she did. And that was the extent of the mutual planning we did.

When Caroline and I finally sat down with Kate and Cecy's collected correspondence, we weren't quite sure what we had (aside from a lot of fun). I don't remember which of us was first to stare at the untidy heap of paper and say, "This is a *book*." Looking at the letters with the sapient eyes of authors, rather than simply as correspondents, we could see places where the timing of events was wrong, important occurrences that were never explained, minor characters who had suddenly become important, and plot threads that had never gone anywhere. We set out to fix these problems.

Revising the letters was nearly as much fun as writing them in the first place. We argued happily about Georgy and Aunt Charlotte and Oliver. Caroline put in Thomas's reminiscing about James's career as A.D.C. to the Duke of Wellington; I retaliated with James's comment about Thomas being mentioned in dispatches. Thomas got to snub Oliver in the park; James was badgered into expanding on Lady Jersey's confused tale about Thomas's brother, Edward. And so it went.

Eventually, we had to admit that we were finished and sent the manuscript off to the kind and farsighted editor who'd bought it. The finished version really isn't very different from the letters we exchanged during that hectic six months; some things are clearer (we hope), and a few things were dropped. Here it is: We hope you enjoy it as much as we did.

Turn the page for a glimpse of
Kate and Cecy's continuing adventures in

THE GRAND TOUR

From the deposition of Mrs. James Tarleton to the Joint Representatives of the British Ministry of Magic, the War Office, and the Foreign Office

I suppose that if I were going to blame our involvement on anyone (which I see no reason to do), I would be compelled to say that it was all Aunt Charlotte's fault. If she had not been in such a dreadful temper over Kate's marriage, Kate and Thomas would not have decided to take their wedding journey on the Continent in preference to remaining in England, and James and I would not have gone with them. And then very likely we would never have known anything about any of it.

Kate is my cousin, and now that she is married she is a Marchioness, which is what put our Aunt Charlotte's nose so dreadfully out of joint. Admittedly, Kate said some awful things to Aunt Charlotte, but after the way Aunt Charlotte treated Kate, she deserved every one of them. She made matters worse by hinting that I ought to be as put out as she, because Kate was going to be Lady Schofield and I was only going to be Mrs. Tarleton. So it is her own fault that none of us wished to stay and listen to her nagging.

At first James was dubious about our joining Kate and Thomas on their wedding journey, though he and Thomas are nearly as great friends as Kate and I. I felt compelled to point out that even if we did not accompany them, they would have Lady Sylvia traveling with them at least until they reached Paris. "And if Kate does not object to having her mama-at-law with them, you ought not to be such a high stickler about our going as well. Besides, she and Thomas invited us."

"You mean you cooked up the idea and talked Kate into it, and she persuaded Thomas," James said. "Sometimes you go too far, Cecy."

"I did not!" I said hotly. Which is not to say that I would not have done so if I had thought of it, but I saw no reason to mention that to James. "Kate came to me, I promise you, and it was Thomas's idea, not hers."

"Thomas wants us on his wedding journey?"

"It's our wedding journey, too," I pointed out, feeling rather annoyed. "And I believe he thinks he is doing us a favor."

"A favor?"

"Aunt Charlotte," I said succinctly.

"I am perfectly capable of handling—" James broke off suddenly, looking rather thoughtful. "You're right," he said after a moment. "That does sound like Thomas."

"If you are quite determined, I can tell Kate to tell Thomas that we have other plans," I said. "But since he already knows perfectly well that we haven't—"

"No, no, I'll talk to him," James said hastily. He turned away, muttering something about keeping me out of it, which I chose not to hear.

Naturally, Aunt Charlotte made a number of shocked and uncomplimentary remarks when she discovered what we were planning. As it was none of her affair, James and I ignored her. After all, Aunt Elizabeth did not see anything amiss about it, and she is at least as high a stickler as Aunt Charlotte. (Well, actually, what Aunt Elizabeth said was that if going on a wedding journey together was the oddest thing the four of us ever did, Aunt Charlotte should be grateful.) Papa, of course, was delighted, and gave Kate and me each a long list of antiquities that he said we must see (most of them quite unsuitable, but I dare say that didn't occur to him).

The wedding was rather small, as we held it barely three weeks after the announcements appeared, but it was most elegant. James and Thomas stood up for each other, and Kate and I were each other's maids of honor, and Papa gave both of us away, since Kate's Papa has been dead these five years. I must confess that at the time I somewhat regretted the haste and the quietness of the ceremony, but I would have gone to much greater lengths in order to be married along with dear Kate. Upon reflection, however, I see that it was a very good thing we were so quick about matters. If we had waited, Aunt Charlotte would probably have unbent and begun speaking to Kate again, and then she would certainly have tried to bully Kate into wearing a wedding gown identical to mine (which was Brussels lace over cream satin), and it would not have done at all. Kate is far too short to look well in the styles I wear, but she was perfectly *stunning* in the white silk brocade that she and I and Lady Sylvia picked out.

Kate was a little nervous before the ceremony started; I believe she was afraid she would trip while she was walking up the aisle, or become entangled in her veil, or tear the hem out of her gown. Nothing of the sort happened, and I am quite sure she forgot to worry as soon as she saw Thomas waiting for her. She looked very happy indeed, and positively *floated* down the aisle. I am afraid I didn't pay too much attention to Kate after that, because it was my turn to walk up the aisle and I was looking at James.

The wedding breakfast afterward was a sumptuous affair. Neither my brother, Oliver, nor Aunt Charlotte could find anything to turn up their noses about, but none of us wished to linger. Finally, a footman came to say that the carriages were at the door, and we said our good-byes. Aunt Elizabeth hugged us both and gave us each a pair of pearl earrings, which she had enchanted so that they would never fall out or get lost. Papa (who was beginning to look vaguely rumpled already) gave me a bottle of brandy (in case any of us should be carriage-sick) and another list of antiquities he had forgotten to include the first time. Oliver, to my complete astonishment, gave me a hug that did severe damage to his cravat and promised James and me one of Thunder's foals. Aunt Charlotte sniffed and said she hoped none of us would regret it, and then presented Kate and me with identical boxes of starched linen handkerchiefs. Kate immediately found a use for one; her sister, Georgina (who has always been something of a watering pot), had already soaked her own handkerchief, and Kate was too kind to let her continue dabbing at her eyelashes with a soggy ball.

We escaped at last, climbed into our carriages, and started off.

Inscribed upon the flyleaf of the commonplace book of the Most Honorable the Marchioness of Schofield

This book was given to me as a wedding gift by my uncle, Arthur Rushton. In it, I am to record my experiences and impressions. Uncle Arthur made a fine speech of presentation in which he admonished me to remember that the thoughts that we record today will become the treasured historical documents of the future. If this is so, I feel sorry for the future. Every other attempt I have made to keep a commonplace book rapidly degenerated into a list of what happened to my pocket money. This time I will try to do better. I intend to write an account of our wedding journey. But I will be astonished if anyone ever considers it a document of historical interest.